PAPER CASTLES

THE QUEEN IS DEAD. THE FIGHT BEGINS NOW.

ELLIE EMBER

Juniperus Press

Paperback: ISBN 979-8-9898701-0-3
eBook: ASIN B0CRPS942P

First paperback edition May 2024.
This book underwent minor line edits in May 2025.
Second cover edition July 2026.

Cover design by Ellie Ember.
No AI was used in the creation of this book.

PAPER CASTLES

To everyone who has felt powerless.

AUTHOR'S NOTE

This book contains scenes of peril and violence, brief descriptions of familial abuse, alcoholism, and suicidal thoughts, and discussions of death (including familial and child death). Please be advised if any of these topics are potentially triggering for you.

The Code of the Kingdom of Kevelda,
Adopted by the Dais of Ministers and
Enforced by the Appointed Mayors...

<u>Article II, Section II</u>

Upon the death of the sovereign, the heir apparent will be announced according to the line of succession. The heir must physically sit on the throne to ascend. Any citizen of Kevelda can challenge the heir prior to the ascension and, if they bring to the Dais proof of the heir apparent's death at their hands, *take the throne themselves...*

PROLOGUE

Evangeline did not hear her father's dying words.

She was not there for his final breath, nor his last rites.

The priest had shot her a glance of pity as she left King Tomas's deathbed to stand outside of the throne room and wait for the Campaign to begin. Evangeline would allow it just this once, but never again would anyone look at her that way once she took her father's throne.

My right, she thought, as she stared at the mahogany doors. *My responsibility.*

Anxiety and excitement warred in her abdomen, gnawing at her stomach with equal fervor. Evangeline would only admit to the latter. The palace walls had seen her grow from a confident child to a determined woman, trained and molded and disciplined to become Kevelda's leader. Her father had ordered the best agents from the king's armed force, the Argentum, to train her for the Campaign. Evangeline knew how to wield weapons from swords and daggers to pistols and shotguns—even a bow and arrow, though that would not aid in the close combat she might face when the throne room doors finally opened. She had even trained in a dress much like the one she wore now, the crimson silk pooling to the floor, a foretaste of the queen she would be.

Her Protector had explained the rules of the Campaign at her father's deathbed, even though she knew them by heart: *When a ruler of Kevelda dies, the heir must sit on the throne to be crowned. Until then, anyone can kill you and take your place to become the new heir of Kevelda.*

There were no laws governing activities in the Campaign, and thus, no repercussions for those who sought her death. From her first steps, her first words, Evangeline had prepared for this.

While the training of the Argentum agents would get her to the throne, her mother's instruction on how to play the court might keep her from having any opponents at all.

"Don't let them decide to fear you or love you," the queen had said, on more occasions than Evangeline could remember, "Make them do both."

Evangeline did not dare to take her eyes off the doors ahead of her, even as her assigned Protector shifted next to her. As much as she tried to shake the thought out of her head, she could not stop thinking about her mother now, the deep red wood reminding her of her mother's loose curls, which were far too often hidden in an updo underneath her silver crown.

Her mother had died four years ago, lost to an illness that destroyed her from the inside out. Evangeline did not visit her mother much in those final months. She did not want to see the woman that held so much power in the court run out of strings to pull. None of the Dais ministers or mayors in her pocket could save her from her own body's betrayal.

Four years, and Evangeline had drawn every one of those leaders to her side, if she had not already done so in her twenty-one years before that. So, Evangeline did not worry about who she would face in the throne room. It would be an untrained mayor's son from one of the smaller cities, or an amateur who wanted the crown to give their family a better life.

Evangeline scoffed. *Easy.*

But it did not make the pit in her stomach go away entirely. The vise gripping her lungs would not dissolve until her Protector gave her the news that her father had officially died, and he opened the throne room doors to reveal who waited for her on the other side.

Was Evangeline sad that her father was dying? She could not say, nor would she give any thought to the impossible question. King Tomas could not have been described as a kind man, but he was not ruthless. He did not show affection, but then again, Evangeline never wanted it. If not explicitly stated by her parents, their actions had taught her to know better. She knew that love, even among family, could be weakness when it came to the power of ruling Kevelda.

Evangeline counted herself lucky that she had no siblings that could fight her for the title of heir.

Not lucky. Evangeline did not like to consider anything to be beyond her control.

Everything in her life led up to this moment. The blood and sweat she had shed while honing her skills for this fight. The tears she had learned to not let fall as she navigated the court.

She deserved this throne, not because she was the only heir, but because she had battled against her nature, whittled herself away so that she could become the ruler Kevelda needed. Queen Evangeline, who would end the war her father had begun, who would bring her people fighting on the island of Thaertos home at last.

No, Evangeline was not sad King Tomas was dying. Not in the slightest.

Footsteps sounded behind her, joined by the sound of uniforms ruffling. On her periphery, her Protector nodded. Evangeline stiffened, gripping tighter the hilt of the sword at her side. She exhaled a long breath, urging her hands to steady as adrenaline coursed through her veins.

"King Tomas is dead," the Protector said in a low voice. "The fight begins now."

The Argentum agent who must have told the Protector the news took her position at the other side of the throne room doors, and together, the two opened them.

A boy, no older than sixteen, stood in the middle of the obsidian floor. The sword in his hands dwarfed him, the prodigious room making him appear even more powerless. No one else stood beside him. The corner of Evangeline's mouth raised in a half-smile at the thought that no one else, none of the Dais or the mayors, had dared to challenge her.

The Protector bowed his head as he backed away. "Good luck, my queen."

"Thank you," Evangeline responded, "but I do not need it."

Evangeline did not bother to run. She strode forward with a steady gait, her shoulders back, her head high. She even removed her hand from her sword, clasping her fingers in front of her as she acknowledged the five ministers seated along the walls to her left and right. Mendoza, her father's Prime Minister—soon to be her own—stood alongside his wife and son, who could not be more than seven years old. The man must not have been worried about letting his son see the bloodshed. In fact, he made the boy watch, tilting his cheek to keep his eyes on the center of the floor.

Perhaps the boy would replace the Prime Minister, one day.

"I'm here to challenge you," the boy with the sword stated loudly, his voice shaking with the effort.

Evangeline waited until she was within an arm's distance of the boy to unsheathe her sword and reply. "No need to shout. I'm right here."

One of the ministers chuckled before stopping himself abruptly.

The boy swung. Metal whistled through the air. Evangeline parried, ducking underneath the strike and twisting until she held her blade against the boy's throat.

"This was never a fair fight," she said in a pseudo-hushed tone, ensuring the Dais, and the microphones broadcasting to the kingdom, could still hear her. "I'll let you try again, if you like."

"I don't need your pity," the boy spit. Evangeline felt a twinge of respect for his lack of begging. "I came here to avenge the people who died for your family's war."

Evangeline pressed the sword tighter, forcing the boy to whisper.

Despite her move, he continued to speak. "I did not expect to survive this. I only hope that it will inspire the next person who fights back."

An unnatural cold enveloped the boy's skin as Evangeline pressed her lips against his ear. "Both of us want this war to end." She anticipated the boy to recoil, but he did not move at all. He may have been afraid to face her, yet he was prepared to die.

Evangeline withdrew her blade and stepped back. The boy gasped for air, clutching the slight red line of blood across his neck. His eyes flickered with confusion.

A martyr is the last thing I need. She turned to face the throne, only five meters away, and began her final steps as the heir apparent.

Those who developed the Campaign, after the Fall had destroyed most other nations, aimed for it to prove that the heir, and as such, the ruler of Kevelda, possessed the strength to handle any possible challengers that could shake the already tenuous political situation. Evangeline justified that nothing displayed strength more than turning her back on an opponent. The world would know that she was not afraid, even as she weighed what this boy's challenge would mean. She would end his rebellion before it began.

A sharp pain seared into her back. She lunged to the side, narrowly dodging the boy's sword coming down on her. "You wanted another try, after all," she hissed through gritted teeth.

The boy responded only by slashing his sword at her again. She blocked with her blade, forcing his backward. Her back burned with every movement. If her heart was not pounding in her ears, she knew she would hear a trickle of blood dripping steadily onto the dark tile. She certainly saw it trailing her as she moved around to the boy's other side. His left–the side he failed to defend.

Evangeline swiped her sword at his legs. He fell to the ground, a scream tearing from his mouth. The tip of her blade dug into his chest as she knelt beside him.

"Both of us want this war to end," she repeated.

She pushed harder against the blade, twisting as it went. The boy could not do more than whimper.

Still, he did not beg.

For a second, Evangeline thought about keeping the boy alive. He would be a valuable ally, if he was on her side. She needed someone with his strength, but not with his willpower. That willpower would be fatal.

Evangeline drew closer to the boy's face, now pale and contorted in agony. "But only *I* am willing to do what it takes to win it."

His death was quick. No one else challenged her.

The ministers could not decide if they feared or loved her.

PART I
THE MAYOR'S DAUGHTER

ONE

Alexandria Redmond decided that throwing up in the bathroom would be better than doing so on stage in front of several hundred people. Or even worse, in front of the cameras broadcasting the monthly Draft to the rest of Kevelda. At least, to those who had televisions.

The other Keveldans who bothered to listen would hear her vomiting over their radios, likely joined by a reporter narrating the sequence of events. Her stomach lurched again at the thought. She fought back the tears that welled up in her eyes. Eventually, they trailed down her cheeks, hot against the chill of the stall.

In her last year of primary school, she and Amira had snuck into this bathroom so that they could avoid the daily track run. Phillip and James had wanted to come with them, but the four knew they would get in far more trouble for skipping the exercise if the boys were found there with them.

She would have laughed at the memory if Phillip was still alive. But he was not. If he was, he would have found a way to tell

Alexandria he was okay. She knew it was useless to hope. No one came back after being drafted. They were never heard from again.

Amira argued with someone in the hallway. Both the concrete walls and the ringing in her ears muffled their voices.

"We will be in the auditorium when the ceremony starts," Amira said sternly, her typically soft voice harsh against the uneasy quiet.

"She does not get special privileges because she is the mayor's daughter," a woman responded.

"Would you say that to the mayor, or only to me?"

Alexandria pushed herself off the ground, wiping the dirt and dust from her hands onto her black pants. She paused to look in the mirror. Red rimmed her eyes, surrounded by dark mascara marks. The water from the sink nearly froze her skin as she rubbed away the smudges. She smoothed out the wrinkles from the rest of her outfit and started into the hallway.

"Don't worry, I'm still here," she said with a forced brightness. She looked at the woman, one of the Argentum agents who was there to make sure that no one ran if the mayor pulled their name.

The woman nodded toward the auditorium doors. Amira gave her one last bitter look before she put her arm through Alexandria's and together they walked toward the room where the ceremony was about to begin.

"Thank you," Alexandria whispered, and this time, her voice matched how she felt. Anxious to hear what names would be pulled this month. Terrified that it would be one of her friends'. Weary because they would have to do it all over again in a few weeks.

"I wouldn't leave you alone," Amira responded. She said it with such conviction that Alexandria almost started crying again.

When they reached the set of wooden doors, she took a deep breath. She closed her eyes, wishing she didn't have to see the rows of seats filled with people she had grown up with, and beyond that, the stage on which she would take her seat next to her father while her mother called out the names of those who would never return to this place.

She would be forced to watch their faces, to look for the person who would let out a shattered sob or a loud curse or simply sit there, resigned to their fate. Not many dared to run, not past the first year of the mandate, when stories emerged across Kevelda of people who had been imprisoned, or worse, for trying to avoid the Draft.

No one wanted to fight for the island of Thaertos, not really. Many of those drafted were far too young to know why the war had even begun; Genea had been their enemy since before they were born. The start of the conflict was the same thing to them as the Fall—ancient history—but they had at least been taught about the Old World bombing itself to bits. Knowing their past was a privilege Alexandria often took for granted, having a history professor for a father and the mayoral records in her mother's office.

Kureya, being one of the larger cities, did not feel the loss of its young as sharply as the other cities did. Some businesses closed, being unable to find workers, and families who lost their primary providers wound up begging on the streets or living in humanitarian homes if they were fortunate. When you're focused on survival, you don't have time to question why you're fighting, only how you'll keep on breathing another day.

Her mother decreed that City Hall would provide free meals once a week, but they could not do more than that. More often than she would like, Alexandria wondered why her mother did not fight for her people. She knew it wouldn't be of much use.

It would not make a difference if Mayor Redmond went to Queen Evangeline and asked for the Draft to end, pleaded for her city's young men and women to not be sent to inevitable slaughter. Still, every time the mayors and their families were invited to a gala at the palace, she waited for her mother to beg the queen.

Alexandria learned to live with the person she became around the court, though she loathed the way she pinned up her hair and put on her most expensive dress to flirt and wink at her peers while James's family lived in City Hall's spare suite because they could not afford housing of their own. She spent weekends building superficial friendships with the mayors' sons and daughters–or if she was lucky, a Dais minister's child–so that her mother would have an advantage in negotiations, only to come back to Kureya having gained nothing but a wine headache and aching feet from the heels that bit into the back of her ankles.

She wished that she had been able to spend more time with the faces in the crowd in front of her, but it did not matter now. It was easier, she supposed, to watch people be sent to die if she had never gotten to know them.

As she sat in the stiff-backed wooden chair set next to her father's, she could only pray that the names pulled from the wooden box on the podium in front of her mother would not include "James Collins" or "Amira Abdul." She did not pray for herself to be spared.

Her peers stared back at her, some with disdain, some with resignation, but all knowing there was a chance they would leave the auditorium with death closer than before. A few sat with their families, with infants in their arms or toddlers squirming in their seats. She found it even harder to breathe when those with spouses or children were named. But everyone would lose a family member, a child or parent or sibling, and she knew it would only make the ceremony more difficult to survive with her soul intact if she dwelled too much on those who would be left behind. Left behind like she had been when the Draft stole Phillip.

The mayor always cried when they went home after the Draft. After all the cameras and microphones were far away, her mother would drop onto the couch, put her face in her hands, and remain there until long after she went to bed. Before Phillip was drafted, Alexandria would sit beside her mother, shedding a few tears of her own as her father rubbed comforting circles on her mother's back. She preferred to be alone now.

For the first few months after Phillip left, she found solace the same way that many others did after the Draft, numbing her thoughts and feelings through any means possible. Amira and James eventually pulled her out of the haze she had thrown herself into, but she still needed these nights alone. It was penance, forcing herself to think about Phillip to deal with the shame of what she had done in her grief.

Her thoughts had enveloped her so thoroughly that she did not notice the crowd had stood to salute the Keveldan flag until her father tapped her shoulder. It must have only been a brief delay before she got to her feet and joined them, but she hoped the cameras did not catch her falter.

When everyone sat again, the mayor reached into the wooden box and pulled out the first name.

And the next.

And the next.

And the next.

A woman cried loudly as another woman next to her reached for her hand, her eyes glazed over without any emotion. Alexandria did not know which of their names were called.

And the next.

And the next.

And the next.

When her mother had named Phillip, he did not cry. Amira did, though. She had let out a choked gasp, covering her mouth with her hand. James had shouted so loudly that the Argentum agents jolted from their posts.

"It has to be a mistake," James had insisted. He looked to the mayor with an anticipating gaze, imploring her with just his eyes to say that she had read the name wrong, to do something to save the boy that had grown up with her daughter, whose birthday parties she had attended since he turned eight years old.

Mayor Redmond did not look in the direction of her daughter's three closest friends. Alexandria had only a moment to study her mother's face before she called the next name. As close as she was, she could see her mother's eyes glistening. Alexandria had fought to keep the same emotionless expression that her family always put on, no matter how much she wanted to scream, to run for Phillip, to shout at Queen Evangeline through the cameras, to crumple inward, to curl into a ball, to clutch her knees to her chest, to never speak to anyone again.

Phillip had smiled. Not his usual bright grin, the one that burned her from the inside out, but the smile of someone who knew that his time was over, and that he had not wasted a moment of it.

The memory clawed at her chest. She could not forget that smile, not when she had to sit in the same seat every month and see the faces of her friends in the audience, only two remaining.

Another name.

And the next.

And the next.

And the next.

Twenty names total. Twenty families who would be forever changed. Twenty empty seats in classrooms and at dinner tables. Twenty people who would never come back.

As the audience cleared out of the auditorium, the Redmonds left through an exit in the back. It was better, safer, for them to avoid the anger and the insults, the tears and the accusations.

One man, after the Draft three months ago, had the audacity to claim that her name was never in the box. Alexandria knew it was. She put in an extra paper with her name on it every single month.

The fact that she was not her parents' biological daughter did not matter to those who hated her family, not until it was in their interest to claim that someone else should inherit the mayor's title after Anastasia Redmond's death.

When she stepped out of the school, the autumn air immediately chilled her down to her bones. Her mother's guards cleared the way to their car. The government-issued vehicle had rust creeping across the roof and hood, obscuring most of the original paint color. A side effect of life in a city next to the sea.

Her parents slid into the backseat, two of the guards taking the front. "Are you coming with us?" her father asked.

"I'll see you at home," Alexandria responded.

The mayor passed her husband a worried glance. "Will we know where to find you?"

A twinge of guilt twisted Alexandria's stomach. In the early months after Phillip was sent to Thaertos, there were nights that she did not come home at all. She would return to embraces from her father and questions from her mother. She knew they cared about her. The regret that she had ever made them think she was in danger would never go away.

"I'll be at the beach," Alexandria said with a small smile. An expression that meant, *I will be okay, I will be safe, but do not come looking for me.*

The mayor sighed, settling back into her seat.

Alexandria was alone on the road after the car drove away. She started her journey to the beach, hugging her arms around her body to keep out the cold. Music sounded in the distance as she neared the heart of downtown. Not for celebration, she knew all too well, but to drown out the thought of the mayor, her mother, announcing who would die. The faint taste of alcohol burned at the back of her throat, and she bit her cheek to stave off the craving.

Despite the pull of the music, she turned left, toward the shoreline. This was a night for memories, good and bad.

She would sit on the rocks that she and Phillip had climbed when they were kids.

She would kneel on the sand where they had a picnic on his last day in Kureya.

She would lie down and look up at the stars they were under that night when she finally admitted that she loved him, far too late.

TWO

Alexandria had the lingering feeling that someone was watching her. She trained her eyes onto the baskets of flowers in front of her, hoping that the tingling sensation along her spine would go away. It did not.

In the city square, a dozen or so vendors set out their wares, hoping to catch the attention of passerby deciding what to do on their days off of work. Surrounded by merchants and their customers, Alexandria was safe at the flower stand. Still, the uneasiness at the perceived attention settled like a weight in her stomach.

Stop being paranoid, she told herself, putting together a bouquet of sun-colored poppies. Amira loved the color yellow, and Alexandria knew the flowers would make a perfect birthday present. She had bought them for her friend every year since they were fifteen, when the only candymaker who produced Amira's favorite candy was drafted. The flowers had not failed her for five years. Alexandria prayed that the cheerful woman behind the stand, Isla, who had been a few years ahead of Alexandria in school, did not face the same fate as the candymaker.

As Alexandria handed the money over to Isla, the woman pulled her in for a hug. The action was unusual not because Isla did not seem like the kind of person to enjoy physical contact–on the contrary, the florist's warm and open nature was well known–but because Alexandria had never spoken to her outside of their transactions. Alexandria yielded to the woman's solid arms wrapping around her shoulders.

"There's a man over by McKinley's who has been staring at you since you walked over here. Do you know him?" Isla said softly.

Alexandria pulled away and pretended to drop a coin on the ground. When she turned around to pick it up, she noticed a tall man with pitch-black hair who seemed far too focused on the packaged cut of meat in his hand. The butcher, engaged in a conversation with another patron, did not notice the man standing there.

"Black hair?" Alexandria asked.

Isla nodded.

Alexandria tried to piece together where she might have seen him before, but her mind went blank. She had a prickling instinct that if she dug deeper, she would remember. "I don't know him. Thank you for pointing it out," she said.

Isla smiled in response but kept her eyes on the man over Alexandria's shoulder. "We all have to stick together, don't we?"

Alexandria dipped her head in farewell and started for City Hall. Looking back at McKinley's, she found the man had disappeared. Anxiety gripped her stomach. It did not dissolve until she walked through the door of the residential wing and locked it quickly behind her.

James's older sister, Elsie, was already in the kitchen preparing for Amira's birthday dinner. Amira worked until evening with Taylor, the mechanic, and though she tried to convince the group and their families to not bother themselves with any festivities, the mayor offered to host the celebration. It was not difficult to gather everyone, considering that James, Elsie, and their mother lived on the other side of the residential wing, and Amira and her sixteen-year-old brother, Sam, had an apartment ten minutes away.

After Phillip was drafted, Alexandria still invited his parents and two sisters to these gatherings, but a year of polite declines later, she did not know whether to continue. She had not seen them beyond a passing conversation at the market in the year since.

The scent of spices drifted through the air, warming Alexandria instantly. "That smells amazing," she said. She hung her coat on the hook by the door and ventured into the kitchen.

Elsie pressed her lips together. "I'm not entirely sure I made it right, but I'll take your word for it." She dipped a wooden ladle into the pot of what appeared to be beef stew and passed it to Alexandria.

The first sip of broth burned so much that Alexandria checked to make sure she did not lose a layer of skin from the roof of her mouth. She carefully blew on the ladle until she had enough courage to try again. Excessive salt stung her wind-chapped lips, but the meat was tender. Just the bite made Alexandria realize she was hungrier than she thought.

"It's perfect," she said. "How long have you been working on it?"

Elsie sighed in relief. "A few hours. You know my mother normally does the cooking, but she's still downstairs helping serve the weekly meal. Perfect time for me to decipher her handwriting for this recipe, when I have to make food for a party."

Alexandria chuckled, handing the ladle back to her. "Well, it worked." She scanned the mess of ingredients on the countertop. "I'll help you clean this up."

The woman looked like she wanted to argue, but eventually yielded to the assistance. They worked around each other, Alexandria placing cans of broth and cornstarch on shelves, and Elsie running back and forth between the stove, sink, and oven.

James interrupted their intricate rhythm when he walked into the kitchen, carrying a rectangle wrapped in printed paper in one hand and patting Elsie on the head with the other. Even though she was seven years his senior, he towered over her. He was not exceptionally tall; rather, she was particularly short. Their only similarity was the bright red hair that they shared, falling in loose waves past her shoulders and draping just under his ears.

"Hello, ladies," he said with a grin. He held up the wrapped rectangle. "I come bearing gifts."

Alexandria remembered with a jolt that she had not yet put the flowers in a vase. She hurried to grab them from the entryway table where she had left them, right before the door opened again, Mrs. Collins and Alexandria's father walking through.

Mrs. Collins immediately sniffed the air. "Elsie, did you remember the oregano?"

"Definitely," Elsie replied, sneaking the jar from the cabinet and sprinkling a few dried leaves—less than the recipe called for—into the pot on the stove. Production at the greenhouses had dipped in recent months as more trained workers were sent to Thaertos; soon, the spices would be impossible to find in the market.

Alexandria's father kissed her on the forehead before hanging up his coat. "Your mother is held up with work. Something important going on in Regia, I presume." His face morphed into what Alexandria could only describe as his "scholar" expression, the way he raised his eyebrows and widened his eyes conspiratorially when he was explaining an interesting piece of Keveldan history to his students. "She ordered us to 'not stop the festivities because the Dais stopped her,' in her words."

"The Dais?" It would not have been surprising for her mother to have to handle a crisis in Kureya on her day off, but a call from the group that served as the queen's advisors, all the way from the capital, was shocking. The queen hardly consulted the mayors for anything, only sending her ministers and head agents to check in on the state of each city every so often. "Did she mention anything else?"

Her father shook his head. "Unfortunately, no. But if Genea was attacking again, we would have heard more, I'm sure."

His assurance only slowed her nervous heartbeat a fraction. Seven years ago, Genea had launched attacks across Regia, killing hundreds of civilians. They must have placed agents in the capital years prior and waited for the right moment to ambush the city. Over half of the Dais ministers had died when bombs exploded in their homes. Darius Mendoza, the Prime Minister, lost his entire family on that day.

When Queen Evangeline decided it was appropriate to host another gala, a memorial of the attacks on their anniversary, the few friends Alexandria had made in the capital were either dead or forever changed. Even the mayors' children, who did not face the attacks firsthand, were eternally on edge. The sliver of friendship that they had begun to share amongst themselves had shattered. Alexandria was only thirteen, and though she knew that her peers were far too young to have caused the killings, it was hard to look at anyone in Regia and not question who had given the Genean agents a way in.

It was her first real taste of what it meant to be Mayor Redmond's daughter, and though she knew that she might be appointed by the queen to take her mother's place one day, she dreaded having to face anyone in the court, knowing that they trusted her as much as she trusted them: not at all.

James, Amira, and their families were the only people who did not seem to care what position her mother held. Maybe their parents did at first, but after watching their children become close friends over the course of primary and secondary school, they decided it would be fruitless to attempt to break those bonds.

Alexandria forced her face into a neutral expression, attempting to erase the fear rising like bile in her throat. It was Amira's birthday, and Alexandria would not let anything mar it. Not when she already had to ignore the empty seat where Phillip would have sat next to her, his arm slung over the back of her chair to make space at the crowded table.

She always longed for that close proximity to him while he was alive, but now that he was gone, the yearning for him to even be in the same room as her was enough to rip a hole in her chest that could never be filled.

Nearly two years, and she could not think about Phillip without tears burning her eyes. Though she was certain that she would never see him again, it was harder not knowing what had happened. If she knew for *certain*, had an official letter or a body in a bag, she could grieve and be done. It would still come in waves, hitting her like a summer rain, right when she least expected it. But she would emerge, not be held under by the chains of "what if."

Alexandria's father passed through to the living space, patting her shoulder twice on his way, as if he could sense the storm brewing in her mind. Squaring her shoulders and plastering on a smile, she took the bouquet, grabbed a vase from the cupboard, and went to work.

~

Sam spoke first as he came through the front door, breaking the group out of their respective tasks.

Alexandria and James, setting out plates and silverware for the eight who now fit perfectly at the table.

Elsie and Mrs. Collins, weaving through the kitchen, taking a cake out of the oven and stirring the stew.

Alexandria's father, grading papers from a stack settled next to him on the brown leather couch.

"It's not my fault the answers were written in the back of the book. The teacher never told us we couldn't look." Sam's low voice echoed through the entryway.

Alexandria looked to find Amira shaking her head in exasperation. Mrs. Collins met them first, pulling Amira into a firm embrace with a "happy birthday" before turning to Sam and scolding him for whatever he had done at school. A sheepish expression blossomed on his face.

After Amira and Sam's parents had passed away, their father volunteering to fight in the war years before the Draft and their mother falling ill five summers ago, Mrs. Collins and Alexandria's parents made sure the two were cared for until Amira graduated secondary school. Mrs. Collins especially made sure that Sam stayed in line, though it was impossible to miss the love that she had for the boy and his sister.

Alexandria often wondered if all their parents had made a pact, when the three–four, including Phillip–were still young, to take care of each other's children as their own.

Once Amira shrugged off her coat, Alexandria wrapped her arms around her friend. Amira's long hair twisted into a bun at the nape of her neck. A smudge of what must have been dirt or grease stained a patch of the brown skin near her temple, a line along her jaw. She had an edge of weariness about her, a day gone wrong in a week already tinged with sadness. They all bore the weight of the world in the few days after a Draft, but caring for a brother who was aging too quickly, nearing a year until his name would be put in the mayor's box, Alexandria knew that Amira felt it the most.

Alexandria held her friend until Amira pulled away. "A car nearly exploded on me today," she said with a hint of a laugh.

Her occupation had many hazards, and since Amira was the best at handcrafting the parts the old vehicles needed, she was first in line for the most volatile jobs. Not many people had a brain that worked like hers, able to visualize exactly which piece of scrap metal should be used and how it needed to be shaped and what coil it might be compatible with.

"Goodness," Alexandria replied, weaving her arm through Amira's, "You need some cake."

"I'll wait until after dinner. If I told Sam he couldn't eat dessert first, then I should follow my own rules."

"It'll be our secret, I promise."

Amira grinned brightly. "If you insist."

Dinner began, the group gathering around the table, sharing stories of their younger years. Alexandria did her best to ignore the slight pause each time someone mentioned Phillip's name, avoiding Amira's subtle glances. Amira was the only one who knew the confessions that she and Phillip had made the day that he left. James could have figured it out, but if he had, he never mentioned it.

A seat remained empty next to Alexandria, this one for her mother, who still had not joined them, held up by whatever business the Dais had with her. Tapping her fingers against her knee was the only thing Alexandria could do to keep herself from thinking the worst: that they were no longer safe in Kureya, that Kevelda was under attack, that they would all share Phillip's fate.

Death did not scare Alexandria, not in the way that she questioned what awaited her on the other side, but she would rather face it in a warm bed, surrounded by those she loved and who loved her, than at the end of a blade or with the bite of a bullet. Even worse was the thought of her family, by both adoption and the bond of friendship, facing the same pain.

The door creaked as it opened. Alexandria straightened, arms tingling with anxious impatience, waiting for her mother to tell them what had happened, though Alexandria knew the mayor was likely sworn to secrecy.

To her surprise, her mother immediately met her stare, not moving to take off her coat. "Alexandria, can I speak with you?"

Her mother's tone reminded her of what it was like to be a child. It was not cold or angry, but serious. A call to do what she said without question. A voice that had not been used since Alexandria was in secondary school.

Something was very, very wrong.

Alexandria met her father's eyes, but he looked as confused and worried as she felt on the inside. She stood and started around the table but did not get far before an alarm blared over the radio. Amira jumped in her seat.

"Citizens of Kevelda," Mendoza's voice announced, tinny and crackling, "It is with a heavy heart that I speak with you today. Queen Evangeline has died after fifteen years of serving her people with courage and compassion."

Metal scraped against wood as a fork fell to the floor. Alexandria grabbed onto the back of a chair, a lifeline tethering her to reality. *The queen is dead.*

Alexandria did not like the woman. When she thought about all the lives that had been lost in her war, Alexandria began to hate her, though she tried her best to push away that anger. It would do nothing besides get her in trouble, especially as Mayor Redmond's daughter, to hold contempt for the queen.

If Queen Evangeline was dead...

The queen had no heirs, no siblings. As far as Alexandria knew, the woman did not have any cousins nor any distant relations. *Would Mendoza take her place?*

The thought sent a shiver down her spine. Her only close interaction with the man had given her nightmares about the coldness behind his eyes. It made sense, after his family was killed, for him to grow cruel in the fight with Genea. But Alexandria had found herself down hallways she was not meant to explore, experiencing firsthand the control he held over his son and wife, far before they met their demise.

He never let the boy and the woman speak to anyone in the court. They stood silently next to him when he gave speeches, and then disappeared. Alexandria thought it might be for the best, that they were not pressured to build alliances, but then realized being a perfect statue had pressures of its own.

"Alexandria–" Her mother was cut off again by the Prime Minister.

"The investigation into the queen's death is ongoing. In the meantime, we will continue with the Campaign. To remind you all, the rules of the Campaign are simple. The heir must sit on the throne to ascend. If anyone wishes to challenge for the crown, they must come to the throne with proof that they have killed the heir apparent. There will be no repercussions for this action. Whoever wins their fight against the heir and makes it to the throne will become the heir ascendant and will be coronated accordingly."

Alexandria was five years old during the last Campaign. She did not recall Queen Evangeline's fight to the throne as it happened, but her mother had told her about it years after, a story she had overheard during one of the queen's galas, to prepare her for the kind of woman she would meet when she went to the palace.

Queen Evangeline, who showed mercy on a boy who sought to challenge her. Queen Evangeline, who turned her back on an enemy. Queen Evangeline, who drove her sword through that boy's chest without a second thought.

A strong queen, if the Campaign proved anything.

It's not strength if you only have to walk across the room to claim your throne, Alexandria thought.

The Campaign meant nothing, not really, when every heir was stationed within throwing distance of the throne before it even began. It was simply a show of cruelty, a means to give the people some hope that they could win the crown, but they were always the victim, never the victor. After all, the fight was on the heir's home field.

"This Campaign is unprecedented. Because the heir is not currently in the palace, the Dais has instated a new rule. The heir must be treated as a fugitive in order to encourage a quick ascension. As such, if anyone is caught harbouring the heir, they will be punished to the fullest extent of the law."

She held her breath, pitying whoever Mendoza would name.

"You may have questions about who the heir is. Rest assured, we received her name from Queen Evangeline before she died. They were her last words."

Alexandria did not know if Mendoza's voice cracked, or if it was just the radio.

Her mother stared at her, eyes wide with an emotion Alexandria couldn't place.

"Alexandria Redmond, your fight begins now. I hope to see you in the throne room soon."

As if he wanted to twist the knife he just lodged in Alexandria's sternum, Mendoza added, "Good luck."

THREE

*N*o.

The last time Alexandria visited the palace, she vowed to never return.

It was a month after Phillip had been sent to Thaertos, and Alexandria did not speak a word the entire time. If she had said what was on her mind, she would have been arrested. Or worse.

The Mayor of Lyrica's daughter, Marlowe, who was as close as she had to a friend in the court, could not get a word in before Alexandria headed straight for the wine tower, took a glass, and sat silently in the corner until it was appropriate to return to her room.

Alexandria regretted that last encounter with Marlowe now. She needed allies among the court, and Marlowe was the only person she could think of who might not immediately try to kill her and take the throne for herself. The girl always knew the palace gossip and maintaining connections was the only way to do so.

Alexandria's current position would be the perfect opportunity for Marlowe to have the ear of the most powerful person in Kevelda—or to become that person.

I'm going to die, I'm going to die, I'm going to die.

"No," Alexandria said, aloud this time. She dropped back into her chair. The faces of her friends and family were blurry, their words muffled as if they were trying to reach her from a different dimension altogether.

She tried to ask, "How?" She was not sure if the word even came out, but she saw her mother's mouth move in response.

Her parents had adopted her at birth. That much Alexandria knew for sure. She had never wondered who her biological parents were, not beyond a casual interest. Not even when she and her parents fought, or when the local newspaper ran an article questioning whether Queen Evangeline would appoint her as the Mayor of Kureya once Anastasia retired, since she was not a Redmond by blood.

It never mattered to her. She was Alexandria Redmond. No matter who had given her up right after her birth, she was a *Redmond.*

Now, she was forced to acknowledge that her parents might not have told her the full story. That, while she thought they had been honest with her as early as they could, they had kept a sliver of a secret, one that would surface twenty years later. One that would kill her.

She would not survive the Campaign. If one of the mayors' children had a mere second of combat training, they would have the advantage. Her mother had never wanted her to be the type who would kill the heir to take the throne, and Alexandria would not have desired that anyway.

A queen had stolen her love away from her. Becoming the queen would be a betrayal of everything Alexandria believed about herself. Power *always* corrupts, no matter who it is.

I don't have to worry about that, she thought. *I'll be dead by morning.*

The ringing subsided. Her father was saying something, but she could not comprehend the words. She was faintly aware of Amira's hand on her shoulder, James sitting by her side.

"Did you know?" she asked quietly.

Her mother met her father's eyes, a look with such grief that Alexandria almost felt guilty for asking. Almost. "No," the mayor responded. "Not until they called earlier."

Her mother had been trying to tell her before the radio alert. Alexandria slumped back against the chair. "How?" she asked again. She wasn't sure what she meant by the question.

How am I related to Queen Evangeline?

How could I be the queen?

How will I keep everyone from killing me the second I walk out of these doors?

"We don't know. They never told us anything. The Dais wouldn't answer my questions." A sharp heat boiled under the surface of her words, not directed toward Alexandria, she knew, but toward her mother's own helplessness.

The mayor could do nothing to stop the Campaign. To save her daughter. Just as she could not save thousands of Kureyans from the Draft, from the war.

Alexandria could sit there and let a thronehunter come for her. She could make it easy for them. Let someone else ascend, take the throne, rule Kevelda.

But her family was here, and if someone came to kill her, would they try to protect her? Would they die for her?

She turned to her friends and their families. "You need to leave. It's not safe for you here." The words sliced through her heart like a blade. She needed her friends now more than ever.

Amira opened her mouth to argue but closed it in an instant. She nodded solemnly, standing from her chair. "Sam," she said to her brother, "go start the car. Take Mrs. Collins and Elsie to the apartment. James and I will meet you there."

Alexandria shook her head. "You can't stay. You'll get hurt."

Her friend's eyes held a fierceness she had never seen. "We're not leaving until you have a plan. Right, James?"

"I like a plan," James replied. His brows furrowed together as if he was already working through the situation, scouring his mind for ways that she would make it through unscathed.

Mrs. Collins gave Alexandria a long hug and kiss on the cheek. Alexandria said her goodbyes to Elsie and Sam, ruffling the boy's hair, even though he was far too old for it now.

If she ever saw them again, nothing would be the same. No more birthday dinners with their families. No more picnics on the beach. No more reminiscing about when Phillip was with them. If she survived, she would be a new person.

She would be the queen.

Will I even recognize myself?

The thought made Alexandria want to curl up on the ground and never get up.

She locked the door behind them, turning to face her parents, James, and Amira once more. Keeping her heart rate steady was her first battle. She had to focus. She could not think about all the ways she might die. She had to determine how she would live.

"I'm not going," she said at last. "They'll find someone else to be their heir."

"It's not that simple–" her mother started, before Alexandria interrupted.

"I don't want to be the queen. I'm not even qualified. I have not trained, or studied what the ruler does or how to handle international affairs. Let alone if I survive the Campaign."

"I have watched you hold the attention of the mayors' children. You have been playing court politics since you were a child, Alexandria, even if you did not recognize it."

Alexandria fought to keep her voice calm. "That's just it. We were children. At best, I rallied a group of intoxicated teenagers. The others may have been building their courts, but I was simply trying to find an ally to get me through the trip, so that I could make it back home to my real friends in one piece."

"I know you're scared, Alexandria," her father interjected, his eyes soft, "but you are more prepared than you know."

"It doesn't even matter if I can handle the court, figure out how to keep the mayors and the Dais happy. How do I survive my challengers? The entire kingdom has been set against me. Any person I come across could be my killer. *They* could be your new ruler," Alexandria spat out. Her mind moved faster than her words, setting her up for a spiral.

"You're making up excuses," James said, his tone like ice. Amira's teeth snapped together. Alexandria's father shot James a wary glance.

Alexandria felt shame then, if only for a second.

He continued, "You have the opportunity to save us all. You are the only person I trust to get us out of the mess that Queen Evangeline put us in."

"I can't save anyone." Her voice came out like a whisper, not with the same conviction that she believed the words.

James must have known exactly who she was thinking of. "Phillip needed someone to fight for him. To say that enough was enough. People shouldn't be forced to fight in a war they don't believe in."

The world spun around her. She tried to ground herself with anything, everything, but all she felt was the edge of the countertop digging into the palm of her hand.

"Phillip would want you to save people like him."

His words cracked something in her chest. Perhaps it was her heart, because it began to beat out of control. Maybe her diaphragm, because her lungs would not fill.

"Don't you *dare* bring him into this," Alexandria demanded.

James stood, leaning over the table. "That's exactly the anger you need to get through this alive."

"Hold on a second," the mayor commanded. "Now is not the time for you to hash out whatever this is."

Amira's voice startled Alexandria and James out of their staring contest. "You aren't the only one who lost him," she said to Alexandria, in a voice that was soft but strong nonetheless.

Alexandria's shoulders slumped. Guilt clawed at her chest. Her friends had mourned Phillip, but Alexandria numbed those feelings until she could never fully rid herself of them. She had forgotten that they missed him too.

"What do you want me to do?" Alexandria asked with none of her former fire.

The question was not to Amira, not really. It was to all of her family, to herself. To God.

"Don't decide today," her father said. "We'll keep you safe."

His eyebrows knitted together, harsh lines forming beneath them. Glassy liquid lined the bottom of his eyes. The expression wilted the last bit of stubbornness that Alexandria had. She knew there was more to his sentence. *For as long as we can. Until someone hurts us as we stand in their way.*

She had to find somewhere to go. But the look on her mother's face told Alexandria that she agreed with her father, and there would be no arguing about it tonight.

"It's best if you two go to the apartment," the mayor said to Amira and James. They both had known the woman long enough to not debate her, either.

Alexandria hugged her friends tightly. She and James nodded at each other, acknowledging that apologies were unnecessary. James had always been opinionated about the queen–even about the mayors, at times–and this was not their first clash. Especially since they had lived across the residential wing from each other for the past five years, becoming more like siblings. Alexandria prayed that she would live for them to have another argument.

She held onto their hands as if they were life preservers in a storm. Once she let go, she knew she would be pulled under the waves, and she might never resurface. She may never again hear Amira's melodic laugh, so rare now, or watch James bicker with his sister.

"I love you both," she said. Tears rolled down her cheeks, and she did not try to stop them. Not this time.

She wished she had never kept walls up between them. That she had not shut them out when Phillip was drafted. Amira was right: Alexandria was not the only one who lost him.

If she lived, she would ask them what those first few months were like for them, how they felt, and what she could do to make up for that missing time.

They both embraced her one last time.

"Don't forget who you're fighting for," James whispered, and before she could ask him what he meant, the two had already shut the door behind them.

She stared at the door for a moment, imagining that her friends were still there, that this was all her imagination, and that Amira and James and Mrs. Collins and Sam and Elsie would walk back in to celebrate Amira's birthday once more.

Alexandria's knees gave out before she could turn around completely. Her mother ran to her side, rubbing her back the same way she did when Alexandria had hurt herself as a child.

This was not a skinned knee or a bump on the head, and a bandage would not remedy her wound.

This was the fight of Alexandria's life, and the only thing she could do was cry.

FOUR

You have to find another heir," Mayor Redmond said. She was in no position to make demands of the Dais, and Alexandria was shocked at the force with which her mother did exactly that.

"Anastasia, I know that this comes as a surprise. It certainly was to the rest of us," Priyanka Agate, the Minister of Development, said through the phone connected to the wall in the mayor's office. "But we cannot change the rules of the Campaign."

Minister Agate was one of the few who took any real interest in the mayors beyond ensuring that they bowed to the wishes of Queen Evangeline and her Dais. Alexandria remembered her warm smile, the way she always made sure that she greeted everyone at the queen's galas.

"She is *my* daughter. *My* family. Her Majesty never took an interest in her over the past twenty years. No one has given us any information about how they're related, but the Dais expects me to just take their word for it." The conviction nearly brought Alexandria to tears. Rather, sent those tears beyond her eyelids. Alexandria had barely recovered from her breakdown four hours ago, when she had to say goodbye, perhaps for the last time, to her closest friends.

The mayor ran her hand through her curls, pacing as much as she could with the wired phone in her hand. She had the volume turned as loud as it could be, but part of Alexandria wished she could not hear the woman on the other line at all.

There would be no saving her from the Campaign. This was a waste of time.

"*We* do not have any information. Queen Evangeline never mentioned Alexandria at all, aside from passing comments when your family visited the palace. Trust me, if we had any inkling that Alexandria was not the true heir, we would not put you in this position."

This was true for Minister Agate because she did not want to put someone in danger unnecessarily, but Alexandria knew better than to assume the same of the others: The Dais would not want her to run the Campaign if she was not the heir purely because that would put the throne at risk. If Alexandria somehow made it to the throne under false pretenses, a true heir could come and challenge her later, at an even more volatile time. Even worse, another imposter could exploit the questions about her heritage and gain power for themselves.

Muffled sounds echoed from the line.

"Yes, this is her–" the minister said before being cut off by a man's voice.

"Mayor Redmond," Mendoza spoke, his words igniting the sense of dread in Alexandria's bones like a flame set on dry leaves. Surprise widened her mother's eyes, as if she too could not believe that the Prime Minister himself would want to speak with her. "Need I remind you that you are harboring a fugitive?"

Alexandria tensed where she was sitting in the chair behind her mother's desk.

Without seeing his face, the man did not carry any of his usual charm. Alexandria learned to see past the way he smiled out at audiences after she caught him hitting his son in the palace hallway, noting that his grin never reached his eyes. His golden-brown eyes and fatherly expression made him seem trustworthy, but Alexandria could not believe a word he said. Especially when he praised Kevelda's performance in the war with Genea, or when he thanked those who "bravely fought," even though they did not have a choice in the matter.

"I mean no disrespect, sir, but I am protecting my daughter." Being in the same room as her mother's gritted teeth, Alexandria knew that her mother meant all disrespect. "I would do anything to keep her safe. You must know how that feels."

Fingers clutching the seat beneath her, Alexandria leaned closer to the phone, desperate to hear Mendoza's next words. She shot her mother a warning glance, but the woman stared at the other side of the room.

"I know exactly how that feels." A dangerous pause. "I know how it feels to carry my boy bleeding from the one place that he was supposed to be safe. I know how it feels to bury a child. This is why we need an heir on the throne–to keep Kevelda safe." It was almost convincing enough to believe the pain in his voice. Almost.

A young boy being smacked across the cheek. A woman standing in silence.

"Let me speak to Alexandria," he said.

Every diplomatic grace that the mayor had taught Alexandria disappeared as the woman spoke. "You have nothing to say to her."

"Mayor Redmond, would you like to lose your daughter *and* your position?"

It was not a threat. It was simply the truth. She toed the line of treason with her questions and demands, her insubordination.

"Give me the phone," Alexandria said, working the device from her mother's hands, her fingers now slack around it. "Hello, Prime Minister." She fought to keep her voice steady as she screamed in her thoughts.

"Alexandria," he said, too cheerfully. The persona disappeared soon after. "If you do not begin to make your way to Regia, your friends and family will be caught in the crossfire."

"I presume you'll make that happen."

"It seems I have to remind both of the Redmond women to watch their tones."

Her blood boiled. The Prime Minister could do nothing to her, not when she was already condemned to be hunted and slaughtered like an animal. "If you have nothing new to say, I have more important things to do."

She slammed the phone back onto its hook and pressed the palms of her hands against her temples for a moment before walking out of the mayor's office.

"What did he say to you?" her mother called after her, but Alexandria was in no position to answer.

Her chest heaved, desperate to take in a breath. She stormed through the foyer of City Hall on the way to the residential wing. Stars danced across the papered walls. Alexandria had to make it there before she passed out. Her legs had already begun to shake, the lack of oxygen making her limbs tingle.

A force slammed into her left side. Her head nearly collided with the wall, shoulder and elbow taking the brunt of the crash. She twisted toward whatever hit her, only to find a man.

He was not much taller than her, but his arms were packed with muscle. A factory worker, or maybe one of those men who cut down trees for the winter firewood. She could not decide whether his hair was primarily gray or brown. She did not care once she saw the knife in his hand.

With one second to decide her next move, she pushed to her feet and dodged his lunge. The blade sliced across the back of her arm. She screamed as she ran past him, half for help, half in blinding pain.

He caught her by her hair, twisting it in his fist as he pulled her head back. To her surprise, he didn't immediately plunge the knife into her back. His chest pressed flat against her spine.

"My son was eighteen when your mother called his name. It was his first Draft." Alexandria flinched at the spit that landed on her cheek. "I don't trust any one of you to bring him back."

Even in his fury, the man hesitated. Alexandria took the chance to speak, rambling to give herself a few more moments alive. "My best friend was nineteen. I loved him. He could have done so much more with his life, but he was sent to die. I would rather him be here, rather him live a life and get married to someone else and have children and grow old, and I be the one dead in Thaertos. Actually, I would much rather join him now. So go ahead, kill m–"

Glass shattered, and Alexandria stumbled forward.

Her mother stood where the two had previously been, the man slumped on the ground. Shards of glass scattered around him. Blood trickled from the back of his head. Gripped in her mother's hands was the bottom of a vase, edges jagged from where it struck him.

The two shared a heavy glance. A weight tugged at Alexandria's core. Her mother had heard everything.

"Promise me that you will fight," her mother said, a plea and an imperative. "Not because I need you to be the queen, but because I need you alive."

Alexandria said nothing at all as they hurried to the residential wing and locked the door behind them.

~

Sheer desperation forced Alexandria out of bed. Her parents were sleeping, though she knew their rest would be as fitful as her own. She packed a backpack as quietly as she could, gathering an extra pair of clothes, some canned vegetables and dried meat from the pantry, and a canteen of water.

Her parents had vowed to protect her, even in light of the threat that came with Mendoza's warning. The mayor asking her guards to escort the man who attacked Alexandria off the property signaled to the Dais that she would shelter her daughter despite the rules against it. The law dictated that they could not harbour her, not if they wanted to keep their positions. Not if they didn't want to be imprisoned or face a much crueler punishment. Shielding her from the Campaign was an act of treason.

Kevelda needed an heir on the throne, whether it was her or whoever would eventually kill her.

The Dais would not rest until she was on the run.

Reporters would follow her as best as they could to give the public their best chance at finding her. Alexandria did not doubt that the Dais had scouts of their own to leak her location at any given moment.

The Campaign may have been created to show the heir's strength, but for someone who did not grow up in the palace, was not trained in combat, and had to travel across the entire kingdom to make it to the throne, it was destined to kill her.

At best, Alexandria prayed that it would be quick. She prayed that her death would be painless. She prayed for a way out, even though the chances of that seemed slimmer by the second.

Though Alexandria did not understand the reason that she was still alive, that she was put in this position, she knew she could not remain at City Hall. She had to keep moving, take one step and then another. Her parents were not safe while she hid under their roof. Neither were her friends if the reports placed her in Kureya.

She had to leave, and there was only one place she could think to go.

Passed down among the generations in her father's family was a cabin on the outskirts of Hult, a small town a few hours southwest of Kureya. The town was not even large enough to have its own mayor, just a Chief Agent from the Argentum to oversee whether its people adhered to Kevelda's laws.

The cabin would be her haven. Its four walls would keep her from having to fight at all. She could survive, a certainly lonely existence, but it would be survival nonetheless. She would not face death surrounded by those she loved, but she also would not face it at the end of a blade.

Her family would be safe. She would sacrifice everything for that. Any chance of falling in love again, of celebrating birthdays with her friends. She would give it up if it meant that they would not be accused of treason or targeted by thronehunters.

She did not have a plan for what she would eat, or how she would pass her time. All she needed was a next step.

She was halfway across the threshold, keys to the mayor's vehicle in hand, when she thought to write a note. She let the door click softly closed while she found a piece of paper and a pencil.

Tears dripped onto the paper as she wrote down her final goodbyes.

To all those I love,

I am so grateful for everything you've done for me. For the time we've spent together. I love you more than words can say. I cannot tell you where I'll be, but I promise I'll be safe. You may not hear from me again, but I will always think of you. Please, keep going.

Though she knew the next words were not true, she wrote them anyway.

Mom, I will fight. I promise.

FIVE

As if her willpower had not already been tested enough, the car was almost out of fuel before she even began to drive.

Alexandria nearly slammed her head into the steering wheel, but she figured that wouldn't be very productive. She needed to move. Quickly.

Lights flickered as the city woke up around her. Only a few people were outside at this hour, mostly factory workers on the early shift and Argentum agents patrolling the area. One looked in her direction. Recognition flashed across his face before she sped through the intersection.

Even those agents were free to kill her. They were supposed to protect everyone, and she could not trust them.

In the rearview mirror, the agent stared back at her. He watched her until she rounded a corner, making her way to the fuel station at the edge of the city.

The densely packed white plaster buildings gave way to uniform, multi-colored houses, and finally, to sparse wooden cabins interspersed with tall, bending trees. The mountains loomed in front of her, but she would trail to the left before reaching them. Her journey would have her skirting the Icelands, a region of barren, icy plains, where few still lived. Marlowe's city, Lyrica, bordered the Icelands, albeit further south than Alexandria intended to travel.

She would drive to Hult, and she would not make detours—besides stopping to refuel, a task Alexandria hoped would not inevitably end in her death.

The rusted metal overhang of the fuel station swayed in the wind. Dirt stained the once-white building behind it, which did not seem to be faring much better.

Pain trickled along the cut on her arm as she pulled her coat on. Her hood did not do much to hide her face, but she prayed it would be enough as she walked into the building and made her way to the attendant.

Wrinkles lined his forehead, a scruffy beard trailing his jaw. When he met her eyes, no recognition formed there. If he did know who she was, he did not seem to care much. Alexandria sighed in relief.

"Long trip?" the attendant asked in a gravelly voice, after she handed him enough money to cover a full tank.

"Seeing family," Alexandria responded. She supposed it was true. There would be photographs of her family all over the cabin. Pictures she would look at for the rest of her life and hope that they would be a sufficient replacement for the real thing.

The attendant placed the money into the register and started for her car, picking up a red fuel canister along the way. Alexandria followed him out, careful not to let the wind blow her hood down.

Adrenaline shook her limbs as she stood there waiting. The attendant went back and forth between her car and the stash of fuel canisters. After the second time, Alexandria nearly jumped out of her skin at every noise.

Another vehicle pulled up to the station, its grey exterior matching the winter atmosphere. Alexandria turned her face toward the mayor's car. She listened for a noise that would signify an approaching person, like fallen leaves crunching or the rustle of fabric, but it never came.

The bell on the front door rang. Out of the corner of her eye, she saw a woman standing in front of the register, waiting for the attendant who had just come outside with the third fuel canister.

She did not watch the man as he funneled the fuel into the tank. Trees danced in the reflections on the car window. The wind whistled in her ears, sounding too human for her comfort.

"Alright–" the attendant began, before he was cut off by a loud thunk.

Alexandria jumped back. The woman stood where the attendant had been, his body now limp on the ground. A metal tack-like contraption stuck out from his neck. His chest rose and fell, alive but asleep.

The woman's voice was low and controlled as she said Alexandria's name.

Alexandria had already started to run.

She circled around the building, attempting to find a storage entry that she could blockade herself in. Rust kept the single door shut tight.

The woman gained on her, only ten steps behind her, but Alexandria's strides were longer.

How pathetic would it be if I died before I even left Kureya?

Her only solution was to topple the metal case of fuel canisters as she passed it. It was heavier than she thought it would be. Rusted flakes chipped off onto her hands as she pulled on its side and sprinted away.

A crash sounded, followed by several pops and thuds and a second of vivid cursing.

Alexandria would have smiled if she hadn't been scared for her life and quickly running out of breath. She panted, ignoring the stitch forming in her side.

Once the mayor's vehicle was back in sight, she used her final push of energy to bolt toward it. She crashed against it, her arms forcing her to a stop.

Her pocket was empty.

Alexandria shoved her hand into the other, scraping the lining of her coat. She fought down a wave of panic, kneeling to check the ground underneath the vehicle.

The keys were gone.

She pulled violently on the handle, hoping that she had forgotten to lock it, but she knew she had not.

Alexandria whipped around to find that the woman was catching up, though limping slightly. Dark stains splattered across her clothing. At least the fuel canisters had done something, though they had not been entirely helpful, given that Alexandria had nowhere to go, nothing to do.

Until she remembered the attendant and the metal in his neck.

A tranquilizer, she thought, already racing around the vehicle to where he laid.

His face was peaceful as she took the device out of his skin, crimson blood on the silver needle that had been embedded there.

She gripped it in her hand as the woman came to stand in front of her.

Dark strands of stick-straight hair staggered across her face, blown out of the tie that held the rest of her hair back during the chase. Her umber eyes squinted, stark against her pale skin, in an expression that mirrored confusion.

She thought I wouldn't put up a fight.

It was a decent assumption, given the fact that Alexandria's only training was a few self-defense lessons her mother hired an Argentum agent to give her after the Draft was enacted.

"Alexandria," the woman said again.

Alexandria lunged forward and lodged the dart in the woman's arm.

Those umber eyes rolled as she dropped to the ground.

Alexandria fell back against the vehicle, cold metal stinging her hands. She drew in a deep breath, and then another, and yet another still, before the temptation to faint ceased. Her heart thudded against her chest so forcefully that it hurt.

The sparse landscape inspired no ideas, gave no avenue of protection against the sight of those who sought the throne.

She could either run to the nearest train station, nearly a half hour away on foot, or she could find her keys.

Though she was hesitant to remain in the area any longer than she had to, especially with the woman passed out steps away from her, she chose the latter.

She wished that she and Amira had not skipped the daily lap around the track when they were children.

Her nerves did not rest as she circled the building. She scoured the patchy grass and weed-infested sidewalks, but the keys were nowhere to be found. When she came to the pile of fuel canisters, she rolled her eyes, dropped to her knees, and began to dig through them.

Arms burning, she pushed aside the canisters, not caring about the damage that she did as she threw them. Only after she remembered that the liquid inside was flammable did she treat them a bit more carefully. It would be ironic if *she* was the one to get herself killed by causing an explosion.

She briefly wondered how the palace would put someone on the throne if that happened, before she shook the thought out of her head.

By the time Alexandria reached the center of the pile, she knew it was hopeless. The keys were not there. She would have to run to the train, then.

She would deal with the problem of having to hide from the people in the seats next to her once she got there. Maybe she would disappear into the bathroom and remain there the entire trip to Hult.

The hair on the back of her neck stood on end. It brought her back to the flower stand, to the feeling of eyes on her.

Jolting up and twisting around, Alexandria swung a fuel canister at whoever was behind her. She hit nothing but air, and the velocity of the canister sent her falling back into the pile.

A man stood before her, black hair like an ink blot against the blue-grey sky.

Not just any young man, she realized. The same one from the market, staring at her now just as he had been from the butcher's cart.

She used the canister as a shield, holding it against her body.

"What are you going to do, throw that at me?" he laughed, a sound as deep and melodic as his voice.

He held out a hand to her, beckoning her to take it.

His laughter, joined by the gesture, caught Alexandria so off guard that she lowered the canister. It would not protect her, anyways. She might as well face death standing.

She ignored his hand, instead pushing up off the ground, scraping her palms against the rough concrete. Her feet moved into a fighting stance, arms in front of her, hands in fists. She forgot whether she was supposed to tuck her thumbs in or not, but she supposed it did not matter.

Broken thumbs would not bother her as long as she made it out of this alive.

"I'm not going to hurt you," he said. He put his hands out in front of him like a peace offering. "I'm your Protector."

"Does that line normally work for you?" Her voice shook more than she would have liked.

He smiled, a dimple appearing on the left side of his mouth. "Is it working for you?"

"No. Not at all."

"In that case," he said as he pulled a folded piece of paper out of his coat pocket, "maybe this will convince you."

A moment passed with her standing completely still, before her curiosity got the best of her. It did not seem like he was going to attack her, and even if she was prepared, she doubted she would make it very long. He was but a few centimeters taller than her, yet he looked like someone who had been training to fight his entire life.

The paper was thick and new, without the telltale yellowing of older documents in the mayor's office. Its creases were flexible, as if it had been folded and unfolded a couple of times. When she opened it, she noticed her mother's signature immediately.

This letter certifies that Agent Carter is Alexandria Redmond's Protector for the duration of the Campaign. The Protector is prohibited from pursuing the title of heir ascendant. Any harm to the heir caused by the Protector will be punishable by death.

It was signed first by Darius Mendoza in sprawling, elaborate lettering. The second signature was nearly illegible, but

Alexandria assumed it was that of the man in front of her–Agent Carter. On a third line, which looked to be drawn in later than the first two, read her mother's signature.

"I figured you wouldn't trust me, so I went to get your mother's signature, just in case."

Alexandria looked up from the page to face Carter, still unsure. But she could not ignore her mother's signature, which was signed exactly how she had seen it a hundred times. If the mayor was under duress, she would have left some kind of clue for Alexandria to unravel.

She took a deep breath and handed the letter back to Carter. "Good call," she replied curtly.

It would be good to have someone to help her stay alive, yet Alexandria had the feeling that the Protector would force her to go to the one place she refused to travel. Regia would kill her whether or not Carter was by her side.

She already had a plan. She did not need him to ruin it.

Alexandria turned away, walking without a destination. The keys had to be there. She prayed that she would find them quickly before the woman woke up from the tranquilizer.

"Where are you going?" Carter called, coming up beside her.

"Nowhere with you." She tried to outpace him, but he kept catching up.

"In case you've forgotten the letter you *just* read, it's my assignment to protect you."

"I don't need you to protect me."

"Clearly. Using her own tranquilizer against her was an excellent idea."

She stopped sharply, Carter almost crashing into her. "You were watching?"

"Of course."

"And you did nothing?"

He smirked, though not in a cruel way. "I had to see how hard my assignment was going to be."

Her hands clenched back into a fist. "What makes you think I want you to come with me?"

"I don't think that at all, actually." He peered over her shoulder toward where the vehicle was. She pushed away the urge to follow his gaze, not wanting to give him any of the attention he seemed to desire. "But I do like a challenge."

"You're insufferable."

"Well, you'll have to suffer me a little bit longer, because dart lady is waking up."

Alexandria looked back and saw what he had been staring at. The woman stirred, pushing slowly onto her knees.

"What's it going to be, Lex? Her or me?" He stood with crossed arms and an expression that told her he already knew the answer.

She huffed, grabbing him by the wrist. "Follow me," she said, "and don't call me 'Lex' ever again."

SIX

"Lexie?" "Lexa?" "Alex?" "Al?"

Alexandria had begun to ignore Carter's questions. She pulled her hood further over her face, training her gaze on the ground. The train station was not busy, but the few people who *were* rushing around made her lungs tight.

"You have to have a nickname," he said, leaning back against the wall.

She already regretted bringing him along. She could have made it on her own, though she did not doubt that he would have followed her if she had attempted to go alone. "No, I don't."

"Then I'll give you one. How about 'princess'?"

"There's nothing in the contract that says I can't hurt *you*."

"You're right," he sighed, though Alexandria knew he had that insufferable grin on his face as he said it. "That one's overused."

No one told her she would have a Protector. Her mother had not mentioned it the countless times she recounted Queen Evangeline's Campaign. And Alexandria definitely did not sign up to spend the rest of her life with a man who made her want to rip her hair out thirty minutes into knowing him. She tapped her foot against the floor, wishing that time would move faster.

The next train to Hult would arrive in two days, which was much too far away. Some thronehunter would recognize her, especially if reporters noticed the pair sitting in the train station for forty-eight hours. There were only three options: Regia–Alexandria had threatened to leave Carter if he bought those tickets–Lyrica, and Kirsk. Kirsk was in the opposite direction of both the places they each wanted to go, and though Alexandria was nervous about the reception she would receive in Lyrica, she held onto the slight hope that Marlowe would harbour them, if only for a few days while they waited for a train to Hult.

"Is 'Carter' your first or last name?" she asked, wanting to turn the attention away from herself. Although she had vowed never to speak to him unless she had to, she was tempted to find a topic of conversation that would rile him up, that would push his buttons the way he already so expertly knew how to push hers.

"Not your business," he replied. She faced him simply so that he would see her roll her eyes. He had already been staring at her.

"It's exactly my business. Everyone in this kingdom is trying to kill me, and you're supposedly the one person who's not. Give me a reason to trust you beyond a piece of paper."

She was not usually this forward, but being hunted warranted a change in character. It was hard to not think about what Phillip would be doing in that moment, how he would hold her hand as they waited for the train, how he would promise his life to hers.

In her heart, she knew she would not have let him give up everything he had in Kureya to come with her. He still had a family, a home, and though she did, too, she did not have a choice in the matter of leaving. She would not have taken away his ability to decide, even though the queen had stolen it first when she shipped him off to Thaertos.

"Call me whatever you want."

She would have to ask forgiveness for the only names she could come up with, so she kept her mouth shut and tried to think of anything else.

That train of thought led her back home, to the people she would never see again. She wondered what would become of her friends and family, what kind of lives they would lead. In her imagination, Amira would eventually come to inherit the mechanic's business. The current owner had no children, and she loved Amira like a daughter. James would get married to another teacher as he taught at the secondary school, and Mrs. Collins would love being a grandmother.

Alexandria smiled as tears sprang to her eyes. *They will be happy. That's all that matters.*

Even as the knife twisted in her chest at the thought of what she could never, ever have.

If she somehow survived the streets packed full of Regian citizens, who would be armed to the teeth and itching to get their chance at challenging her, and made it to the throne, she would not have a normal life. She would marry for political gain, if at all. Queen Evangeline never married, and Alexandria could understand why. Many kings and queens had met their downfall at the hands of their spouses.

No, there would be no love waiting for her in Regia. At least in the cabin she would have the memories of her parents to carry her forward into oblivion.

Carter's voice broke through her thoughts. "Train's here."

She slung her backpack over her shoulder and followed him outside to where a line of people waited to board. Nervous energy buzzed through her arms. She flexed her fingers to absorb it, but every movement generated more. Soon, her whole body would be shaking.

Carter took her hand. She jerked it away immediately, but he reached for her a second time. He leaned in and whispered, "Your fidgeting looks suspicious."

He was right: A few people were looking at her for a bit too long, trying to peer under her hood. She closed her eyes, took a breath, and laced her fingers in his, praying that the line would move before someone pulled a knife.

Carter had the wisdom to not make any further remarks, though Alexandria guessed that it took all his willpower not to do so.

When they reached the front of the line, Alexandria realized too late that the conductor was not just tallying passengers but was asking for names. Likely for the manifest, in case an accident happened on the train. Her fingers wrapped tighter around Carter's hand. She forced herself to breathe, to not let her voice shake.

"Name?" the conductor asked.

"Carter Kingston," Carter responded, and Alexandria stowed that information away for later. She wondered whether it was the truth or a lie.

She ransacked her brain for a name, anxiety making her mind go fuzzy. Carter squeezed her hand once, twice, as the conductor inclined his head in question.

"Gwen," she finally breathed. "Gwen Brooks."

Carter stepped onto the train first. Alexandria pulled her hand out of his as soon as she boarded. She followed him to one of the private cars, where they found seats behind a clouded sliding glass door.

"No one will bother us in here," Carter commented, tossing his coat onto one of the cushioned benches. Alexandria sat down on the bench that lined the other wall, embarrassed that she had not thought of this solution on her own. She assumed that she would have to keep her head down the entire time in the public car, not that she would have a chance to breathe before she would have to put her guard up again.

Yet her feelings about Carter were still undecided, and she imagined this journey to Lyrica would be anything but peaceful.

She took off her coat to use as a makeshift pillow as she spread across the bench and resolved to close her eyes.

Carter did not like the silence, however. "You don't talk very much."

She kept her eyes closed. "I can't imagine why."

"Aren't the mayors' children supposed to be diplomatic?"

Alexandria pushed herself upright, hoping to end this conversation before it began. She did not want to talk about being Mayor Redmond's daughter, not when she would never see her mother again. "Diplomacy has never given me anything but a headache."

He shrugged. "Allies are important. Especially for a future queen."

"You have a lot of faith that I'll make it to the throne."

"I have a lot of confidence in myself, actually." His brown eyes turned gold in the faint light streaming through the window, and they burned into her skin as if he was reading her thoughts. If he was, he obviously did not get the memo that she did not want to be talking to him, not even a little bit.

She had hardly slept in twenty-four hours, and she was not going to let him distract her from getting safely to Hult.

"I'm not going to Regia. Final answer," she snapped.

"You're afraid to die, I get that," he sighed, "but I promise that I won't let that happen." He cringed a bit as he said it, as if he knew he could make no such oaths.

"I'm not afraid to die."

Carter leaned forward, elbows on knees. "What is it, then? What is keeping you from fighting for the throne?"

She watched the landscape transition from sparse trees to flat land stretched out to the horizon. Shadows of mountains rose in the distance, blending into the clouds. Her teeth ground together, not out of anger, but because Alexandria did not trust herself to keep the question unanswered. She longed to justify her decision, to have someone understand.

It had been far too long since she had been vulnerable with anyone, and all her instincts told her that Carter was not the person she would start with.

"If you're intent on bothering me, ask a better question." It did not come out with the fire she wanted to feel.

He rested against the back of the bench with arms crossed, kicking out his legs in front of him. Alexandria shifted her body so that they would not touch in the small space.

"What would you have done if you were not the heir?"

She laughed bitterly, the force of it shocking her. "I didn't exactly have the time to figure that out."

"The fact that you can even say that is a luxury." Alexandria could not tell if he was joking, but the pointedly neutral expression on his face was enough for her to know that he wasn't. "Most people have to provide for their families. They don't get to think about what they want to do. They just do it."

"You're from Regia. Don't pretend that you had it any harder than I did." Talking about her life in the past tense made her want to scream.

"I signed up for the Argentum when I was fifteen." He still had that neutral expression, no emotions crossing his face. Alexandria admired it, desired that much control.

She resisted the urge to make a snarky response. Watching her tongue, she responded carefully, "I've been the mayor's daughter since birth. I likely would have been named her replacement by Queen Evangeline and become the Mayor of Kureya myself. If I had tried to figure out what I wanted to do, it wouldn't have mattered. I wouldn't disgrace my mother's name by denying that call."

She didn't tell him that she gave up envisioning the future when Phillip was drafted.

His grim smile did not reach his eyes. "Anything for family."

A solemn understanding passed between them. Alexandria's heart softened slightly, though she fought to keep her annoyance alive. He did not make it very hard.

"The best thing you could do for your family is take the throne," he said.

An angry noise erupted from Alexandria's throat. She laid her head back down on the coat and turned toward the back of her bench, facing away from him.

"See you in Lyrica," she said as she closed her eyes.

She did not fall asleep, waiting to hear Carter move. He never did.

The tingling feeling on the back of her neck remained, as if he was watching her the whole time.

SEVEN

Alexandria was still unsure how she felt about Carter as they made their way across Lyrica on foot, avoiding the gazes of the townspeople and each other. At least, Alexandria was doing her best not to acknowledge Carter's presence beside her. The Protector kept his head on a swivel, looking out for threats. It was possible that he was not thinking of her at all beyond keeping her alive.

When compared on a map, Kureya dominated the small town they were traveling through. Lyrica was hardly half the larger city's size, and with Lyrica's City Hall set dead center, walking from the train station would take a half hour at most. That is, unless they were attacked along the way.

Alexandria had never been to Lyrica, though Marlowe regaled her with stories of the city whenever they spoke at the queen's galas. Marlowe was a few years younger than her, not yet even old enough for the Draft, so Alexandria often evaluated her words as though they were a child's fantasies, or perhaps exaggeration.

As soon as she entered the city square, she knew her former assumptions to be a mistake. The City Hall was a white plastered brick building with a pointed red roof, dusted with light snow. In fact, the white powder coated everything around her, which made the entire city seem softer. Mismatched buildings spread out around the mayor's hall, an assortment of heights, sizes, and colors. Each was trimmed with golden lights, the kind that Alexandria only saw on Kureya's City Hall during the winter holidays. Beyond the buildings to the south spread a beach covered in black sand, a story of Marlowe's that she had written off before she witnessed it with her own eyes.

Kureya was beautiful in its own way, the hustle and bustle of the city creating its own rhythm, but Alexandria could only describe Lyrica as magical.

She must have made a sound of surprise, because Carter asked, "Never been here?"

"There wasn't any reason to make a trip," she responded, still in awe of the city. A group of children sat in a circle around a woman reading out of a book in the middle of a grassy square. A couple walked hand-in-hand, the man carrying a young child on his opposite hip. The sight tugged on Alexandria's heart, eliciting another bittersweet memory.

Amira had slumped down beside her onto the wooden bench in the middle of Tolan Park, which was positioned so that those who sat on it could look out over the sea. A line of fishing boats had docked along the marina, with more coming in as the sun began to set. It was five years ago, when Alexandria had her curls cut above her shoulders, the summer sun transforming her usually light brown skin a richer, deeper shade. She would try to cover the freckles on her nose and cheeks with powders she took from her mother's cabinet; they did nothing but cast her unnaturally pale.

"Taylor's going to let me come on as an apprentice," Amira had said. It would have been good news if she had not sounded so tired. Alexandria knew that with her mother being sick, Amira could not find much joy in anything. Worry aged her features well beyond her sixteen years.

"That's good," Alexandria had commented, "The woman needs help."

Amira did not respond. She had sunk back against the bench, eyes on the water. Alexandria nudged her shoulder with her own. Amira merely rested her head against her.

"The experience will help you get into university. Maybe even one in Regia," she had continued, wrapping her arm around her friend.

Amira sighed. "I'm not going to university."

"Why not? You're the smartest person I know." It was the truth, not just a platitude. Amira had been fixing everything from the mayor's telephone to the Abduls' vehicle for as long as Alexandria could remember.

"Mother isn't getting better, and Sam–" She had choked on the words. "I'm all he has left."

Alexandria held her friend tighter. Uncertainty had frozen her tongue. She had never been the best at comforting people, likely a result of having few real friends aside from the three who had adopted her into their circle.

The two sat there in silence until Alexandria said, "Yes, he has you, but you also have *us*. We will take care of you both." She was making promises on the behalf of her family, who she knew would agree, but even if it was only her alone, Alexandria would always protect her friend and her brother. They would always have a home with her, she had vowed.

If that meant taking care of Sam while Amira attended university to learn more about technology, or better yet, while she made a name for herself in Regia, Alexandria would do it in a heartbeat. Amira would never ask for that, though. She would bear every burden the world put on her, even when her friends fought to carry them alongside her.

Amira's mother died two weeks later, buried on the last warm day of the year.

The children in the park ran in circles now, oblivious to the two hooded strangers who walked past them. Alexandria cleared her throat, taking in City Hall once more.

"Have you been to Lyrica?" Alexandria asked.

"Once," Carter responded. He did not explain and did not seem to want to. But that had never stopped him from asking her questions she did not want to answer, and she was curious as to why the Argentum agent from Regia had traveled so far.

"What for?"

"It was my first post," he answered. To be sent away from home to a place he had never known at fifteen years old–Alexandria could not imagine it. The fear, first of all, but also the longing to return to a home that was no longer his. Contracted to the queen's commands.

When she was quiet, he continued sarcastically, "Come on, Lex, it's not a tragic story."

"Forgive me for thinking you're capable of emotional depth," she muttered.

He shrugged. "That's rich coming from the woman who has only displayed one emotion over the past twelve hours, that being complete disdain for the person who's here to protect her."

"That's not true," she argued, hoisting her backpack higher onto her shoulder. "I've also been tired."

Carter laughed. "Is that humor I sense?" he said. "Besides, 'tired' isn't an emotion. It's a state of being."

"I wish you would find another *state of being* far away from me."

Carter only laughed more. Alexandria fought the smile creeping onto her own face.

It was not difficult to do so once they reached the steps of City Hall and Alexandria remembered why she was there. Marlowe could very well try to kill her or tell the reporters her location. From what she remembered of the girl, it would much more likely be the latter. Marlowe would kick back and watch as thronehunters descended on her.

Marlowe was not vicious like some of the other mayors' children. While they would gather information on other families to give their parents an edge in the court–given the mayors' general lack of control in any kingdom matters, this typically included uncovering information that the mayors could whisper into the ear of one of the Dais ministers–Marlowe would spread gossip about the children's personal lives, stir up some drama that usually only lasted until everyone went home. Alexandria once again attributed that to her age, but now that Marlowe was older, would her desire for power over the court's social dynamics translate into a hunger for the throne?

Alexandria prayed that she would find a friend in the girl and not a bitter enemy.

I only need to survive the night, she thought. *Then I'll be on my way to Hult, and none of this will matter.*

Though most of her interactions with Carter had made her want to scream, the inevitability of being alone for the rest of her life made her want to ask him to come with her. He wouldn't, she knew. She was his assignment, and the Argentum would not look favorably upon one of their agents disappearing with the heir. That is, if he even wanted to go with her. It was much more probable that he would drag her to Regia if he knew where she planned to go.

Alexandria began to formulate a plan for leaving in the middle of the night while Carter asked for Marlowe. She hid in the shadows on the side of City Hall, shrouded by snow-dusted bushes. It was a terrible hiding place. If anyone saw her sitting there on the ground, they would think it more suspicious that she was crouched in the greenery than if she was standing.

She was pondering whether to move when someone grabbed her arm.

Alexandria swung her fist right into Carter's nose.

"I'm so sorry," she apologized profusely, hands over her mouth. She fought the urge to laugh, not knowing how else to react.

He held his nose, ignoring the small trickle of blood running onto his upper lip. "Don't worry about it," he said as he grimaced. "Nice punch."

"Why did you sneak up on me like that?" Though Carter did not seem mad, Alexandria's cheeks were hot against the cold wind.

"Did you want me to shout your name to the whole city?" He wiped away the blood with his coat sleeve. "I guess this assignment will be harder than I thought."

You have no idea.

"Anyways," he continued, voice a bit nasally, "I talked to Marlowe. She's going to meet us in the basement."

"And you know where that is?"

"You ask so many questions."

"You would too, if it was your life on the line."

"My life *is* on the line."

Alexandria stopped short. She had not thought about it before, but Carter's words struck a nerve. If he did not bring her to Regia, what would happen to him? She presumed that if she was killed, it wouldn't matter–that was the point of the Campaign, the chance to prove the heir apparent's strength. Yet if he disappeared *with* her, would the Dais hunt *him* too?

There was also a real possibility that he could die protecting her. Every step they took put him just as much at risk as it did her. Though he was assigned to be her Protector and his actions were not entirely of his own accord, Alexandria filed that information away, adding it to the collection of confused feelings she had about him.

Carter led her around the building to a square of wooden slats protruding from the ground. He pulled on one side, revealing a set of concrete stairs leading into darkness below. Alexandria beckoned him to go first. She refused to venture into the pitch-black basement without knowing what would meet her there.

He must have found a light switch, because the rest of the steps illuminated as Alexandria entered the basement and closed the wooden panel behind her.

The basement was built of even more concrete, spanning what must have been the entire length of the building above. Rows of metal shelves took up the center. Packages of dried meats lined them alongside boxes of grains and canned vegetables.

Alexandria pressed deeper into the space, wondering how Lyrica had this massive of a stockpile. Her mother kept a small storage of winter provisions in Kureya, but it was only enough to provide a few days' worth of food to those who needed it most. She had watched the mayor apologetically turn hungry people down in the heart of winter because they had run out of extra food.

A bitter taste filled her mouth. Marlowe's family had to have made some kind of deal with another official. Alexandria could not think of a reason for them to have this much stockpiled otherwise.

She would have been content if she knew that it was being given to starving citizens as their crops froze over, but labels stating that the food had been packaged years ago indicated that the Mayor of Lyrica kept the provisions for himself.

Alexandria froze in shock at the sight of rows upon rows of ammunition boxes, with weapons of different shapes and sizes hanging on hooks above them.

"Alexandria!" Marlowe squealed from behind her. Alexandria turned just in time to face the brunt of Marlowe's excited embrace. She had not expected such a kind reunion, and after taking in the storage space, her shaky trust in the girl wavered even more.

When the girl pulled away, Alexandria could not help but ask, "Where did you get all of this stuff?"

Marlowe's smile dropped at her tone. "*I* didn't get it anywhere, and I wouldn't know where it came from."

"'Wouldn't know,' or didn't ask?"

The girl's facade faded almost as soon as it had started. "Look, I'm just the mayor's daughter. You think he told me anything about this?" She pushed a lock of her long blonde hair over her shoulder. "And you can't tell me your mother isn't preparing for war. We all are."

Alexandria's mother was not preparing for war, at least not like this. Not that Alexandria knew of. And she was not going to let Marlowe convince her that the mayor was keeping something from her.

"So, you keep all of this here, even if your people need it?"

"My people don't need it." She leaned against the shelf nonchalantly, as if she would not care either way.

Carter sidled up to Alexandria's side. Marlowe's gaze flickered to him with an expression that Alexandria could not read.

"Anyways, you two can stay here, as long as you stop prying into Lyrica's affairs." The last part of Marlowe's statement was paired with a look that shot daggers at Alexandria. "But I wouldn't stay long. It's only a matter of time before Queen Evangeline's assassin finds you, and I'd rather not be caught in the crossfire."

Alexandria's stomach dropped at the words. *Queen Evangeline's assassin.*

She scolded herself for not thinking about it before. Mendoza had said that Queen Evangeline's death was under investigation, but Alexandria was too concerned with survival to connect the dots.

A smile formed on Marlowe's face. She knew exactly what Alexandria was thinking. That was what Marlowe did–stir the pot, control people's emotions. Marlowe could leave any situation with more power than she entered it with.

Alexandria stepped closer to the girl, who did not move a centimeter in response. She just smirked knowingly.

Marlowe had been Alexandria's closest friend in the court because Alexandria never thought she needed allies. She trusted the girl because she thought that Marlowe could never do any real damage, not with her gossipmongering and whispering.

But Marlowe had been the real danger the whole time.

She might not share political secrets, but she knew them. Whether she overheard or simply charmed others enough to tell her, the seventeen-year-old in front of Alexandria would either be the reason she survived or her downfall. It all relied on how she played her cards.

"Who assassinated Queen Evangeline?" Alexandria pressed.

Marlowe feigned shock, clutching her hands to her chest. "I don't know." Her eyes darted between Carter and Alexandria. She dropped her arms and deadpanned. "But don't trust anyone, Alexandria. Not me, not *him*," she inclined her head toward Carter and came up to Alexandria's ear to whisper, "not even yourself."

Alexandria stared at Carter, whose mouth hung open. He shrugged, mouthing, *I don't know what she's talking about.*

Since Carter had not killed her yet, even though she had most definitely provoked him enough to do so, Alexandria took the girl's words with a grain of salt. She couldn't help but feel, however, that Marlowe knew exactly who was going to try to kill her next.

EIGHT

It only took five minutes after Marlowe disappeared up the stairs for Carter and Alexandria to get into another argument.

"Are you seriously considering running for the rest of your life?" Carter seemed more shaken up about Marlowe's comment than she was. Though it was not apparent in his movements or expression, his tone was elevated, argumentative where it was usually laced with a joke.

"Regia was a death trap for me before, but now that I know the queen's assassin is out there, do you really think I'll just waltz into the capital?" Alexandria whisper-shouted back at him. She did not want anyone to suspect that they were down there, to hear voices and have curiosity get the best of them.

Truthfully, Alexandria's plan to hide at the cabin for the rest of her life was falling further out of reach with every passing second. If the queen's assassin wanted to kill her, too, then it would only be a matter of time before she was found. She wouldn't stand a chance if she was alone, not with her minimal combat experience.

The risk of going to Regia still outweighed any chance she would be attacked in the cabin. She had no leads on who the queen's assassin was, nor any indication that they were looking for her. Other than Marlowe's veiled statements, which she knew she shouldn't write off so quickly.

Alexandria needed Carter if she was going to survive. The thought of requiring his help made her want to rip her hair out.

"You must have a plan," he said, "One that's worth risking *my* position over."

She bit her lip, debating whether she should play the last card she had, or hold it to her chest for a moment longer.

When she hesitated, he continued, "Your only chance at surviving is making it to the throne. It's only a matter of time before someone kills you out here. Not *if,* but *when.* Would you rather die fighting for your crown or be killed like a coward?"

Rubbing her temples, Alexandria forced herself to take a breath. "Train me, then."

Carter stumbled as if he was not expecting her to concede anything in the argument. "We don't have time for that."

"I'm just supposed to trust that you'll protect me as I wander into a city where everyone wants to challenge me? No, thank you." She pointed her finger at his chest. "If you want me to go to Regia, then you'll prepare me for it. You *will* train me. Show me how to fight."

"Spoken like a true queen. Already commanding your soldiers."

The words rubbed Alexandria the wrong way. She did not want to be like Queen Evangeline. Not at all.

It was one of the reasons why she had to betray her entire nature to say, "Train me, and I'll go to Regia with you."

"We'll have to find a safe place to stay." He locked his eyes onto hers, studying her expression. Alexandria forced herself not to back away. "I assume you know exactly where that is."

She nodded silently.

"Where?"

"You'll see when we get there." She would not tell him yet, not when he could report it to his superiors. Alexandria did not think he would, with the queen's assassin possibly being among his ranks, but she could not risk it. Not until she trusted him more.

"I'll give you one week. Then we'll go to Regia."

"Give me two."

"Fine." Carter ran his hand through his hair and walked away without another word. He disappeared into the rows of shelves, heading back toward the entrance of the basement.

Alexandria roamed through the rows again. She was no longer curious about what they held; she just needed to get away from Carter.

He thinks he knows everything, she thought, *but this is my life, and I get to choose how I survive.*

Never mind that it was his assignment. If she was going to make it out of this without losing herself, she could not go to Regia. She could not risk becoming anything like the woman who had gotten Phillip, and countless other Keveldans, killed. She would not have that weight on her shoulders.

Having to live with the burden of those dead soldiers on her conscience would be worse than a slow, painful death.

By the time she reached the opposite wall, the tears in her eyes nearly blinded her. They rolled down her cheeks in an unrelenting wave. She muffled her sobs with her hand. The only thing worse than crying in that moment would be Carter hearing her doing it.

Becoming the queen meant nothing to her, because it still did not give her the power to bring Phillip back. Even if he was alive, the war was not over. Genea and Kevelda were still fighting over Thaertos. Queen Natania may also be a new queen, but Alexandria did not know if she would be willing to put their predecessors' fight behind them. If she was not, Alexandria would be forced to continue to make impossible decisions.

After the Fall, Genea thrived in ways Kevelda could not. Thousands of powerful individuals from the Old World had built shelters in Genea before the bombs destroyed their former countries, and while Kevelda had not been damaged by the fallout, Genea had the advantage of insurmountable technological wealth on its side. The fact that Kevelda still managed to hold off Genea in Thaertos stunned Alexandria, especially now that Kevelda's surviving allies, Duarmme and Victori, had joined the Genean Coalition. She wondered how much longer they could stand to fight against the more advanced kingdom.

The full weight of what it would mean if she sat on the throne hit her in that moment.

She would either be Kevelda's savior or their villain. The war would end at her hands, or countless more of her people would die. Alexandria would not–could not–face those odds.

No matter what it took, Alexandria would convince Carter to stay in Hult with her after the two weeks were over. She would need someone to watch her back if the queen's assassin or another thronehunter ever located her.

Cool concrete brushed Alexandria's skin as she slid to the floor. Though she was indoors, the basement did not keep out the winter chill. She hugged her knees to her chest, wrapping her hands into her sleeves. The tears had subsided, giving way to a numbness that Alexandria had not yet felt in the twenty-four hours since she was named the heir. There would be no changing her fate. She could only let reality settle onto her bones like a funeral shroud.

Fatigue finally caught up with her.

~

Something cold clamped across her mouth and nose, stifling her ability to breathe. A hand.

She stared into Marlowe's face, the girl's grey eyes squinting in concentration. Alexandria tried to scream. The sound came out only as a muffled whimper.

"Sorry, Alexandria," Marlowe smirked, "You're my only way to the throne."

Desperation surged into Alexandria's chest as it failed to fill with air. She drove her knee into Marlowe's stomach, forcing the girl off her. As she jumped to her feet, head still light from lack of oxygen, Marlowe gripped her leg, pulling her back down again.

"Carter!" Alexandria shouted. It was completely possible that he could not hear her across the length of the building. She should have stayed by him. She should have–

Her boot struck Marlowe's throat. The girl growled in exasperation, spitting strands of hair out of her mouth. Alexandria kicked again and Marlowe released her ankle.

Alexandria wove through the stacks. Footsteps echoed loudly behind her, gaining speed. The girl might not be as strong as Alexandria, but she moved faster.

She remembered the weapons stash too late.

Three short knives stabbed into her back, shoulder, and arm. Searing, burning pain followed a moment later, her entire body cramping as if it was being crushed inwards. Alexandria let out a low scream.

The pain dragged on for an eternity. Her arms spasmed, legs kicking against the floor she now laid on. She did not remember falling, only the heat of the sun gripping her veins.

Alexandria sobbed as the fire subsided. An unnatural soreness threaded her muscles. The stabbing in her back remained, though not nearly as agonizing as it had been.

Her nails dug into the concrete as she inched forward. "Carter," she whispered, dragging herself along the floor.

"Doesn't look like he's coming to get you," Marlowe commented calmly, "How unfortunate."

Alexandria remembered her promise to her mother. *I will fight*. She had not expected to actually keep it, but deep inside, she knew this was not the end. She did not want this to be her end.

Her muscles groaned as she flipped around. She tensed for another attack by Marlowe's device, but the strings still attached to her back did not seem able to do any more damage. Slowly, she pulled the blades from her back, finding small darts instead.

Marlowe kneeled on Alexandria's legs, holding her immobile. Alexandria pulled the closest object from the shelf next to her and threw it at Marlowe.

The girl was not fazed. She picked the item up and looked at it. "Dried fruit. That's the best you could do?"

She lunged for Alexandria's neck and wrapped her thin cold fingers around it. Marlowe was not strong enough to break her windpipe, but sheer motivation gave the girl enough willpower to cut off Alexandria's airflow. Her lungs throbbed as she struggled against Marlowe's grip.

A soft click sounded from above her. Alexandria opened her eyes to find a gun trained at Marlowe's head.

"Get off of her," Carter demanded. Upside down, Alexandria noted the stream of blood flowing from a short gash in Carter's forehead.

Marlowe pouted and released her grip, backing onto her knees. "I thought I hit you hard enough."

"Obviously not." Carter brought the gun closer to the girl, his finger on the trigger.

Alexandria struggled to inhale. "Don't–" she started, interrupted by her own choking.

"She tried to kill you. And me, by the way."

"She's a child," Alexandria wheezed.

"Murderous intent isn't something you grow out of." Her words must have had an impact, because he lowered the gun and glared at Marlowe. "Leave. Don't come back until we're gone."

Marlowe sighed, brushing out her hair with her fingers. "Fine." She looked down at Alexandria. "Don't forget me when you're queen."

Alexandria muttered, "Certainly won't." Muscles on fire, she pushed onto her hands, ignoring the tears that dropped from her face onto the floor. She prayed she would never feel that pain again.

She picked up the device that Marlowe attacked her with. "What is this?" she asked breathlessly. "And can you find me one?"

Carter nodded and reached out his arm toward her. She slumped against him. They supported each other as they crossed the basement, stocking up on food and weapons along the way.

"I could use that safe place right about now," Carter laughed tiredly.

Alexandria agreed.

NINE

They would have taken the train if the woman from the fuel station had not been talking to the clerk at the ticket booth.

Alexandria jumped back around the corner, dragging Carter to the doors. Once they were outside, Alexandria said, "She's here."

"'She' who?" Carter asked, trying to find the woman through the glass.

"From the fuel station."

"The woman you tranquilized?"

"Yes, Carter. We haven't been to another fuel station, have we?"

Carter threw his hands up. "I was just making sure." Though the wound on his forehead had already closed, red still stained the area around it. She softened thinking about what he had done to protect her, and then bristled as she remembered that she was currently in the need of protection.

"We have to find another way." Alexandria swore under her breath.

They both scoured their surroundings. The train station sat in the middle of a field, flanked by trees that grew denser farther from the city. It was their only option to make it to Hult, unless they could survive a hundred-kilometer hike in near-freezing temperatures with nothing but the clothes on their backs and the food they had taken from Marlowe's father's storage. Which they could not.

Carter started toward the parking lot. "I have an idea."

Alexandria followed close behind, praying that it was a good one.

When he reached a rusted silver car with an off-kilter bumper, he rammed his elbow into the driver-side window, sending shattered glass flying onto the ground. Alexandria took in a sharp breath.

"You're stealing a car?" she asked, glancing around to see if anyone heard or witnessed the break-in.

"*We're* stealing a car."

"That's not any better." Cars were not easy to come by, and most people could not afford them. Amira's mother had bought one with the meager money Queen Evangeline gave families of dead soldiers before the Draft, and Alexandria's family had been given one for official business. Whoever owned the car Carter was currently hotwiring might need it and not be able to pay for another one.

"You're going to have to do far worse things over the next few weeks. Save your guilt," he commented flatly. His eyes narrowed as he focused, connecting and twisting wires until the car came to life.

"I can ask forgiveness for multiple things at once," she replied. Alexandria looked around once more before she opened the passenger door and slid into the seat.

Though Carter asked again where they were headed, Alexandria only gave him one direction at a time. She was not entirely sure how to get to Hult from Lyrica herself, but the map of Kevelda she had taken from her mother's office provided some insight once they made it onto the highway.

It would not make any significant difference if Carter knew where they were going now as opposed to when they got to the cabin, but Alexandria stubbornly held onto the last piece of control she had.

She could trust Carter, she presumed, but she could not trust the people he worked for. The queen's assassin could be anyone in the Argentum; they would have access to the palace and would not be questioned for being close to the queen. If Carter was the queen's assassin, he would have killed her already.

Yet there was someone else who had found her twice...

"That woman could be the queen's assassin," she said to no one in particular.

Carter side-eyed her as he drove. "What makes you think that?"

"She seems awfully set on finding and killing me."

"Everyone is, Lex. That's kind of the whole point of the Campaign."

His use of the nickname grated her less and less each time. It was starting to grow on her, though she was loath to admit it. "What about the darts? No regular citizen has those."

He shrugged and tilted his head from side to side as if weighing the statement. "That's fair." He was silent for a moment. "A veterinarian could."

"I'm more inclined to believe that the woman who nearly killed me is an Argentum agent than an animal doctor."

"You're making a lot of assumptions here. For starters, you don't know that the queen's assassin is an Argentum agent, or if the woman from the fuel station is either of those things."

Alexandria sighed and fiddled with the map. "I know. I can't explain it. I just want it to all make sense. Everything seems more manageable if I can connect it, somehow."

"You need someone to blame. I get that. But as soon as you get distracted looking for connections where there are none, you're dead."

She dropped the paper into her lap. "I don't need you to remind me that I could be killed at any moment."

"Don't worry," he said with a wink, "that's what I'm here for."

"Reminding me of my impending death, or protecting me from it?"

"Both."

Alexandria folded the map up as neatly as she could–it would never get back into the shape it originally was–and stowed it in her backpack. Minutes stretched into hours, the silence accompanied by snowy plains and ice-covered mountains. While the view was beautiful, Alexandria quickly became bored of staring out of the window. She could not let her mind think itself into another spiral.

"Why were you assigned to me?" she asked at last.

Carter did not respond, and Alexandria thought he might not have heard her until he said, "What happens in the Argentum stays in the Argentum."

She laughed. "Oh, come on. I'm the heir. I have a right to know why they chose *you* above everyone else."

"You really want to know?"

Alexandria beckoned for him to continue.

"I was the best they had, obviously." His grin turned into a grimace as Alexandria hit his arm. "You have to stop punching me. Where's the contract? We need to add 'no harming your Protector' as a rule."

Alexandria rolled her eyes. "I'll stop when you start telling the truth."

"I've never lied to you."

"You're seriously the best agent in the Argentum? Queen Evangeline should've focused more on fixing that than fighting over Thaertos."

Carter feigned offense. "I can't work in these conditions. I'll tell them right now that I'm forfeiting the mission."

"Seriously, Carter." Alexandria tried to use her most forceful tone, but her words were still trimmed with a smile. In the safety of the moving car, Alexandria finally had a chance to relax. Carter might not be such a bad companion, after all.

Her thoughts wandered once more to how she would convince him to stay in hiding with her longer than two weeks.

"I worked my way up," Carter said. "Enlisted at fifteen, trained any chance I had. I took every special mission, even the mundane ones. Until one day, the queen made me a part of her personal guard."

"You were on the Queen's Guard?" Alexandria was shocked at first, but when she thought about it, the information did not surprise her at all. It made sense that the Protector would be someone who worked with the former queen. But if he was on the Queen's Guard, he had to know more about the queen's assassin. More than he was letting on.

"Yes, I was." He straightened his shoulders and turned his attention back to the road. Alexandria knew she had hit a wall with him. A topic that he would not speak about. She supposed she would act the same if he asked her about her past.

They had already evaded death twice–thrice if she counted the close call at the train station–by each other's side, but they had only known each other for a day and a half. Alexandria trusted Carter with her life, not with her story. She could not imagine ever telling him about Phillip, especially not about how deep their feelings for each other had truly gone.

She scoured her mind for another topic but could not ignore the nagging feeling that Carter was neglecting to tell her something important.

Two hours later, they drove past a sign with "Hult" written in block letters. The scenery did not change at all, no indication that they had entered the town beyond the post. Snow-covered trees lined the road so densely that light hardly shone through them. Only two or three rows of trees were visible, but the forest went much deeper. Alexandria counted on that.

An offshoot of the road trailed into the forest on their right, and she motioned for Carter to turn. The gravel path wound further and further until the main road was no longer visible.

"Stop here," she said as they neared a rectangular patch of packed dirt. It was a makeshift parking area for people who came to these woods to hunt or hike, if they had the leisure time.

"Now would be a great time to tell me where we're going," Carter commented. He searched the area cautiously, as if a thronehunter–or a bear, for that matter–might jump out at any moment.

Alexandria reached into her backpack for the map and a pencil. She tore off a corner of the map and wrote directions on it. "When you enter the trail, keep right. Follow it until you pass the ravine and make a left on the unmarked path. There should be a bunch of rocks. That's how you'll know to turn. The cabin is at the end of the path."

Carter studied her handwriting. "Why are you telling me this as if I won't be with you?"

"Because someone has to go get us food," she said. The one thing she had not accounted for when planning to stay at the cabin alone was finding ways to sustain herself without being seen. Carter solved that problem. "There's a market in town. Just go back the way we came and take the road until you find it. There should be a sign."

"I thought I was going to be the one in charge. I guess I underestimated you." He folded up the torn piece of paper and put it in his pocket.

Alexandria pat his shoulder in mock reassurance. "You'll get there eventually. Besides, it gives you the chance to lose anyone who might be on our trail." She opened the car door and jumped outside into the chilly air.

"Anything else? Or will there be more surprises?" Carter leaned on the center console and asked through the opening.

"You tell me everything from now on, and I'll be completely honest with you in return."

She expected him to laugh it off, but he reached out his hand. "Deal." Alexandria took his hand with her own and shook it.

"Deal," she replied.

She started into the forest, looking back only at the sound of the car rumbling as Carter drove away.

TEN

The forest grew so dense that it would have been impossible to differentiate which direction a person was headed in if the trail had not already been carved out. Alexandria strode forward, careful not to slip on the icy rocks. If it had been further into the winter, the area might have been unnavigable. Hult had not received much precipitation, and the path was rough enough that she would remain upright if she paid attention and trekked slowly.

Alexandria and her parents had hiked this path numerous times. Her father inherited the cabin, which meant that he spent many seasons exploring the wilderness around it. While they did not regularly hike from the trail to get to the cabin, since they could just take the gravel road a ways down to get to the cabin's actual driveway, her father had noted where the official trail connected to the one that his family had worn down for generations.

Longing clawed at her chest. She missed being here with her parents, yearned to be anywhere with them at all. Only two days had gone by. How would she make it the rest of her life without them?

She hoped it would get easier, but thought that it might feel more like grief. The pain would never go away; it would just become more manageable. She would grow into it, like a coat she would wear every time the cold came.

It would be the same as losing Phillip: a life without closure, but with the knowledge that she would never get it. That was closure enough, in its own way. She would not know if they lived or died, what happened to them after she left. Amira and James, too. With the mayor, she might hear news of her death on the radio, but for her friends, her father, no one would announce it to the world.

In two weeks, when Carter had left–*if* he left, Alexandria had to remind herself–she might feel it more. She might consider treating them in her mind as if they had already died. Bring on the grief early so that she was not wracked with it in a year or five, so that she would not second-guess her decision then, when the world had already moved on without her.

Mendoza would likely rule in her place. She doubted they could find another heir, not when the Dais could not even explain how *she* was related to Queen Evangeline. If Alexandria emerged in a few years, would the Campaign still continue? Or would she be able to return to a semblance of her normal life? Alexandria prayed that the people of Kevelda would forget about her.

A twig snapped behind her. She whipped around, looking for the source of the noise. There was nothing there. It must have been an animal, something small that could escape into the trees.

Alexandria knew better. The trees were so dense that anyone could be hiding in them. She was not going to take the chance.

Her surroundings blurred into a collage of brown and green as she ran toward the fork in the trail. Footsteps followed her now, the sound of crunching leaves a deafening cacophony as she raced blindly forward.

In a split second, she decided to turn left. Whatever she did, she could not lead her assailant to the cabin. She had to find a way out of this that did not put her future self in danger.

If she had a future self.

She continued down the trail before crashing into the depths of the woods. It would be more difficult for the pursuer to follow her if she made her own path. Her skin stung as branches sliced her high and low.

The sound of footsteps grew distant, but if Alexandria stopped, it would catch right back up to her.

She couldn't run forever. Her legs burned with the effort it took to navigate the roots and stumps and vines on the forest floor. Cold air seized up her chest, her lungs cramping. The ache in her bones from Marlowe's attack earlier in the day still had not subsided.

A tree came up on her right with branches low enough to swing herself onto. She braced herself for what might be the worst decision of her life and began to climb.

The foliage crackled more intensely as Alexandria hoisted herself higher and higher, the bark scraping into her hands. She bit down on her lower lip as a splinter lodged into her palm. Alexandria had only seconds to hide in the boughs and hope that the pursuer would not find her.

Please, she prayed, clutching her chest with one arm and clinging to the tree with the other. *I don't want to die like this.*

She peered down through the branches to the ground ten meters below. A man crashed through the trees, rushing toward where he thought she had gone. She was too high up to distinguish any details about him, other than that he appeared to be of average size and had grey streaks in his hair.

Five minutes passed without another sound. As guilty as she felt about the wish, she hoped that the man was lost in the woods and stayed that way, at least until she was safely in the cabin. She lowered herself branch by branch, arms on the verge of snapping as she made her way to the ground.

Quickly and quietly, she found her way back to the trail and turned toward the way she had come. Her senses were on edge, tuned into every sound and movement. She kept close to the tree line, hoping that would disguise her from anyone who might see her. Her heart raced faster with every passing second, as if the forest was an hourglass filling up with sand and she was about to drown in it.

At the fork, she started in the direction of the cabin. It would only take her ten minutes to reach it, and she felt every second as they stretched into hours of their own. She wondered how the man had found her. She had not noticed any cars following them down the road, though she supposed she had not been paying much attention. Her thoughts had been trained on what Carter might know about who killed the queen, rather than on who might try to kill her next.

Fear drove into her stomach as she remembered Carter. She had only heard one car. Perhaps he was safe, and the trees had silenced the noise of her attackers as they approached.

If they found him first, there was nothing she could do about it. She could only keep herself alive and pray that he would join her later at the cabin, with no knowledge that this had ever happened.

Birds called out to one another. Their chirps grated against her nerves.

Just a little longer, she thought.

Until she turned and saw a man shadowing her.

He was younger than the other, his hair a bright golden blonde. Freckles dotted his face, an indicator that he was far too close to her. The sun glinting off his dagger was another.

She broke into a run without hesitation. Her legs screamed at her to stop.

It was too late for her to change directions. She would lead him right to the cabin if she continued.

The sheathed hunting knife she had taken from Marlowe's stash banged against her thigh. In her backpack was the taser, but Alexandria did not think she would have the chance to reach for it before the man attacked.

When she came up on the ravine, she chose the knife. She planted herself into the ground, taking a fighting stance with her back to the river trickling far below. No one could come up behind her. She did not want the older man to sneak up while she was confronting the younger one.

A cruel gleam flashed in the man's eyes, a smirk slashing his mouth that told Alexandria he would enjoy killing her. For him, it would not just be an attempt to take the crown. No, it would be an excuse for him to justify the violence he had long wanted to inflict on someone, anyone. And she was the perfect victim.

Time stood still as he lunged for her, driving the dagger toward her chest. She gripped his arm to keep the blade from finding its target. Her arms shook in response, only a matter of time before they gave out.

She kicked him in the stomach, forcing him back a few steps. He ran at her again and she dodged to her left. The ravine was to her right now, her back exposed. She twisted to find him upon her once more. He took hold of her knife-wielding arm and pinned it against her back. She smacked his throat hard with her other forearm. He choked and faltered for only a moment, but the second was all she needed.

Alexandria pulled her arm free and drove the knife into his right shoulder. He bellowed in pain, letting go of the dagger. It fell to the ground with a thud.

Without a moment's hesitation, he tore the knife out of his shoulder and threw it over the side of the ravine. A crimson stain spread rapidly across his timeworn shirt. The man did not seem to mind.

That was when Alexandria realized how deeply he desired to kill her.

Her stomach dropped as he rushed toward her, hands splayed. But she had already been nearly strangled today, and she was not going to let it happen again.

She dropped to her knees as he reached her, tripping him over her back. She hardly had a second to stand before he pulled her to the ground.

His arms wrapped around her core as she struggled to free herself. She sent her elbows backwards again and again, to no avail. He breathed heavily in her ear. The sound made her sick.

She thrashed and kicked as he stretched out his hand toward the dagger in front of them. Once he had it, she would be dead within seconds.

The only thing she could think to do was throw them both over the edge of the ravine into the shallow water below.

Colors spun around her as they rolled, sky and ground merging into one. The cliff was steeper than she imagined. The man had let go of her, likely searching for a way to stop his descent, same as she was. She grappled for any kind of purchase, a branch or rock that she could cling to.

A long root jutted out of the dirt. She wrapped both her hands around it long enough to slow her velocity. Digging her heels into the ground, she came to a stop.

The man had not been so fortunate.

He laid at the bottom of the slope, halfway into the water. His body twisted and bent at unnatural angles. Alexandria could not stop herself from sliding the rest of the way down to him.

Red lines drifted into the stream from where his head had struck a large rock.

She hesitated when she noticed his chest moving, but the pattern was uneven and jarring.

These would be his last moments. Alexandria forced back the tears that stung her eyes. This was her fault. He attacked her first, but it was her choice that finally killed him.

She knelt at his side. "Father," the man choked out, and in that second, he looked no older than she was. Perhaps he was younger.

Father. She had forgotten about the older man and now knew exactly who the one in front of her was calling for. She should have run, should have done anything else, but her limbs refused to move.

She sat by the man as his gaze turned distant and his chest ceased to rise. An eternity might have passed before she moved next. Her hand reached out to close his eyes and mouth, but instead, she turned to the river and vomited.

Everything burned—eyes, throat, limbs—as she struggled her way up the side of the ravine. Dirt packed underneath her nails, red scratches covering her hands from the branches she had fought through.

In a daze, she limped to the cabin.

ELEVEN

Alexandria crouched down to grab the spare key from under the mat. It took every last drop of energy that she could muster to do so. Once the door was unlocked, she made her way over to the couch, her vision blurry.

I killed him, she thought, digging the heels of her palms into her eyes. It did not erase the sight of his lifeless stare, the awkward hinge of his jaw as if he was still calling for his father even in death.

Alexandria had become exactly who she feared. She had killed someone. It did not matter if she did it to defend herself. Queen Evangeline had done the same by sending Phillip to die.

Blood covered her fingers, turning sticky as it began to dry. She wanted it off. She needed to be clean.

It smeared on the dusty wood floor as she tried to stand. She could not take her eyes off the red stain. It settled into the grain of the wood, the ridges in her skin. The blood would never come out.

Once the tears came, they did not stop, even when Alexandria streaked her face with blood and dirt trying to dry them.

She had never been so utterly alone.

Her mind wandered back to the ravine, to the man who would never grow old or see his father again. To the father who was still searching for her, but would soon realize that he should have been protecting his son from her instead.

I did what I had to do, she repeated to herself, as if it would atone for her crimes. She would pay the price of taking the man's life for the rest of her own.

If she left the cabin, she might have to kill someone else. No, not *might. Would.* It would be impossible to make it to Regia without taking another life.

She was not willing to pay that price to save herself.

Hands found her shoulders. Alexandria tried to jump to her feet but ended up falling back to the ground.

"What happened?" Carter asked. He came around to crouch in front of her. His eyes were wide with worry, until he registered her tears and set his jaw. "Did someone hurt you?"

"How did you get in?" She could not answer his questions. Not yet.

"The door was unlocked," he replied. Alexandria wiped her nose on her sleeve. She did not know if the dark stain on it came from blood on her face or if it had already been there.

When she did not respond, Carter stood. "I'll be right back."

Alexandria stared at the floor in front of her, not bothering to wonder where he went. Her head felt awfully empty, the resulting fuzziness tempting her to scream just to fill the silence.

He returned with a tan cotton cloth dampened with water. In his other hand, he held a glass.

Carter gave the glass to her and told her to drink it. She took small sips while he blotted away the blood spattered on her skin.

He began with her face, his eyes narrowed in focus. A muscle twitched in his jaw as if he was straining not to ask her any more questions. She held her breath.

"I should have been with you," he said.

Alexandria shook her head, taking hold of his hand to stop him for a moment. "I'm the one who came up with the plan."

"Still, I–"

"Have you ever killed anyone?" Her voice was weak. She hoped he would say "yes," though at the same time, she did not want to know that he had felt this same kind of pain. It was as if a piece of her soul had fractured, a shattered image of the person she thought she was.

He nodded, lowering his head. "I have."

"Who?" It might have been another topic that put his walls up, but she needed him to talk to her. Otherwise, she might fall into a silence she could never climb out of.

A part of her would remain in the ravine, always trying to think her way out.

Carter sighed and sat by her side. "It's part of the job description."

She had not thought of that when she met him, nor did she want to think further about the fact that the man assigned to keep her alive had probably killed numerous people at the queen's orders.

"The first is always the worst," he continued.

"I don't plan to have a second."

He looked at her as if he was finally putting the pieces together. His eyes softened, though the tension in his jaw remained. "I hope you won't have to," he said, and Alexandria knew it was genuine. His plan to take her to Regia would force her into that position, though.

She reached for the cloth, rubbing the scrapes on her hands, but he took over before she could make herself bleed more. He worked across her skin gently, making the crimson stains disappear.

"My first kill was the person who murdered my family," he started, eyes meeting hers before focusing on her skin once more. "He didn't kill them himself, not exactly, but he was the reason why the Genean spies were able to plant the bombs undetected."

"They were killed in the Genean attacks?" She should not have been surprised. He was from Regia. Everyone there had been touched by those attacks.

"They were," he said, and he left it at that. Her hands were clean, but she didn't want him to stop. His touch was the last thing holding her together.

He rubbed his finger over the wet spots on her black coat. His skin came away red. She stared at the stains, realizing just how much blood had gotten on her. The blood from the man's shoulder, where she stabbed him before finally killing him. A shiver ran through her body.

The fabric against her skin suffocated her. Carter helped her take the coat off, sliding it over her wrist to avoid transferring any of the blood back onto her. He offered to clean it, and Alexandria could do nothing but nod until the bloodied coat was out of sight.

When he came back, Alexandria asked, "How did you find him?"

"It was an assignment. A few years after the attacks, the Argentum uncovered communications between him and Genean officers. I took the chance to avenge my family."

Her voice quieted. "Did it take the pain away?"

He stared past her. "No," he said, "it just introduced me to a new kind."

She knew that feeling all too well. Some days, the shame at how she reacted to Phillip's unconfirmed death was more painful than the grief. Both were equally debilitating. She had pushed her friends away, made them worry about her as she drank herself into oblivion, withered from the inside out. Forced her grief onto them when they already had to deal with their own, failing to support them the way they did her.

Yet this pain, the one from losing a core part of herself–the person who would never take a life, never even thought she would have to consider it–was too much to bear. It built up inside of her until the words spilled out of her, no matter how hard she tried to keep them in.

"I killed a man today," she whispered. "He attacked me. We both fell into the ravine. Only I came out."

Carter tentatively wrapped his arm around her shoulder. She leaned into his side, knowing that this would be rare. Once the shock had worn off, they would go back to their distance, their opposing sides. He would tell her to go to Regia, and she would try to convince him to stay.

"It was an accident. You were protecting yourself."

"That doesn't change the fact that he's no longer breathing, and that I'm the one who caused it."

"Nothing I say will make a difference. I know that because I lived it. When you're ready for forgiveness, I'll be the first person to give it to you." He held her closer for a moment before letting go. His hand grazed the bandage on her arm, peeking out from her shirt sleeve. "What's this?"

Her mother had bandaged the cut from the man's blade back at City Hall. Fortunately for Alexandria, the wound was shallow. Nothing like the pain of Marlowe's taser. "My first challenger gave it to me. Before you came."

"I'm sorry I wasn't there." A recurring theme for her Protector.

"But you were in Kureya that morning. You knew where I was."

"The Dais knew about Queen Evangeline's death before they told the rest of Kevelda. I was sent to find you that morning, but I could not contact you until the Campaign was announced."

"Why did you wait until the fuel station?"

"It hardly seemed wise to try to take you to Regia with the mayor protecting you. If I knew you were in danger at City Hall, I would've been there in a heartbeat." He stood and reached a hand down to her. "Help me put the food away?"

Alexandria took a deep breath before letting him help her up. His words seemed genuine, and she was not in the headspace to doubt him.

She was in the middle of stacking cans in the pantry when a knock banged on the door. The cans in her hands fell, clattering against the countertop. Carter held a finger to his mouth and walked out of sight.

A man shouted as the door creaked open. "Where is she?" he screamed. Alexandria squeezed her eyes shut, as if she could make herself smaller. As if she could disappear.

She needed to hear this. The voice of the man's father, the one who had chased her before she killed his son.

"Who?" Carter questioned, his voice unnaturally even.

"The heir. She killed my son." The man's voice cracked, Alexandria's heart along with it. It should matter that they both tried to kill her first. But her heart did not feel the difference between self-defense and premeditation.

"I'll help you find her." Carter's voice trailed off. Footsteps started and grew distant. The door slammed shut.

Her arms shook as she braced herself against the counter. She counted the seconds until Carter returned.

One.

Two.

Three.

Four.

She vowed to go after him if he was not back in five minutes. Three hundred seconds.

Eleven.

Twelve.

Thirteen.

Fourteen.

He could handle himself, she knew. It was his assignment. Carter was to protect her at all costs. The Argentum knew he was capable of bringing her to the palace alive. Still, her stomach twisted into knots as she stood there, the only sounds her echoing heartbeat and the numbers ringing in her head.

Sixty.

Sixty-one.

Sixty-two.

Sixty-three.

I can't be alone again. This was the life she had planned, completely alone, but she wouldn't survive it. There would be nothing remaining of her if she was left to her own thoughts.

At two hundred and fifty seconds, Alexandria was ready to go search for Carter. She had already started for the door when he entered. His face was devoid of expression as he walked to the sink and washed the blood from his hands.

PART II
THE HEIR APPARENT

TWELVE

You're going to have to hit me harder than that if you want to survive Regia," Carter said, holding his arms up in a defensive position.

Alexandria gritted her teeth. "Trust me, if I could hit you harder, *I would*." She tightened her ponytail, brushing aside the dark curls that bounced in her face. She set her right leg slightly in front of her, preparing to throw another fist, only for Carter to block it.

They had wasted no time in starting to train, using the near-empty garage as their arena. Alexandria did not want to sit still and bask in her thoughts for much longer, not when the man in the ravine's lifeless eyes watched her as she tried to sleep, and Carter already had one foot out of the door on his way to Regia.

She had spent the whole night figuring out what her plan would be while Carter had slept in the room that was formerly her parents'. Her room had remained exactly how she left it, a stash of detective novels in the closet and a stray shirt that was about three sizes too small in the back of the drawer. All of this left behind by the girl she was before the Draft, before the small town became less welcoming to the family that came in their government-issued vehicle.

"It's only a threat if you mean it." Carter smirked.

She lunged forward, aiming for his stomach. He blocked the hit with his forearm. Another strike failed and he grabbed her wrist. She launched her other fist at his face. His hand came up right before she made contact with his jaw.

His eyes widened. "A bit overzealous."

With her wrists in his hands, she could not move away. She tilted her head up to meet his gaze. "I'd like to actually be learning something. Besides, I'm sure you can handle it. You've been hit before."

For a brief moment, she swore his expression darkened, even though he laughed it off. "And you're sure of this why?"

"I've been tempted to punch you a hundred times already. You have that effect on people." The corners of her mouth rose, betraying her true feelings. Maybe it was the adrenaline coursing through her veins, but for a moment, she had forgotten both the past and the future and all the worries that plagued her.

He brought both hands behind her back, drawing her closer. Her heart beat faster, and her mind turned again to her plan to make him stay.

She had considered pretending to make no progress as he trained her and using that as an excuse for another few weeks in the cabin. The issue, she decided, was that she would have to come up with a new strategy after that time had ended. He might not even believe it, and then she would have wasted two weeks in which she could have truly learned how to protect herself.

In her current position, all but wrapped in his arms, she could not help but think of an alternative option. Perhaps she could get him to fall in love with her.

A laugh escaped from her lips. Carter's eyebrows furrowed in confusion.

She had read too many romance novels.

Option one, then, she thought. He couldn't force her to go to Regia. The only risk to this plan, at least for the moment, was being alone for the rest of her life, with only her guilt and longing to accompany her. No big deal.

"Something wrong?" he asked, eyes gleaming mischievously.

Alexandria wiped the smile off her face. "No."

He raised an eyebrow. "You sure?"

"It's just"–she sighed a little too dramatically–"It's useless. How can I prepare in two weeks for a fight some of my challengers have been preparing for their entire lives?"

She was not necessarily lying to him. That fear certainly existed in her mind, that she would not be able to survive no matter how much she trained *or* how long she stayed at the cabin.

"You can't," he replied.

She had not expected him to agree so quickly, at least on that front. "Then why are you so adamant that I go to Regia?"

"Because you have no choice," he said, letting go of her wrists. "You are the heir. This is what you must do."

Her voice rose. "The Dais can let someone else rule. I never asked to be the heir, and I refuse to be the queen."

"Life does not care whether you *want* responsibility. You just have to grit your teeth and bear it."

The one moment of peace that she had since being named the heir was officially over. Her body shook as she spoke. "There are hundreds of people who want the throne. I don't care. Let them have it. But I will not be their sacrifice so that they can gain power, and I will certainly not sacrifice myself to become the person that the throne will make me." She stormed toward the door into the house. "Tell Mendoza he can crown himself, for all I care."

"The Dais would not see him as legitimate if he bypassed the Campaign, and neither would other kingdoms," he argued, even though she pretended to be out of earshot as she entered the kitchen.

Cold water melted away the invisible dust on her hands as she stood over the sink. "I have no doubt he would make them bow anyways," she whispered to herself.

"What is that supposed to mean?" Carter asked from behind her. She jumped, not knowing that he had followed her inside.

She chose her words carefully, knowing that even if she was the heir apparent, Mendoza was currently the closest person in the palace to a king. "I saw the way he interacted with his family before they were killed. He acted the role of a loving husband and father, but he controlled his wife and son like they were pawns. If he could do that, who's to say he isn't playing a much larger game with all of us?"

Though she knew what she had seen that night in the palace all those years ago, she had no evidence. To accuse him of anything beyond that, of hiding a bigger scheme, was a baseless allegation. The only crimes he could claim were supporting Queen Evangeline as she sent her people to die and manipulating the kingdom into believing that the queen's war was for their benefit.

"You don't know what you're talking about." He faced the wall, leaning against the counter opposite of her.

"Do you?" she asked, even though he likely knew the Prime Minister far better than her. Her fingers twitched. The argument was futile. She did not even care about Mendoza; she just wanted to feel something other than fear, and she yearned for a way out of the fight she had inherited.

Even if Mendoza was as cruel a ruler as he was a man, she would not mind, as long as she was not the one making decisions that would kill those she loved. There would be no escaping the war with Genea, and as queen Alexandria would either have to surrender or send more of her people to their inevitable deaths. And if she stopped fighting for Thaertos, Alexandria doubted that Genea would let the matter rest. Queen Natania would send her armies to take over Kevelda. No one would be able to stop her then, not with the Coalition on her side. It was an impossible situation that she'd rather Mendoza be responsible for.

The creaky hinge on the cabinet door broke the tense silence as she reached up to grab a pot. She ignored Carter the best she could on her way to the pantry, bringing a can of soup over to the stove. The metal lid opened with a pop as she twisted it off the glass jar.

"If you're so convinced you're going to die, don't delay the inevitable." His words dripped with such conviction that she broke her vow to not look at him. "Go to Regia. Survive, or don't. Whatever you do, just get it over with."

She set the can on the counter with a clang that echoed through the room. "I apologize for the inconvenience of continuing to breathe."

His hand went to his forehead. "That's not what I meant."

Her anger bubbled out into scornful laughter. "Don't backtrack now. You'd rather I die so that you can go back to your life in Regia." Blood rushed into her cheeks as she realized how naive she was. "I can't believe I didn't think of it before. You're not a noble soldier trying to bring his queen to her throne. You're not even a good agent attempting to fulfill his duty. You just want me off of your hands."

He opened his mouth to speak, but Alexandria continued, "What, is there a woman back home? Some promotion you're looking forward to? Tell me, what's so important that you won't even pretend that you want me to live?"

The roaring in her ears blared so loudly that she did not hear whatever Carter muttered as he walked through the back door, slamming it behind him.

As she turned back to the soup boiling on the stove, a weight lifted off her chest. She should feel despair at the knowledge that Carter would never truly stay by her side, and perhaps she would soon enough, but in that second, she was grateful that she would no longer have to waste her energy on him. She built a wall around her heart, forcing herself to remember that she was nothing but an assignment to Carter.

That was what she told herself as she took fish out of the icebox and sliced through it with a knife.

Alexandria closed her eyes and leaned into the memory it evoked.

Phillip's fingers had closed over hers as she gripped the handle. "Let me help," he had said, resting his hand on her lower back. It was the day before he was sent to Genea, and Alexandria had prepared a picnic for her and her three friends to send him off.

It had been impossible not to think of everything they did as the last time they would do it with him.

He'll be the one to come back, she thought, more like a prayer than a prediction.

"I've got it," she said. "Go keep Amira and James company."

While Alexandria and James were usually the ones to clash, and Amira the one to dissolve the tension, her friends had been bickering the whole morning. James, in his hot-headed way, kept attempting to come up with ways to keep Phillip home, and Amira had rebutted that she would rather make the most of the time they had left with their friend. James had told her she was not trying hard enough. Amira had told him that he would regret not embracing this day for what it was.

"I'd rather let them fight it out." Phillip wrapped his arms across her chest, pressing his head against hers.

Alexandria relaxed back into him. She had been so frightened of her feelings for him all those years, that he would not feel the same way and things between them would never be the same. At the end of it all, she was going to lose him anyways. It was far too late for her to tell him that she loved him. It would only make goodbyes much harder for them both.

A tear dripped down her cheek onto his arm. He did not pull away. Instead, he kissed her cheek, his lips as warm as the summer sun. Alexandria had pretended to ignore it, even as her stomach somersaulted.

She finished cutting the bread and stowed it into a wicker basket lined with a faded tablecloth. Her fingers wrapped around his wrist, the touch sending shivers up her arm. It was the most difficult thing she had ever done, pulling away from him. The choice she would always regret the most.

The basket was as heavy as her heart when she set it into the crook of her elbow and said, "Let's go."

Alexandria could not bear to remember more, not as the soup boiled over the side of the pot and salty tears slid into her mouth. She dug her nails into her palms in an attempt to clear her head, but the red scratches she found there only reminded her of Carter. Of the way he had cleaned the blood off her skin with such gentleness and care.

She wondered if he did really care about her, or if he had only seen himself in that moment when she asked him about his first kill.

The handles burnt her hands as she moved the pot off the stovetop. She pulled two bowls out from under the counter and filled them both to the brim. Steam emanated from the soup as she carried the bowls outside to where Carter sat on the wooden deck.

He jumped as the door opened. "Here," she said abruptly, handing him a bowl. Carter nodded his thanks as he took it. "Once you're done, show me how to block like you do."

The edge of his mouth lifted in a sheepish smile. "Deal."

THIRTEEN

You're still holding back," Carter said, holding Alexandria's arms fast behind her back.

She struggled, wrenching herself free from his grip. "You're still insufferable."

"I know you can land a punch. My recurring nose bleeds tell me that much."

"You weren't prepared for me to hit you. I wasn't either." Alexandria tried not to feel bad that he was still recovering from her punching him in Lyrica. It was an accident. She also did not like him very much at the moment, not after their argument last night. Needing him to help her survive and enjoying his company were two vastly different things.

"Don't let your opponent prepare, then."

"How do you suppose I do that?"

"You're tall. Longer steps mean you move faster. Use it to your advantage."

"The few centimeters I have on the average woman won't make that much difference, and it certainly won't for any man I have to fight."

Carter shook his head. "You're missing the point. None of your challengers think you can win. You don't have their training. You're not as strong or coordinated as them."

"Keep going. You're really boosting my ego."

"You can't win, not if you try to beat them with their own strategy. But you're a surprise, Lex. You have been since Mendoza announced your name. Act like it. Hit them where they least expect it. It's the only chance you've got."

Alexandria kicked him in the stomach. He caught her ankle and she stumbled to the side. Her knee cracked against the floor, a sharp pain jolting up her thigh. She sucked air in through her teeth.

"Not enough of a surprise," she said.

"I've been trained to expect them. Plus, I know you more than your challengers will."

"You've known me for three days."

"You're easy to read." He extended his hand down to help her up.

She took it, the callouses on his palm rough against her skin. "Am I?" Without a moment's notice, Alexandria yanked him down to the ground. The momentum sent her sprawling onto her back.

He caught himself on his elbow beside her. A laugh bubbled out of her mouth before she could stop it. It died as soon as he joined in. Carter was not her friend, and it was necessary for her to remember that.

"Show me how to survive," she said at last. Gritting her teeth against her sore limbs, she rose to her feet. She did not give him the same help he had offered her as he stood. "You were fifteen when you entered the Argentum. What training did they give you?"

"It's been seven years. You can't learn all of that in two weeks." He tilted his head to the side as if weighing his options. "My first few years were painful. Lots of bruises, cuts, and a fractured bone or two."

Alexandria grimaced instinctively.

He continued, "But if I were to teach you what I know, without those injuries, of course, I would start with strength training. Do you have an ax?"

"There should be one in here somewhere, but I don't understand how that's related at all. Forgive me for not wanting to give you an ax."

"I should be the worried one."

"How so?"

"Either purposefully or not, the chances of you whacking me with it are high."

"Are you implying I have bad aim? Just add it to the list of insults you've thrown at me today."

"No, I'm implying you hold grudges."

Alexandria rolled her eyes and crossed her arms. "You basically said you don't care whether I live or die. That's concerning, coming from the one person who's forbidden from hurting me."

"I care about getting you to Regia. You have to be alive for that to happen."

"That makes me feel so much better."

"Don't take your anger out on me. I'm not the one you're really mad at."

"But you're the one who's here. Mendoza's not. Evangeline sure isn't." Carter flinched. "Sorry," Alexandria continued sarcastically, "*Her Majesty.*" She investigated a stack of boxes in the corner, pulling the ax out from behind it. It was not heavy, though swinging it might be a problem with the cuts on her arms and palms.

Carter took it from her and weighed it in his hands. "Picture their faces on a log. Maybe it'll make you aim better."

"You've got to be kidding me." Alexandria's father had always chopped the wood for the fireplace, or her parents bought bundles of firewood in town. Neither of those were options now. When the snow started piling up, they would need the wood to keep themselves warm. Eventually, she would have to do it on her own. Her muscles protested at the thought.

Handing the ax back to her, Carter backed away as she gripped it tightly. "Lead the way," he said. He remained a safe distance from her as she put on her coat and set out into the forest.

A light layer of snow coated the ground outside the cabin. Only a few centimeters deep at most. Winter would come soon enough. She would have to convince Carter to stock up on food again before he left for Regia, in a way that didn't raise questions about her plan to stay. Alexandria added it to the list of things she needed to figure out.

As they trudged through the tree line in search of downed trees and logs, the silence set Alexandria's nerves on fire. Birds chirped and leaves rustled, but every noise transformed into the sound of footsteps as they spun around in her head. Echoes of the man in the ravine, of his father, of the woman from the fuel station.

"What's it like, being in the Argentum?" she asked, breaking through the deafening quiet.

Carter tucked a small log under his arm. "Constant training and briefings, standing around for hours, waiting for an attack to occur." His voice fell flat. "Fascinating stuff."

"What will you do now that the queen is dead?" She tried to search his expression, understand his feelings about the queen, but he looked in the opposite direction.

Why do you even care? she asked herself. He would be gone in two weeks. A blip on the timeline of her life.

"Protect the next one. If you'll have me on your guard, that is."

"I'll think about it." She would never have to make that decision, anyways. "Tell me more about the Argentum."

"Are you asking for information about your future guard, or about me?"

"Whichever one." Her pace quickened as she took a log in her arms. "This should be good enough." They started their journey back to the cabin. When she spotted it through a break in the trees, the tension in her chest eased.

Carter began his story as Alexandria set out a log on a stump and swung the ax down against it.

"The second I joined the Argentum, I was no longer a child. Even before then. When the Genean bombs went off, actually."

Alexandria kept her gaze locked onto the wood in front of her. Her arms strained with every swing. The cut from the man's dagger stretched painfully. She focused on Carter's voice, ignoring the warmth running down her sleeve.

"I spent two years training before I was sent to Lyrica. The instructors made us fight against each other, and in my first match, they set me up with a girl a few years older than me who had already been training for a year. Wanted to watch me struggle, I guess. No surprise that I lost."

"Would have loved to see that," she said through gritted teeth. Her words came out in a staccato, every breath a punctuation mark as she swung.

Carter laughed. "I don't feel bad about making you chop the rest of this wood."

"And I'm the one who holds grudges?"

"I have a few of my own," he said. "I never had to be strong before I joined the Argentum. Not physically. Sometimes I wanted to, to protect myself and my mother, but it wouldn't have made much difference. After that first fight, I changed. I knew that it would take everything I had to work my way up, to punish the people responsible for my family's murders."

She paused, resting the ax on the wood in front of her. "Why are you telling me this?" He had told her about his family, about him killing the man who took them from him, but that was before their argument. There was no reason for him to open up to her now. Not when it would make her pity him.

"You asked."

"I needed something to block out the noise." She winced at how cryptic the sentence sounded.

"Maybe I want you to understand the choices I've had to make."

"I don't want to understand."

He covered her hand with his own before she could pick up the ax and swing again. "Take a breather. You'll hurt yourself if you're not careful."

She let him take the ax and dropped down onto the deck. The chill seeped through her pants. Alexandria did not realize how forcefully she had been swinging the ax until she stopped. Fire ran through her limbs, lancing up her back. If only she could figure out how to give herself a massage.

The blade whistled as Carter swung the ax through the air, splitting the log with a crack. "I thought you were going to make me chop the rest of it," she said.

"I'm not as cruel as my instructors."

Alexandria watched as he chopped the rest of the wood in silence. He moved efficiently, years of serving the queen giving him more control over his muscles than Alexandria would have in her lifetime. She caught herself staring and shifted her attention to the ground before he noticed.

They each carried a bundle of wood inside, stacking them next to the fireplace.

The rest of the night passed quietly. Alexandria predicted that the remainder of the two weeks Carter promised would go similarly. It would be uncomfortable, but it was for the best. She could not allow herself to hope that he would stay, nor would she grow attached to him.

They both retreated into their rooms after dinner. In the hallway, standing against her parents' door, he caught her attention. "More training tomorrow. Bright and early." His eyes displayed the strain of his smile.

Alexandria nodded quickly and twisted her doorknob. "See you in the morning, Carter."

Sleep never came.

FOURTEEN

Every morning for a week, Carter knocked on Alexandria's door at sunrise. His apology for what he had said to her in the kitchen that second night: giving her a real chance at surviving. She still did not plan to go to Regia, but she feared she would have to protect herself in the cabin at some point. Carter's training eased those worries, at least slightly.

While she would have previously put a pillow over her head and gone back to sleep, the night could not end soon enough. She barely slept at all, tossing and turning while she mulled over everything that she had left and lost.

Phillip's touch. The dead man's eyes. Her father's smile.

Even worse was the anxiety that gnawed at her stomach when she thought of the queen's assassin having not been caught. Regardless of whether the woman from the fuel station was the assassin as Alexandria feared, she was a threat. The woman had found them twice already, and if the reporters tracked Alexandria to Hult through surveillance footage or interviews with civilians, she had no doubt the woman would locate her and Carter again.

Her mind lingered on the assassin as Carter softly rapped his knuckles against the door. Alexandria threw back the covers and jumped to her feet. She pulled on a jacket and her mother's snow boots, secured her hair in a ponytail, and opened the door.

"Good morning," he said, his voice gruff. His eyes were less alert than usual, rimmed red around the edges.

"Early morning?" she asked.

He leaned against the doorframe. "The lack of sleep is finally catching up to me. How about we sleep in tomorrow?"

She would not be catching any extra hours of sleep either way, but she supposed she could distract herself until he was rested. "You're the one who wakes me up at sunrise."

"You never said you were opposed." A strand of black hair fell into his eyes, and she was tempted to brush it away, but figured that would be a strange thing to do. She stared at it a little longer before forcing her eyes elsewhere.

"We all have things that keep us up at night." It was intended as a joke, but her tone fell flat.

Carter finally swept his hair back, then grazed the stubble on his jaw with the back of his hand. "Sunrise it is, then."

Alexandria did not argue with that. She belted on the sheath with her dagger–a replacement for the one the man had thrown into the ravine–and followed Carter outside.

They had slowly expanded their perimeter over the past few days, recognizing that Alexandria could not stay inside forever. No one had found them yet, and they had encountered no danger in the woods surrounding the cabin. Snow piled on the trails, and while that would not stop a thronehunter that was truly invested in killing her, Alexandria was hopeful that it would deter at least some people from their searches, if the reporters had pointed them to that part of Hult at all.

Freezing wind bit at her face, but she did not mind when she saw the way the rising sun reflected off the snow. It cast the field around the cabin in golden-yellow light, the sun peeking over the tops of the trees. Her heart swelled with gratitude that she had survived to see another morning.

When Alexandria stepped off the last step into the snow, she sank to her ankle. "I don't think we'll be going far today," she called back to Carter, who soon joined her on the ground. "I hope this doesn't ruin your plans."

He touched the snow with his gloved hand. "I think I have a new one," he said.

Snow exploded off her arm. Her jaw dropped. "Not fair!" She knelt down and packed snow in her hands, cranked her arm back, and launched it as hard as she could at his chest.

Carter clutched his heart as if he had been shot. "If only you threw punches like that," he started, before reaching to make another snowball after he noticed her doing the same.

She dodged his throw, falling to her knees. The snow chilled her legs up to her thighs. Elbow deep, she pushed back off the ground.

"Here, let me help." Carter offered out a hand. Alexandria reached as if she would take it, but instead hit him on the cheek with the snowball she had clutched with the other.

"Not fair," he mimicked, his eyes bright with laughter.

Alexandria chuckled in response. "This is war, Carter."

"Is it really? I seem to have forgotten who the enemy is."

"Let me remind you." She prepared to toss another ball of snow when a crack sounded behind her. Carter threw his arms out between her and the noise as they both dropped.

Alexandria unsheathed the dagger at her waist. It nearly slipped from her slick leather gloves.

They waited in silence, the forest eerily quiet as the seconds trickled by. After several minutes with the only movement coming from a bird flying through the trees, Carter stood. Alexandria came to her feet, brushing snow from her pants, dagger still in hand.

When Carter had locked the back door behind them, they both peeled off their coats and boots. Alexandria immediately began to shiver.

Carter was the first to break the tension. "Your lips are blue," he said with a hint of a grin.

Alexandria laughed, her nerves still jumbled up. "It was worth it."

"I'm proud of you. You finally got in a *good* hit." He tossed the quilt hanging over the side of the couch at her. She wrapped it around her shoulders, but it did not stop her shaking. She was starting to think that it was not just because of the snow.

Worry grew like a parasite, worming its way into her brain. What if she was not safe in the cabin, after all? The sound in the woods could have been anything. It could have come from the bird that they saw. But it also could have been an assailant waiting for the right moment to strike.

"When you took care of the man who came here, did you hide his body well?" The question had been plaguing her ever since she watched him wash the blood off his hands, but there had never been a good moment to ask. They had been caught in an unsteady truce, and she feared that any serious topic would have sent them back into an argument. Yet there was something about the snowball fight that had relieved some of the tension, even if it did end in fear of an attack.

Carter's smile fell. He went over to the fireplace and kneeled to stack the logs. "Yes, I did. No one will be able to find it, not unless they're looking for him. They especially won't be able to trace it back to us." She sat next to him, crossing her legs in front of her. His eyes met hers, hands fiddling with a match. "You're safe."

"How can you be sure?" she asked.

"I can't say with absolute certainty that someone won't find us here." He brushed against her arm as he leaned back onto his elbows. "But even if they did, I have confidence that you'd survive."

Alexandria let out a sound somewhere between choking and laughter. "I'd place your bets on something safer."

"Don't count yourself out. You're too stubborn to die."

"Is that so?" She was starting to feel lighter, pushing her fears into the depths of her mind.

"You have an incredible will to live."

She toyed with the edge of the rug. His words were not entirely true, but she was not going to correct him. It would be much easier if she died. She longed to be with Phillip, yearned for the peace of eternity. She did not, however, want to be gutted or otherwise dismembered by a thronehunter with something to prove. "I suppose you're right," she replied at last.

"If you want to be sure, I can bring you to where I left him. I wish I'd had time to bury him, but with the ice..." He stared into the burgeoning flames, shaking his head. "No one deserves to be left like that."

"Help me bring his son to him." It was the only thing she could do for the man she killed. She could not bring him back. She was not sure she would if she could. He would still be a threat to her if he was alive.

Carter gave her an apologetic look. "The ravine will be dangerous. We might not be able to reach the bottom, let alone get back up."

"Please," she whispered.

He owed her nothing, but she needed him to do this with her. It was naive of her to ask, especially since their partnership was held together only by a contract.

His eyes softened, flickering with an emotion that Alexandria could not explain. "Okay."

They left the fire burning, knowing that there would be a chill in their bones when they returned, not solely from the weather. Alexandria led the way to the ravine, trudging through the thick snow. She listened for the sounds of anyone trailing them but heard nothing beyond the chirping of birds and rustling of leaves.

An icy sheen coated the slope that she and the man had fallen down. The river at the bottom had frozen over, the slow-moving trickle ceasing completely. Her breath caught as she saw the man's body, caught halfway into the ice.

From where she stood, his skin was pale, almost as white as the snow around him. His eyes stared right at her. He looked as if he was going to speak to her, to scream at her. If she got closer, she imagined she would hear him whispering: *Father*.

She moved closer to the edge, crouching, waiting for him to move. If it had been warmer, his body likely would have decomposed more. She had prepared herself to find him like that, half-eaten by maggots, but this was far worse. Then, it would only be a body. Now, it was her worst memory preserved.

Bile rose in her throat. The world swayed beneath her feet.

And then the ground disappeared as she stumbled toward the ravine.

Carter's hand caught hers as she choked out a scream. She kicked for a foothold, but the dirt was frozen solid. A nagging voice in her head demanded that she let go and join the man below. She looked down at the man once more, the distance making her head spin.

"Don't let go, Alexandria," Carter said, taking hold of her wrist with his other hand. She wondered if he could read her thoughts, or if he had seen her choice in his eyes.

His muscles twitched as she grabbed his arm with both hands, pushing up on the cliff as he pulled her over the edge onto solid ground. Oxygen rushed back into her lungs. She panted, choking on the cold air.

Her legs shook as she stood. Carter supported her by her elbows. She would not be able to get to the man's body, let alone bring it up the side of the ravine.

Alexandria broke into sobs. Carter caught her as her knees buckled. He wrapped his arms around her, holding her tight, whispering softly into her ear.

"I need to bury him. We can't just leave him here," she cried.

All her attempts to stop made her chest heave harder. She tried to picture the man as he lunged for her, the violence with which he approached her, but when she imagined his blonde hair, the only face that appeared was Phillip's. The man's family would have no body, no burial, no closure, just like she had none of her own. It broke her to know that she would cause his loved ones the same agony that she suffered by Queen Evangeline's hands.

"This isn't just about the body, is it." A statement more than a question.

She could not respond, fighting to breathe. If she could speak, she was not sure what she would have said. She simply clutched his back tighter, as if he was the only thing keeping her tethered to the ground.

"My mother had no funeral," he whispered. "There was nothing left of her to bury."

His words shocked her into a semblance of calm. Tears scoured hot paths against her skin. She sniffed, blinking back the ones that still threatened to fall past her eyelids. Her fingers were stiff with cold as she relaxed her grip on his coat.

He held her for a second longer before letting her go. As soon as he did, Alexandria bristled against the chill that he left behind. "I'm sorry," she said, her voice thick with the lump that lodged there.

In their eyes passed the understanding that once they went back to the cabin, things would be different. They could not erase what had happened there. It might never be mentioned again, the way they let their walls down, but it would always hold a place in the back of their minds.

They had a new contract, one that went far deeper than paper, and Alexandria did not know how she would react when Carter left her behind.

FIFTEEN

Alexandria lunged, pressing her forearm into Carter's chest.

They were practicing fighting with knives, using spoons from the kitchen drawer to avoid any actual injuries. She grabbed his dominant wrist in an attempt to wrench the spoon out of his grip. He pulled his arm free and twisted away.

Her next strike aimed at his side. He pushed his arm against hers to deflect the blow, knocking the spoon out of her hand.

Carter grinned as he rushed at her, narrowly missing as she dodged and rolled to the side. She came back to her feet in a split second. Instead of blocking, she swiped past him, picking her spoon up from the ground. With each step, her breathing became heavier.

"Good," he said, barely fazed.

She gritted her teeth, waiting for him to strike again. Their eyes met. His eyes always narrowed slightly right before he attacked. As soon as they did, she tensed, ready for the move.

He drove the spoon at her chest. She caught his arm and twisted it, pulling him so that she stood behind him, with his arm bent behind his back.

"Very good," he said, definitely fazed now.

Alexandria smiled, holding her spoon up to his neck. It was too soon to celebrate her victory, however.

He threw back his elbow, sending a jolt of pain up her side. She faltered just long enough for him to duck under her arm, wrench the spoon out of her hand, and pull her against him. She writhed, trying to break free of his grip, but his arms wrapped too tightly around her. He wouldn't budge.

"I win," he breathed against her ear. Her heart skipped a beat in response.

Alexandria escaped his grip immediately, putting as much distance between them as she could.

She tried not to sound breathless, but she had already been panting before. "I won before you did. If these were real knives, you'd be dead."

"If you say so," he smirked. Alexandria accepted the small victory. Against a real challenger, she still might have hesitated to strike a killing blow, but if it was a matter of life and death, the fight would have inevitably ended with her blade against a thronehunter's neck. She was excited to make progress, though she reminded herself that it was not necessary.

Only two days remained until their deal was over, and Carter had not mentioned anything about Regia.

Alexandria did not know whether to be worried or relieved. She certainly was not going to be the one to bring up the subject of going to the capital. Though she wavered on her decision to stay more and more as time went on, she was not excited to leave the cabin. Restlessness nagged at her, rather than a true desire to take the throne.

Carter tossed the spoon at her, and she caught it. "Again?" he asked.

"Let's take a break," she said. She needed a second out of the cramped garage to clear her head. "Stop while you're ahead."

"So you admit I'm ahead?"

She could not keep herself from smiling. "Whatever."

~

Alexandria shot up, staring straight ahead into the darkness of her room. The stale air nearly suffocated her. She needed to forget her dream, erase the image of her friends being killed one by one.

Phillip went down first, then Amira, then James. All killed by bullets from Genean guns.

A bitter taste crept into her mouth as she drew her door open. The quiet click as the knob twisted set her teeth on edge. The last thing she needed was for Carter to hear her and ask why she was awake.

Something always stopped her from telling him about Phillip. Maybe it was because she was afraid of saying anything critical about the Draft to an Argentum agent. She supposed she could get over that fear as the heir apparent. Even if she was not the heir, Carter did not seem like the type who would report her for such a thing.

No, telling Carter about Phillip would be a betrayal to herself, because she could not explain who Phillip was to her without breaking her own heart all over again.

Carter had asked who the people in the pictures on the wall were. There were a few of her father's father, and his father before him, all faded by time. But her parents had hung pictures of themselves with her, and of her with her friends on the couple of trips to Hult that they had joined her family on.

One displayed her and Amira sharing a cone of shaved ice during a particularly hot summer when they were eleven. She could not help but laugh as she explained to Carter that the cone ended up melting and bleeding through the paper around it, staining her hands purple from the berry juice that colored it.

She told him about James and Amira, about Sam and Elsie and Mrs. Collins, and even shared that her mother was particularly capable at fishing, and that she had taught Alexandria how to salt and preserve the fish they caught from the lake down the trail.

But never Phillip. Whenever he pointed to the boy with bright blonde hair and an even brighter smile, she changed the subject.

She had made a promise to herself, the night before Phillip left, that no one would ever know how she had loved–still loved–him. The pity in her parents' eyes whenever Phillip was mentioned in her vicinity was already too much to bear; if they knew she had wanted to spend the rest of her life with him as more than just her best friend, she could not imagine how they would react.

Especially since she hardly had the chance to express her feelings to *him* before he was gone.

The four of them had eaten their picnic that day on the beach, reminiscing about their failed secondary school dates and most memorable birthday parties. Phillip had lost a tooth at Amira's ninth birthday after biting into a slightly overcooked cake.

"It was already loose," he assured her as they sat by the sea, and while he had smiled, sadness settled in his eyes. They all laughed in a similar way.

Amira shivered. "I can't believe mother let me help her bake it. A big mistake, obviously."

They continued talking until sunset, and then Amira had to leave to pick Sam up from his apprenticeship. James left with her, avoiding an emotional farewell.

Amira had hugged Phillip hard and fast, a tear sliding down her cheek. She sniffed and brushed it away, hiding her eyes until she got in the car. James shook Phillip's hand and appeared to be ready to leave, then turned and wrapped his friend in a hug.

"Come home, okay?" His voice cracked.

Phillip nodded solemnly. "I will," he promised, though Alexandria knew it was a lie.

When Amira's car faded from view, Phillip reached for Alexandria's hand, and she did not hesitate to take it. They had never talked about their feelings for one another, but the words had always hung unspoken between the two. Alexandria was too afraid that it would change things between them and their friends, and she could not imagine losing any of them if her and Phillip did not work out.

Now, she was losing him, and none of those fears mattered. All she could do was regret the lost time.

They walked along the beach in silence. Waves crashed against the shore. A storm would likely come soon. She hoped that one would, and that it would be so turbulent that he could not leave. She would give anything to have another day with him.

Phillip sat down on the sand near the marina, the last of the fishing boats docking for the night. He patted the sand next to him, motioning for her to join. Their legs pressed together as she sat by his side.

She avoided his eyes, instead staring into the fading sunlight.

He brushed a curl behind her ear. "What's wrong?" he asked.

"Nothing," she said. Her laugh was agonizing. "Everything. I'm just scared, that's all."

"Scared of what?"

She finally met his gaze. His blue eyes glistened. He knew exactly what she was afraid of. "What's going to happen." Her fingers fidgeted with the end of her white cotton dress.

"Nothing's going to happen." It sounded like he was reassuring himself more than her.

She glanced back up at him. He was worried, but he would never admit it. That's not what Philip did.

"You're not afraid?"

He paused before answering. "I'm coming back."

She did not want to argue. He was lying to himself, to everyone, to her. No one came back from Thaertos. Her eyes welled up with tears, and she looked away to hide them from him. It would only hurt him to see her cry.

A radio played from one of the fishing boats as its owner anchored to the pier. She was glad for the music because it would keep Phillip from hearing her sniffle.

"Do you want to dance?" he asked.

"Now?"

He nodded with a smile. *His* smile, the one that lit up every room he entered.

She took the hand that he reached down to her. They put their arms around each other, not dancing so much as embracing and swaying. Alexandria longed to hold him forever. It would ruin her, how much she cared about him. But she couldn't stop. She would love him for the rest of her life, no matter how far he went, even if death separated them. That night would be the last time she could say it.

"I love you," she whispered, so softly that she was not even sure if he could hear her.

He tilted up her chin with his finger, holding her gaze. A single tear dropped from his eye onto her cheek, following the path traced by her own. His lips pressed softly against hers, a thousand unspoken words exchanged in the kiss.

It was every "I love you" they would have said for the rest of their lives, if only he was allowed to live it.

She moved her hand to the back of his head, pulling him in closer. He kissed her like there was no tomorrow, because they would not get one. Her heart raced and broke all at once, started anew in each second that passed.

When they pulled apart at last, he rested his forehead against hers.

"I'm coming back for you," he whispered, and she knew she would never be okay again.

~

Alexandria jumped out of her memories when she saw Carter sitting on the couch, an old book of her mother's in his hand, the fireplace lit in front of him. She nearly turned back to her room, but he saw her over the top of the page.

"Couldn't sleep?" he asked, closing the book.

"No," she whispered, even though no one else was asleep in the house.

"That makes two of us. Want to talk about it?"

She fiddled with the end of her hair. "Not particularly. You?"

"No." He shifted over, leaving room for her to sit next to him.

While her thoughts ran in a million directions at once, her legs carried her over to the couch, and she dropped down onto it. His wavy hair flicked up at the edges. He probably had not thought she would find him out here this late–or early, depending on what time it was.

His stubble was gone, however. A new cut slashed red against his jaw. He followed her gaze. "Knives don't make good razors."

She chuckled softly. "I could have told you that." Her fingers twitched to run across the scratch. "Did you put anything on it?"

He shook his head, and she went into her room to grab the first aid kit out of her backpack. It was small, with only a roll of bandages and some antibiotic ointment, but that was all she needed. She dabbed some of the off-white cream onto the cut, letting it dry for a moment. It took all her willpower to move her hand away. She was tempted to try to bandage the cut so that she could touch him again, but it was so minor that any further care was unnecessary.

Remembering Phillip had obviously impaired her ability to think clearly.

Carter cleared his throat and she realized that she had been staring at him. Her face burned as she moved to put the kit away. He caught her arm, her breath hitching in response.

"Are you sure you don't want to talk about it?" She heard the hint of laughter in his voice, as if he knew what was going on in her head, when she did not even know herself.

The last thing she wanted to do was talk about Phillip. She longed for Phillip to be there, for them to live happily ever after in this cabin, heir or not. Yet neither of them would get their happy ending.

Today was the last day that Alexandria could pretend that the Campaign did not exist. She would either leave with Carter the next day, or she would be left once more. He still had not mentioned their deal, but she could not imagine that the day would pass without him telling her his plan. Their peace would be broken, and her last illusion of safety would vanish.

"No," she said. "I mean, yes, I'm sure."

"Okay."

Her voice shook with the fear of being alone again. "Just stay," she whispered. Pleaded.

"Okay," he repeated, softer this time, as he pulled her against him. She did not know what his response meant, if he would stay with her forever or only be by her side for the night.

It did not matter to her as she rested against him and drifted off to sleep.

She woke to the sound of the radio's emergency alarm blaring through the living room.

SIXTEEN

Carter untangled his arms from hers and looked around, bewildered by the noise.

The sun lit the room through the slits in the curtains. *We slept past sunrise*, Alexandria thought. She would have smiled at the idea if the radio was not currently splitting her head open.

"This is the Prime Minister, Darius Mendoza," he spoke through the crackling radio, as if people would not recognize him by his voice alone.

Carter's eyes widened with an expression like fear. She squeezed his hand, though her heart crashed against her chest.

"Many of you are excited for Alexandria Redmond to reach the throne or are patiently waiting for the chance to challenge her yourself. I am here to let you know that you will not have to wait much longer."

Her stomach dropped. She had no idea what he could possibly mean, only that it would not turn out well for her.

"Alexandria Redmond," he paused briefly, as if speaking directly to her, "has two weeks to make it to the throne. If she does not appear, her parents will be executed as traitors for hindering Kevelda from claiming a leader. Anastasia Redmond, the former Mayor of Kureya, has been stripped of her position until these charges can be cleared."

This time, it was not her saying "no," but Carter. He muttered the words under his breath as if he did not want her to hear.

"He's going to execute them," she said, the sound muffled by the blood rushing in her ears. Her world had been flipped upside down. Everything around her seemed *wrong*, even Carter's hand in hers.

She let go and jumped to her feet. The light was too bright, the radio deafening, her clothes suffocating. Her legs carried her to the wall, but no further. It scratched against her as she slid to the floor.

Her thoughts raced. She needed a plan, and quickly. Regia was her only option now. There would be no hiding in the cabin, having a lonely, yet peaceful, life. Though she had learned how to protect herself better over her time training with Carter, she still would not withstand an attack from someone stronger or faster than her.

If she did not go to Regia, her parents would die. If she did, she would be killed.

It was the easiest choice Alexandria had ever made.

"We're leaving today," she said, forcing herself onto her feet. The room spun around her, but she set her jaw and prowled into her room.

"We can't," Carter argued as he followed her. "You're not ready."

"I appreciate the confidence," she replied. Hands shaking, she packed her extra clothes back into her backpack, stashed the first aid kit, and rounded up the extra weapons. She walked into the kitchen, Carter still trailing behind, and shoved the packages of dried fish into the open zipper. Her empty canteen of water was still sitting in the side. She filled it under the tap and stowed it in its pouch.

"You'll be killed."

"You didn't seem to care about that when you were ordering me to go to Regia before," she snapped.

"I care now." She paused only to understand what had made his voice crack. Whatever the emotion was, he neutralized it immediately. "It's my assignment to protect you, and I cannot protect you if you go to Regia."

"Who's going to protect my parents, Carter?"

"I don't know."

"Exactly!" She rushed toward the door, not entirely sure where she was going or what her next steps would be. The only thought in her mind was to get to Regia, save her parents, and hopefully live long enough to give Mendoza a piece of her mind.

She had been right about him. He was up to something, was playing a game with her life. And she would have none of it. It was impossible that he wanted her to go to Regia for her to take the throne; no, he had to have another plan for her. But for now, if the heir was what he wanted, he was going to get her.

Alexandria vowed to make him regret that he ever knew the Redmond name.

The wind whipped her hair as she stormed outside. She did not know where she was going, only that she had to move. She couldn't hide inside the cabin when her parents only had two weeks before their execution. Carter called after her, but she pretended not to hear.

Her feet took her into the forest in the direction of the trails. Branches scoured a new set of scratches into her palms. The stabbing pain in her chest hurt much worse. She kept moving, even as the snow soaked through her pants and her uncovered fingers went numb from cold. If she died from exposure and someone took proof to Regia, perhaps it would save her family.

By the time her legs gave out, knees too frozen to move, she could not tell which direction would take her back to the cabin. She couldn't go back, not even if she wanted to. Carter would try to convince her to stay, despite arguing for her to go just over a week ago. She couldn't wrap her head around the sudden change. Did he really care so much more about her now that he would admit Regia was a death trap?

It didn't matter. Her mind had gone as numb as her limbs. She fell to her knees, then onto her hands.

I'm going to die either way. Whether she was killed by a vicious thronehunter or she ascended the throne, Alexandria Redmond would no longer exist.

She loathed Queen Evangeline for how she stole Phillip from her. But she could not say for certain that she would not make the choices the dead queen had. She did not know how to win a war. What if the throne turned her into a person her loved ones did not recognize?

She longed to believe that she would make the right choices. She could pray and fight and hope for the best answer, but every step she took would have consequences. As someone who suffered because of Queen Evangeline's actions, she did not want to be in that position at all.

The only way her parents would live was if she sacrificed herself: either her life or the person she hoped to be.

Ice bit into her hands as she pressed them into the ground. And then she screamed, a low, shattered sound. Every ounce of heartbreak and fear and pain that she had felt over the past two years tore from her lungs. A river of misery pouring from her throat, drowning and freeing her all at once.

She screamed until her voice failed, and then the world went black.

~

Warmth kissed her face, a tingling sensation rising from her fingertips into her core. Bright light burned her eyes. She squeezed them shut again. A soft fabric was being rubbed up and down her arms.

She forced her eyes to adjust and saw that the quilt had been wrapped around her shoulders. A second later, she realized that Carter was holding it there, holding *her* steady, pressing the heat into her skin. Her teeth chattered loudly.

Despite the shaking in her limbs, she tried to get up. Her legs protested against the movement.

"Stay still," Carter said. "You're freezing."

"Let– me– go," she demanded through her clacking jaw.

He began to say something, then released her. She regretted it as the cold threatened to freeze her from the inside out. Her head pounded as she stood. As she stumbled around the couch, running into it a few times, she found her backpack and picked it up. It weighed double what it had before. She gritted her teeth, forcing them to stay shut, and started for the door, ready to face the cold again.

Regia. Regia was the only thing on her mind when she fell against the door, her hand steadying her.

"Don't leave." Carter grabbed her wrist, just as he did only last night. She hated the way that it made her feel, a thousand volts of electricity lighting up her bones. If he did not let her go, then she would have to forget everything they had gone through and distance herself from him again.

"You can't make me stay," she hissed.

"I know. Stay for a moment and we can work out a plan. You'll die before you make it out of Hult if you leave in this condition."

Her shoulders relaxed slightly. She wanted to go right that second, but he was right. Going to Regia without a strategy would mean her death. Even *with* a strategy, facing Regia would be a death sentence.

"Okay," she resigned. She shrugged the backpack off her shoulder and sat on the couch.

"Sometimes I think you just like to argue with me."

"You make it very easy." Her usual sarcasm was stilted by the anxiety that creeped into her stomach and the pounding that knocked against her skull.

He supported her with his arm and led her to the fireplace. She did not fight as he laid the quilt back over her shoulders, nor as he put his legs on either side of her and pulled her back against his chest. Her thoughts stitched themselves together slowly as the heat reentered her body. His fingers drew lines of warmth on her face, brushing her curls out of her eyes.

She coughed, half from the cold that still settled in her lungs, half to break the silence. "I have to go to Regia."

"I figured that out when you buried yourself in the snow." He didn't bother to laugh.

"We'll have to find another car. I'm sure someone has checked the surveillance footage at the train station by now and knows which one we took."

"I can drive into town tonight and find one that looks like it won't be missed."

She fidgeted with the blanket. "They'll all be missed here."

"We'll just have to get to Regia quickly, then."

She took her eyes of off the flames and looked back at him. "Thank you, Carter."

"Don't thank me yet," he muttered. She elbowed him in the stomach. "What was that for?"

"No sarcastic comments? Your solemnity will kill me before anyone in Regia can even think to."

The corner of his mouth lifted in a smile that didn't reach his eyes. "Believe it or not, Lex, I don't want you to die. Sometimes."

She turned back toward the fire. "Much better." He started stroking her hair again, so naturally that she wondered if he even registered he was doing it.

Her mother used to braid her hair in front of this fireplace, her fingers working deftly through the texture that was much different from her own. While the mayor had loose waves that cascaded down her back when she removed the pins from her usual updos, Alexandria's curls bounced in spirals. It was something she shared with Queen Evangeline.

The thought was a knife to her chest. She still had no answers about how she was the heir, but with that similarity...

She did not want to think about the possibility of her relation to the queen being close. Like a daughter.

Her shoulders tensed as the word rang through her mind. *Daughter.* No, she was Anastasia and Henry Redmond's daughter. It did not matter how her blood tied her to the queen. Her bond would always be with the people that raised her. They had done far more for her than the queen ever would.

And now that Queen Evangeline was dead, it mattered even less. She would never be able to ask the queen about their connection. If she could, Alexandria was not sure that she even would.

She chewed on her bottom lip and relaxed into Carter's arms. It would benefit her none to worry about the queen now. Regia was the first priority.

A knock rang through the cabin. Alexandria jumped at the sound. Her eyes met Carter's, and she was sure her face betrayed her panic. His jaw set in an intentional calm. He unwound himself from her and made his way to the door.

When it opened, a man's surprised voice asked, "Who are you?"

Alexandria knew that voice.

James.

SEVENTEEN

Before Carter could draw his knife, she shouted, "Wait!"

She hurried as fast as she could to the entrance, her muscles becoming accustomed to moving again. When Alexandria stepped into sight of the door, James's eyes softened.

"Alexandria," he said, pushing past Carter. For a moment, she was worried that Carter was going to stop him.

She ran to James and threw her arms around him as he squeezed her in response. He nearly lifted her off the ground with the force of his embrace. "What are you doing here?" she asked, her voice tight.

He pulled away, looking between her and Carter. A glance of evaluation as he decided whether to trust the man who had been close to drawing a weapon on him. "They took Amira."

Alexandria's smile and stomach both dropped at the same time. "Who? Why? Where is she?"

"I don't know, but I'm assuming it has to do with getting you to the palace." He peered at Carter again. "I came to help. This was the only place your parents could think that you would hide."

The way he said "hide" sent blood rushing to her face in shame. She had spent the past two weeks here, in relative safety and comfort, while her family was being threatened and her closest friend had been kidnapped.

She was already making choices that hurt the people she loved.

James came up next to her, resting a hand on her shoulder. "Who is he?" he questioned pointedly.

"I'm her Protector," Carter said, forcing a smile. "And you must be James. I've seen your pictures."

"'Protector.' That's a bit pretentious."

Alexandria choked on a laugh. "He was assigned by the Argentum to help me get to the throne safely."

"Argentum?" James raised his eyebrows at her. "That's even worse. You're sure about him?"

"He hasn't killed me yet."

"She has tempted me quite a few times," Carter said lightly. Alexandria punched his shoulder and he winced.

"What do you know about Amira?" Alexandria asked James.

"Sam came to City Hall in a panic. He said that three people dressed in black had barged into the apartment and took her." James shook his head. "He felt guilty about hiding in the closet. I asked if he had seen anything else, but that's all he knew."

Alexandria leaned against the wall to keep herself steady. "It was Mendoza. Everything points back to Mendoza. I can't explain it, but it does."

Carter stiffened. "We can't prove any of it. Yes, he threatened to execute your parents, but to the rest of Kevelda, your parents are traitors. Beyond that, we have nothing."

"I know what I saw–"

"You saw a man hit his son. He might be a bad man, but that does not mean he's a mastermind. You might be right, but until there's hard evidence, no one will believe you. Even as the queen."

"As the queen, I will make sure that no one like him holds power," she said. Her voice faltered as she realized the implication. "*If.* If I become queen."

"I, for one, would like to believe it really is Mendoza behind all of this. Because if it isn't him, that means there's a bigger threat out there, and we have no clue who it is," James added.

"You're right." She looked back to Carter. "He's right."

"We don't need to worry about this right now," he responded. "We'll focus on getting you to Regia."

His statement was true, though she did not want to admit it. Amira's kidnappers, Mendoza's plan, Evangeline's bloodline, the queen's assassin–questions circled in her head, with no real answers for any of them. The only step she could take was forward to the throne.

She pushed off the wall. "I'm ready when you are." Almost immediately, her leg gave out, but she righted herself before she could fall.

Carter twitched as if he would catch her and then decided against it as James looked him over again. Her friend was not threatening, but he was easy to read: right now, he had a general air of disapproval and distrust.

"I'll go find us a way to get there. Pack up and we'll leave as soon as I get back." Carter sounded almost relieved to get out of James's presence, or maybe he was excited to finally be in control of a plan. Alexandria grimaced thinking about the last time she had left him uninformed.

"Be careful," Alexandria said as Carter shrugged on his coat.

"What's the fun in that?" he quipped and walked out the door. Alexandria rolled her eyes and gestured for James to follow her to the couch.

He dropped next to her with a sigh, putting his head in his hands. "I can't believe they just took her. I mean, why Amira? Why not me?"

"I don't know," Alexandria whispered. It was a good question, and an impossible one to answer, among all the others. Everything in her screamed to go look for Amira. She pushed away the lingering thought that Amira might not be in Regia. What then? Where would she start?

What if whoever took Amira had already killed her?

Alexandria could not lose another friend. The thought alone made her heart race. She forced herself to breathe. "Carter was right. We can't worry about it now. Our only lead is Regia."

James clenched his jaw and Alexandria prepared herself for an argument. His face softened when he met her eyes. "I'm so glad you're still alive."

"I had a few close calls," she laughed quietly. Eventually, she would tell him about Marlowe and the woman from the fuel station and the man in City Hall. No one else would know about the men in the woods, the body she left in the ravine. That would stay between her and Carter.

"I would thank Carter, but I have full faith you could've survived on your own."

"I'll take that as a compliment."

"It was intended as such." His grin was brief before it disappeared. "I don't trust him."

While she had assumed this moment would come, it did not prevent the bitterness rising in her throat. "You don't know him."

"Do you?"

She threw her hands in the air. "He has had every chance to kill me."

"It's only been two weeks."

"You have no clue what I have been through in that time," she gritted out. "He has been the only one by my side."

He winced. "Do you think Amira and I *wanted* to leave you alone? We have families to protect."

"So do I!" she shouted, moving away from him. "Carter is the only chance I have to make it to Regia and keep Mendoza from executing my parents."

"He could be working for Mendoza. The Argentum is under his control now."

She shook her head, trying to prevent the thought from taking root. "No. I refuse to believe that."

"Why?"

"James, I know you're trying to protect me. I appreciate that, I really do. But there are much bigger threats here that I can't even begin to explain. Don't get distracted by thinking Carter's the enemy when he's the whole reason I'm still breathing." Her voice began to shake as she was reminded of him pulling her back up from the ravine, telling her not to let go.

James faced her again, pressing his lips together. "I trust you," he said at last. "If that means giving Carter a chance, I will."

"Thank you," she sighed, relaxing back into the couch. James laughed, loud and bright. Alexandria startled at the noise. "What's so funny?"

"We really do fight like siblings."

She couldn't help but grin in response. "I suppose that happens when you live in the same house."

"Not anymore. Some agents came and forced us out of City Hall after Mendoza made that announcement."

Her stomach twisted. "Right. My mother's not the mayor anymore." What would that mean for her parents while they awaited their execution? Could they afford to eat? "Where are you all staying?" was the only question she could get out.

"The deputy mayor put us all in a hotel," he said, "though I'm not sure if Mendoza knows about it."

She exhaled a breath of relief. "Good. It's better if he doesn't know."

Alexandria rose to her feet and strode over to where her backpack laid on the ground. It was still packed from earlier, and while the exterior was a bit damp from the snow, the waterproof lining kept everything inside completely dry.

"See if you can fit anything else from the pantry in your bag," she ordered James. From all of the knives and daggers in her bag, she handed him a spare. "You might need this."

He flipped it once in his hand. "Thanks."

She nodded and dove back into the backpack, digging out the taser. It was lighter than she expected, and when she clipped its holster onto her belt, she hardly noticed that the device was there. Perhaps she would actually be able to use it the next time someone attacked her.

Carter had explained that the cartridges would need to be switched out, and that it would only work two or three times. The device became much less exciting after that, and more a reminder of the excruciating pain she had endured for the brief minute it had been used on her. Yet it would be helpful in disorienting her attackers rather than killing them. Something she prayed she would never have to do again.

While James raided the pantry for anything useful she had left behind, Alexandria went to grab Carter's backpack from her parents' room. It seemed like an invasion of privacy, but neither of them had the chance to personalize their space over the past two weeks. She wanted to get everything put together so that they could leave immediately when he came back.

His backpack had not been emptied at all. It hardly looked like he had been in the room. The bed was made, a habit she did not expect from him. She supposed it made sense; he had gone through training to become an Argentum agent and spent time in the palace barracks, after all.

The zipper was open on the backpack, and when she picked it up, a few items fell out. She stashed his dagger and the box of ammo back into the compartment. When she stooped to pick up the third item, she froze.

There on the ground laid the keys that she had lost at the fuel station.

Why do you have these, Carter? The question repeated itself in her mind. She stowed the keys in the bottom of the bag, wanting nothing more than to get them out of her sight.

Carter had kept her from leaving the fuel station. But why?

It had to be a misunderstanding. James's comments were getting to her, undermining everything she knew about her Protector. Carter had saved her, she reminded herself. He promised to do his best to keep her alive.

Someone knocked at the door. Carter couldn't be back already. She zipped up the backpack and threw it over her shoulder, palming her dagger as she crept out of the room.

She and James locked eyes over the kitchen counter. He motioned toward the door, mimicking the action of opening it. Her heart raced as she nodded in response.

He hesitated before making his way over to the door. It creaked open slowly.

Before she could blink, James was on the ground with a dart in his neck.

Alexandria ran back to her parents' room and locked the door behind her. She looked back and forth across the room. Her only escape route was the window, but when she tried to push it open, it wouldn't budge. Rust grew around the lock. She was trapped.

Hiding was her only option, then. She slid over boxes in the bottom of the closet, forced herself into the cramped corner, and shut herself inside. The boxes would be her only shield if the woman found her.

As silently as possible, she took the taser out of its holster. It would give her a longer range than the dagger. She hoped she knew how to use it correctly.

Her breathing echoed in the silence. She clamped a hand over her mouth to muffle the sound, the taser extended with the other. A single tear slid down her cheek. After everything she had gone through, the woman had still found her. She would die in this closet.

No, she could not think like that. Her fingers pressed against the trigger.

The lock on the bedroom door clicked, followed by a soft creak. Footsteps padded against the wood floors. They echoed louder and louder until the closet slammed open, bright light flooding in.

Alexandria pointed and squeezed, sending bolts of electricity toward the woman. She crumpled to the ground, thrashing and tugging against the lines.

PAPER CASTLES

A sharp pain bit into Alexandria's neck. She muttered a garbled mess of words. It was too late.

Her fingers pulled a metal dart from her neck before the world went black.

EIGHTEEN

Her head smacked against something hard as she jolted awake.

She found herself facing a wall of concrete, her shoulder pressed into a bare mattress. It creaked when she rolled over, old springs bouncing beneath her.

Not dead, she thought, *but where am I?*

The mattress was on the side of an expansive room, completely empty save for it, and now, her. A rusted metal railing rose from the ground in the middle of the space.

Pins and needles stabbed at her limbs as she stumbled off the mattress and onto her feet. Cold bit her skin, a drafty wind rustling through the shattered windows on the other end of the room. After checking her waist for her weapons and finding them gone, she crossed her arms over her chest.

The woman had kept her alive. For what reason, Alexandria could not guess. She hoped that James would be okay.

Killing did not seem to be the woman's modus operandi, something Alexandria was grateful for at the moment.

She did not let herself ponder it for too long. As she leaned over the railing, she found that she was on the second story of a building. Below her was another empty space which seemed to expand even further than the one she was in.

A warehouse. She was in a warehouse.

Hult did not produce much, but she recalled seeing a few factories driving into the town as a child. This one could have been abandoned after the Draft began.

If she was even still in Hult at all.

The last remaining daze of the tranquilizer dissipated. In its place rose the violent pounding of her heart.

There was an opening with a ladder on the other side of the railing. She raced toward it. It was connected to the platform by only one screw. The rest had been disintegrated by rust and time.

When she set her foot on the first rung, a sound like a shutter rolling open echoed below.

She jumped back onto the platform as the woman's shadow appeared below. Eyes scanning the room, Alexandria found nothing that would help her defend herself.

She ran soundlessly to the mattress, dropping down onto it and closing her eyes. The ladder clanged as the woman climbed it. Alexandria forced her breathing to still.

"Alexandria," the woman said, the sound coming from right next to her, "I know you're awake."

Alexandria opened her eyes and pressed her back against the wall in a quick movement. "Who are you?" she asked. "How do you keeping finding me?"

"My name is Leianna. I'm your Protector."

Her heart stopped. "I've heard that one before," she snapped, even as her trust in Carter disintegrated further. "Try again."

Leianna crossed her arms. "You're much more trouble than you're worth. It was an honor to be assigned this mission, but I'm starting to think it's a punishment."

"Show me proof."

Leianna's stilted laughter startled her. "Show you proof? What proof could I possibly give to convince you that Carter has been lying to you? Besides not killing you, of course."

"He had a contract," Alexandria muttered.

"A contract? To not kill you?"

"It had Mendoza's signature, as well as my mother's. And I know I can at least trust her."

"I thought Carter was honorable. A little quiet, but always up to a challenge. He did everything our commanders asked. He was promoted to the Queen's Guard, even though I had been in service longer, but now I'm starting to understand why. He always has a plan."

Leianna's words sent her head spinning even as she argued back. "I have no clue what you're talking about. One of you has been protecting me for the past two weeks, and the other has been hunting me. Who would you trust?"

"He played a good game. I'm sure he charmed you, but I'm the one who's going to get you to the palace. This is *my* assignment."

"You've done nothing to convince me."

"I don't need to convince you. If I must knock you out to get you in the car, I will. My duty is to bring you to the throne. If I have to remove *you* as an obstacle, I will." Her dark eyes flashed in a way that told Alexandria she was telling the truth. At least about knocking her out. "He attacked me on my way to find you at the beginning of the Campaign. Kept me from taking you straight from City Hall to the palace. When I got away, you had already left. I found you first. Now I know that Carter was using that time to get his *contract* signed. It meant nothing though, not when you were so desperate to get away from me that you stuck a dart in my neck."

Even though the image she held of Carter was fracturing by the minute, she still had no proof that Leianna was telling the truth. The woman had not killed her yet, but there was nothing to say she would keep Alexandria alive. Not like Carter had.

She had to get out of the warehouse.

"Okay, I believe you," she said. "Why would Carter lie?"

"I plan to find him and make him tell me," Leianna threatened. "Once you're on the throne."

"If I make it to the throne, questioning him will be my job, not yours." Alexandria did not think that Leianna meant to simply ask Carter questions, and even if he had been lying to her, she did not want to see him tortured. She would have to ask him herself.

Everything they had gone through couldn't all be part of a big lie. It just couldn't.

Leianna nodded. "Very well."

Alexandria pushed off the wall and shimmied to her feet. "What now?" she asked, in a voice that she hoped would convince Leianna that she trusted her.

"We drive straight to Regia. No stops. I'll take you right to the palace and make sure you get to the throne room." She reached an arm behind her and pulled car keys out of the black backpack that matched the ensemble she wore. It did not look to be an official uniform, but it was not something a civilian would own, either.

Alexandria immediately thought of the people who kidnapped Amira. James had said that they wore all black. It was not necessarily a sign that Leianna was connected, but it was enough to send adrenaline through Alexandria's veins. There was no escape in sight, so she would have to play along a little longer.

"Let's go. You first," Leianna ordered and motioned toward the ladder.

"Why me?"

"I won't have you tranquilizing me again."

Alexandria cursed in her head. *Smart one.*

"I'll remember you ordering me around," she told Leianna, with as much of a threat as she could muster.

Leianna pointed to the ladder again. "Hopefully you'll also remember me keeping you alive," she deadpanned.

Alexandria pressed her hands into the rungs, trying to hide their shakiness as she descended. She needed a way out, and quickly. Leianna had already moved halfway down the ladder.

The ladder. That was her chance.

She tugged it hard. It shook but did not budge. Her arms strained as she yanked it again.

"What are you doing?" Leianna shouted.

Another pull, and the last screw snapped free.

The ladder fell toward her, Leianna along with it. Alexandria darted out of the way as Leianna hit the ground with a thud. A second later, the ladder crashed next to her.

Leianna's backpack broke her fall, but Alexandria did not wait to see how long it would take the woman to recover. She snatched the keys that had fallen out of Leianna's hand and rushed outside.

Without a coat, the air threatened to freeze her alive. Her joints turned to ice as she hurried to the one vehicle parked outside.

She breathed a sigh of relief when the key fit in the lock and the door opened. Alexandria slammed it shut behind her and hit the lock once more. In her peripheral vision, Leianna stumbled out of the building and raced toward her.

The car started with a shudder. Alexandria did not know where she was going. She did not care as she threw the car into reverse and slammed on the accelerator. Leianna jumped out of the way as the car narrowly missed her. Alexandria felt guilty for a split second when she considered that Leianna might have told her the truth.

"Oh well," she mumbled to herself, shifting into drive and speeding away.

Her knuckles turned white from gripping the steering wheel. The road wound through thick trees, giving her no sense of direction. Maybe she would never find the cabin. She would drive until she ran out of gas and then have to fend for herself on the side of the road.

Her breath ran ragged and heavy. No amount of air would fill her lungs.

If she went back to the cabin, would she face a different Carter than the one she thought she had known?

Leianna had no proof, she reminded herself. No proof, and yet she spoke of Carter like she knew him. They had served in the Argentum together. He had been assigned to the Queen's Guard, and she had not. That was a motive for her to try and get back at him.

Yet the seed of distrust had already taken root. And it was beginning to grow.

He had saved her. He had brought her out of the sea of painful memories that threatened to drown her. He had told her he would stay with her.

He had stolen her car keys.

The past two weeks could not mean nothing. Her heart could not handle another loss. She clenched her teeth and set her eyes on the road.

Five minutes later, she was in the heart of Hult. The small town had been overrun by thronehunters. Cars lined the streets, a spectrum of conditions from rusted and dented to recently polished. None of them were new, but there was a difference between those that came from Regia and those that did not. People who came for fame versus those who came to protect their families from someone who had the chance of being a greater threat than Queen Evangeline, a risk they could not take. She supposed everyone had their reasons for wanting to kill her.

No matter their motives, she was stuck on the "killing her" part.

While the sight of people swarming the streets of Hult unsettled her, she now knew where to go. She turned back in the direction she came.

This town had once been kind to her. The residents knew she was the Mayor of Kureya's daughter, but they had never treated her differently. Not until the Draft began and an Argentum agent came every month to pick off their young people, one by one.

It was a shock when she and her family had returned six months after the Draft began, and already the population had dropped by a quarter. Their Draft quota had to be reduced not long after that, or there would have been no one of drafting age left.

As they had driven through the middle of town, every face turned to look at the government vehicle. Some fell, while others lit up in anger. To them, they were just another official coming to take away their loved ones. Alexandria could not find it in her to be mad at them, only to be furious at the queen.

They had been coming to the town for years, yet her mother had done nothing to help its people. She did not have the power to stop the Draft in her own city, Alexandria knew, and she would have even less of a say in a town that did not have a mayor. But the thought still plagued her.

Alexandria could not save them. The war was still raging, whether or not she was on the throne. Even if she tried to fix things, her people might die, and Hult would not welcome her again.

Perhaps she owed it to them to try.

She shook the thought out of her head. It would be of no use to worry about that until she survived to sit on the throne and save her parents.

When she reached the turn onto the gravel road, she did not bother to park at the entrance to the hunting trails. Instead, she drove further until she reached a snowy strip that led right up to the cabin. They would only be there for a few minutes at most, and if anyone had been tracking her, she, James, and Carter would already be gone by the time they came.

Her mind stuck on Carter. She would have to ask him about Leianna. The woman had mentioned them serving together, but Carter had pretended not to know her after the fuel station.

Even if she could trust him to keep her alive, he was keeping something from her. She could not even begin to imagine what it was. If he wasn't her Protector, then what other motives would he have for helping her survive?

The field in front of the cabin was empty. Either Carter had not been able to steal another car, or he had not returned yet.

She took the keys out of the ignition and sped through the cold up to the door. The wood echoed through the silence as she knocked. Footsteps rustled, and then a voice called, "She's back!" before the door opened to reveal James standing behind it.

"How did you get away?" James asked, pulling her in for a hug.

"I'll tell you on the way to Regia," she responded.

Carter rushed over and wrapped her in his arms. She let herself relax into the embrace for a moment, then another moment longer. He pressed his face against her neck. "I thought we'd lost you," he breathed.

It took all her willpower to pull away. She took his face in her hands and locked eyes with him. "Tell me everything," she commanded. "Tell me the truth."

NINETEEN

Leianna said she's my Protector," Alexandria said. "You had my car keys in your bag. And you were watching me that day in Kureya before the queen was even dead!"

She had nearly forgotten that last part with everything that had happened over the past two weeks. At first, she had believed his excuse that the Dais knew that she would be named soon, but it now compounded everything else that did not add up about Carter.

"I have the contract. That's proof enough that she's lying," Carter argued.

"Why would she lie *and* keep me alive?"

Carter's voice rose. "Why would I? Seriously, Alexandria, do the past two weeks mean nothing to you? We've fought together. I saved you from Marlowe, from the man that came here. I woke up with you every morning at sunrise to train. Some nights,

I didn't even sleep, worrying about how I would protect you if more thronehunters came knocking. I have spent every waking moment thinking my way out of you being killed in Regia, even if it means dying in your place!"

Alexandria stepped back, her heartbeat fluttering. "I didn't know."

He closed his eyes and exhaled slowly. "Queen Evangeline stationed me in Kureya and ordered me to keep an eye on you before she died. *She* told Mendoza to assign me as your Protector. I took your car keys because I knew you wouldn't trust me. Every government vehicle has a positioning system, based on the radio transmitters. If you didn't make it to Regia in one trip, someone would have found you. Someone like Leianna. I was assigned to bring you to Regia, even if it killed you, but *everything* I have done was to keep you alive."

Carter did not guard his face. In his eyes must have been every ounce of fear and worry that he had kept from her since they met. She did not realize that he had moved closer until James cleared his throat.

"I still don't trust you," James commented, looking at Carter, "but it's your call, Alexandria."

Everything that Carter had explained made sense. She still had questions about Queen Evangeline, but there was a chance Carter did not know the reason why the queen had given him those orders. Her heart begged her to trust him. Her head screamed at her not to be naive.

She would be in Regia before nightfall either way.

And even though she had fought it, Carter had made a place in the circle of people she could not bear to lose. At least not now, when he could be the difference between life or death. He broke her trust, but no matter whether he was telling the truth or not, she would not make it to the throne without him.

"Come with us," she said at last.

His shoulders dropped in relief. He grinned when he said, "Good choice."

Something had changed between them once again, a difference in the way he carried himself. Alexandria could not pinpoint exactly what it was, but she hoped that she would not come to regret giving him another chance.

"We have to leave now. If you're right and all government-issued vehicles are tracked, then I just told the whole Argentum where we are," Alexandria said. "Think any of your friends would come to challenge me?"

"I wouldn't call them 'friends,'" Carter replied, "but I could name a few agents who would want the crown."

She tossed Leianna's keys to James. "You drive. I'll be running as soon as we get there. Carter, you'll have to give him directions."

"What are you going to do?" James asked.

Alexandria attached another holster to her belt, securing a dagger in place. She had lost her other dagger and the taser to Leianna. The woman likely still had them in her backpack. She took in a deep breath, battling the anxiety constricting her lungs. "Pray," she finally said, "and plan."

Tension ran thick between the three of them as they secured the last of their belongings and left the cabin. Alexandria could not dwell on the thought that she may not ever see it again. While she was about to step into the fight of her life, she could not deny that her time in the cabin had begun to heal her in some ways. There was always a risk that a thronehunter could find her. Yet she had felt safe with Carter by her side.

Now, she had a mission. She did not want to be the queen, but she would do anything to ensure her family's survival. If she failed to sit on the throne after making it to Regia, at least they would outlive her.

I will fight. Her breath shook as she stepped out under the gray winter sky. *I will fight.*

The hair on her neck stood on end as she started for the car. It was too silent. No birds. No animals. Nothing. Like they were waiting for something bad to happen, too.

James cursed behind her. She swung to face him, following his gaze back to the car.

To the flat tires.

To the slash lining each of them.

Carter unsheathed his knife. It whistled against the eerie silence. Alexandria gripped the handle of her own.

A crack of thunder clapped next to her. She dropped to her knees, arm over her head.

Not thunder. A gunshot.

She twisted as Carter fell to the ground. Her throat burned with a scream.

James stood frozen in shock. She ran up to him, put her arm around his waist, and dragged him to the cover of the cabin's front porch.

A man came around the corner and planted himself in front of them. The barrel of his gun pointed at James.

"Make this easy for me and he lives," the man said. His eyes darkened as his finger brushed the trigger.

Alexandria stood without hesitation, hands in the air. "Okay," she breathed. "Point it at me. Not him." The man did just that. She closed her eyes. The gun cocked. "Wait!" she shouted.

"Yes?" the man asked. She was surprised her exclamation worked. She did not have an actual plan. It took her a moment to come up with a response.

"What's your name?" she asked, rushed and shaky. She opened her eyes and began to move toward him. He backed up, still pointing the gun at her.

He's scared. He doesn't want to do this. It was a dangerous assumption to make, but Alexandria had no alternatives.

"You don't need to know."

"Please," she begged. "I just want to know."

"Jason," he replied. The gun was still trained on her. She stood in the driveway now, a few feet in front of him.

Her next step would be to get him to turn. "You're doing this for Mendoza, aren't you?"

His jaw clenched. "I'm doing this for no one," he gritted out.

"Everyone's chasing me for someone. Themselves. Their families. Tell me, who is your reason?" She swallowed hard. Fear muffled every sound besides her racing heartbeat. Her voice was calm. Yet if he heard her blood pounding, he would know exactly how terrified she was.

The gun followed her as she inched around the man holding it. "My daughter. Petra. I do everything the Dais asks, but there are still days I can't feed her." His finger clenched against the trigger.

Alexandria blinked slowly. *New topic.* "You're Argentum?"

The man nodded, his eyes trained on her movement. He did not seem to care. He still had all the power.

"How did you find me?" she questioned.

"Will told me Lei was assigned to you. He wasn't supposed to tell anyone. She wasn't even supposed to tell him. He just wanted me to know why he would be gone for a while, to help her from home. I've been tracking her since you were named. When she finally moved from that warehouse, I knew she found you. I guess Carter found you first. Makes sense. He's a smart one. What I never expected was that he would keep you alive. Still can't figure that one out."

Queen Evangeline had assigned him personally, Carter had said. If Leianna really *was* assigned to be her Protector by the Dais, that meant that the dead queen and the Dais were not on the same page. There was some disagreement in the palace.

Or maybe, Evangeline had wanted to double Alexandria's chances at surviving. Yet Alexandria could not figure out why the queen wanted *her* to sit on the throne—a woman she had never met.

Alexandria made one last move. "Trust me, I can't figure it out, either."

"You won't have to," Jason replied gruffly. He leveled the gun once more and put his finger on the trigger.

James and Alexandria shared a glance before her friend drove his knife into the back of the man's shoulder.

The gun clattered to the ground. Jason grabbed his shoulder, groaning in agony. His hand came away covered in crimson.

Alexandria dove for the gun. She pointed it at the agent before he could move. He kept his hand pressed against the wound, his other arm limp.

"If you come for us again, I will not be this merciful," she snapped.

She had killed the man in the ravine. It would kill her to do that again. Her eyes found Carter on the ground, curled around a growing red patch of snow. The sight alone convinced her that she would do what she had to.

Another scream rose in her throat. "Do you hear me?" she shouted.

Jason nodded. His grimace hardened into something darker. She would not let it fester.

"Then leave. Now." Her voice began to break. She had to hold it together, if only for a few more moments.

Jason turned and walked down the driveway to a vehicle parked just along the edge of the forest. The trees and snow hid it, but she chastised herself for not noticing it before.

When the vehicle disappeared from sight, she rushed over to Carter.

"Please be okay," Alexandria said, a whisper and a prayer. James kneeled next to them.

"I got shot," Carter groaned through clenched teeth.

"I see that," she replied. She almost smiled at his response, knowing that he was still alive. Her face fell when she noticed the red stain growing larger. "James, help me carry him inside."

The two each took one of Carter's arms. He sucked in air sharply through his teeth at every movement. "It'll be over soon," she murmured, "I promise."

Once inside, they settled him onto the ground. Alexandria pulled the first aid kit out of her backpack, wishing that she had more than the minimal supplies. She was naive, and unprepared, and she was going to be the reason Carter died protecting her.

James helped him sit up against the wall while she took the coat off his shoulders. She lifted the hem of his shirt. A mess of blood covered the tan skin along his side.

"How bad is it?" Carter asked.

"Not bad," she lied. "Just a scratch."

She was in way over her head. She didn't know the first thing about caring for a gunshot wound. The first thing she did was run to the kitchen and dampen a towel under the faucet. Her mind raced as she hurried back to him.

She wiped the blood from around the wound as best as she could, even as more erupted from the gash. The bullet had grazed him. It did not look like it had struck too deep, but again, she had never seen a real bullet wound.

James handed her the roll of bandages from the kit. She pressed a wad against Carter's side, ignoring his yelp of pain. Her fingers trembled as she wrapped the white cloth tightly around his torso.

"I should've cleaned that," she said. "I–I don't know. Should I do it again?"

Carter gripped her hand. "Please don't." He forced a grin. His laugh sent him clutching his side again.

"We can't stay here, but you're in no condition to go to Regia."

James was blurry from behind her tears. She blinked them back. He put his hand on her shoulder. "Jason said that Leianna was assigned to you, right?"

"Yes," she replied, and then she put together what he was going to say next. "She won't help us. You don't know what I did to her."

James's eyebrows knit together in confusion, and then his eyes widened. "Did you kill her?"

"No," Alexandria bit out, more sharply than she intended to, "but I didn't exactly leave her unharmed."

"There must be something she would want from the future queen. Make a deal."

Alexandria studied Carter's face, his eyes closed tightly. "Don't," he whispered. "She'll do anything to get ahead."

And in that second, Alexandria knew exactly how to get Leianna to help them.

TWENTY

Alexandria ran the two miles to the warehouse as fast as she could. The cold stabbed her skin, tore into her lungs. Her eyes burned from the tears streaming down her cheeks.

Carter had begun to bleed through the bandages. If they made it to Regia soon, he would be fine. Leianna would be the only way for them to get there. She did not have a car thanks to Alexandria, but she might be able to call for some kind of backup.

Backup that might try to kill Alexandria. She would not let Carter die trying to protect her.

She had to make it to Regia, though. Her parents' lives balanced on whether she did. Leianna might not be able to help at all, and Alexandria was to blame.

Tears had formed icy flakes on her cheeks by the time she reached the warehouse. She gripped her knees, panting. The chill stung her throat like thousands of tiny blades.

Leianna had pulled the metal shuttered door back down since Alexandria had stolen her car and drove away. As her hand rose to knock, she hesitated. She wondered if she should draw her weapon. Their last meeting had not entirely been pleasant.

She decided against it. It was better to not look like a threat. With her eyes red and curls swept across her face, she doubted that she came off threatening at all.

When she knocked, she heard fabric rustling from the other side of the door. The sound of footsteps grew louder, then the door shook as it retracted upwards.

Leianna was on the other side, pulling the metal chain that made the door move. Three-quarters open, she dropped it and said, "I knew you'd come back. Carter's not the person you thought he was, was he?"

Alexandria forced herself to stop shaking. "We need your help to get to Regia."

"I won't help you if he's involved," Leianna scoffed.

"Please," Alexandria pleaded, "He's hurt. An Argentum agent attacked us. Jason."

Leianna's eyes widened so briefly that Alexandria wondered if she imagined it. "How did he find you?"

"I'll explain later. Please, just help us. We can't make it with him injured, and I–I don't know how to fix him." Alexandria shivered as a gust of wind brushed past her.

"Why should I help him? He pushed me off track for two weeks."

"I'll give you all the credit when I sit on the throne. You'll be promoted to the Queen's Guard."

It only took a second for Leianna to think about it. "Okay. What's your plan?"

"I don't have one."

"I don't like walking in blind."

"You're going to have to!" Alexandria clenched her hands to keep from shaking. Every moment they stood here was another moment longer Carter was bleeding on the floor.

Leianna must have sensed that her grip on their deal was slipping, because she picked up her backpack and hoisted it on her shoulder. "Lead the way."

They walked in a tense silence all the way back to the cabin. Alexandria wished she could run, but her legs were already burnt out. She did not know if her lungs could take any more. It took everything in her to keep herself calm when her fears swirled around her head the entire two miles.

What if he's dead when we get there?

The bullet had not hit him that deep, she reminded herself. Carter would be fine, at least for a while longer.

What if I don't make it to Regia and Mendoza kills my parents?"

That was a more valid worry. They had twelve, thirteen days to get her on the throne. They currently had no car and no way to get one. As they trekked through the woods alongside the road, Alexandria had an idea.

One that she did not particularly enjoy.

~

Upon seeing Carter, Leianna's first action was to hold a knife against his throat.

Alexandria lunged at her. James caught her arm.

"If you even think about jeopardizing my mission any further, I will not hesitate to send you home in a body bag. Is that clear?" Leianna threatened a bleeding Carter.

Carter nodded, a strained smile on his pale lips.

"What's so funny?" Leianna asked. She slipped the knife into her belt.

"If you don't stitch me up, I might go home in a body bag anyways."

Leianna sent Alexandria a look that she interpreted as *I'm only doing this for that promotion. Your Majesty.* Alexandria held her gaze with as much steel as possible.

"Get the bottle of alcohol out of my bag," Leianna commanded no one and everyone.

James moved first, letting go of Alexandria's arm to reach into the backpack next to Leianna. Leianna tugged up the hem of Carter's shirt. Alexandria stood frozen, transfixed by the blood-soaked bandages lining his ribs.

Leianna unwound the bandages roughly. She did not flinch as Carter's breaths turned sharp. Alexandria dropped down beside him in a daze. She forced herself to focus on what Leianna was doing, on the metallic scent of blood that tinged the air.

James handed Leianna a clear glass bottle about the size of his palm. She put it up to Carter's mouth and he took a swig. Then, she dumped the rest of the bottle on his wound.

Carter gritted his teeth, a low scream shattering through them. Alexandria jolted out of her shock. She held the back of his head with her hand to keep him from hitting it against the wall.

He gripped her arm tightly as Leianna threaded a needle from her bag and began to stitch up his skin.

By the time she was done, Carter had gone entirely white, even a tad bit green. A few drops of alcohol sat at the bottom of the bottle on the floor, and Alexandria avoided the sight of it, focusing on him instead. She did not let go of his hand.

"Thank you," Carter said, looking at Leianna.

She ignored his gratitude. "We've been here too long. We don't have a car. The reporters just noted a blockade heading toward Regia, so even if we did, we couldn't get past that."

"A blockade?" Alexandria asked.

"Some thronehunters blocked the road. They're checking every car to find you."

Nausea bubbled in Alexandria's stomach. She had not expected getting to Regia to be easy, but it was now hitting her just how difficult it would be. The thought of people crowded in the capital waiting to kill her had scared her enough, when she really should have been worried about getting there at all.

"We'll go on foot," she replied.

"That's a terrible plan," Leianna said.

"It's the only plan we have." Alexandria loosed her grip on Carter and stood. "There are camping supplies in the attic. A tent and sleeping bags."

Carter's voice was gravelly as he said, "I never thought you to be the exploring type."

"She's the most adventurous of all of us," James said. "You should have seen her on those camping trips."

He did not mention that it was a lie. Phillip loved to explore more than her. He just rarely had the chance, with his family's fishing business. When she went camping with him, it was like he was an entirely different person. Not that he was discontent with normal life, because he wasn't, or at least he wanted everyone to believe so. But in the woods, he was free.

Alexandria cleared her throat, "If by adventurous you mean I didn't mind killing the spiders, then by all means, you're right." She addressed Leianna. "This is the plan. Now, can you help us get to Regia?"

Leianna sighed, shoving the supplies back into her bag. "Of course, I can get you there. Just don't let yourself freeze along the way."

They bundled into their coats, scarves, and gloves, each carrying a backpack along with a sleeping bag. They all agreed to take turns carrying the tent. It was large enough for the four of them, though it would be tight. Leianna argued that they would have to take turns on watch, so the four of them would never be in the tent at once, anyways.

Alexandria breathed a sigh of relief when she found enough sleeping bags for the group. One of her friends must have left one long ago. She would not tell James that she had found a web of spiders on some of them. If she did, he might not sleep the entire time it took them to reach Regia.

It would take four days if nothing drastic happened. Alexandria was not going to push her luck and assume it would be an easy journey. Even so, they would be in the palace before the week was over. She would either be sitting on the throne or lying in a pool of her own blood.

Carter could walk, but moving his left side above his ribs made him grimace. James carried his sleeping bag so he did not have to. Alexandria took that as a sign that he was warming up to Carter, at least slightly.

Alexandria walked up to her friend's side as they hiked their way through the trees. "Thank you for saving me."

"That's what friends are for," James replied.

"I think this is a little more than what you bargained for when you invited me to your eighth birthday party."

He laughed. "You have a point."

"I'm sorry you got mixed up in all of this. You *and* Amira," she sighed. Amira, who had her brother to care for. Who had the mechanic shop to run. Who *had* to be alive. Alexandria would not imagine any other alternative.

"We both chose to be your friend, whatever may come. You did the same for us."

"That was back when the only difficulty being my friend was because I was the mayor's daughter. You can still back out."

He nudged her side. "That's not the only difficulty. You have a bit of a temper."

"You're one to talk." She rolled her eyes with a smile. "Let's not get into that right now. This is a nice moment."

"Once again, happy you're alive, but I do remember you sending our teacher evidence that a certain ex-boyfriend had cheated on a test."

"First of all, he cheated on me *and* that test. Not a temper if I have a reason."

James put his hands up in front of him. "Okay, okay. I concede."

"Good," she smirked.

"You'll make a great queen."

"I can't tell if you're being nice or if you're making fun of me."

"Both," he replied, "and I mean it genuinely."

"Glad to see things haven't changed too much while I've been away," she sighed, "but thank you. For everything."

"You make it easy to choose you. Even if you yell at me." He smiled at her.

She couldn't keep herself from grinning in response. It was good to have someone who knew her as well as James by her side again, even if they fought.

Though the more she thought about it, she realized that he did not know anything about what she had gone through since the Campaign began. He couldn't, even if she told him. There were some things she could never explain. Like the way it felt to kill someone. Only Carter could understand that.

They walked side by side, Leianna leading the way and Carter trailing close behind. If someone attacked them from behind, he would only be able to defend with his right side. The image made her slow her pace and join him.

"How are you feeling?" she asked quietly.

"Like I've just been shot," Carter responded. He used his right arm to brace himself against a tree as he maneuvered over a log.

"I assume you've been better," she tried to joke. Her voice still shook at the memory of the earlier attack, of the crimson snow around his body.

"I've also been worse."

"Not your first time being shot?"

Carter shook his head. "Never been shot, but I have had shrapnel lodged in my leg."

"What from?" she asked, and then she remembered how his family died. The attacks on Regia. The bombs. She clamped her mouth shut.

"No sad stories today." He kept his eyes trained on the two walking ahead of them. "What was that I heard about an ex-boyfriend?"

Alexandria did not necessarily want to explain, yet she figured that the man beside her, who knew her deepest regret, could handle the parts of her past that she laughed about around the dinner table.

TWENTY-ONE

A line of cars cut across the road, blocking anyone driving that way from passing through. A woman sat in one of them, another standing along the second car. The man outside searched every vehicle that passed. When he raised his hand, the woman in the car pulled backwards to let the passing car move ahead.

Alexandria's stomach dropped at the sight. Two weeks, and the hunger for her blood had made the thronehunters more desperate with every second.

She tried not to think of them as animals. Yet when she saw the man yank the car doors open, the drivers' eyes widening with fear, it was impossible to remember that most of the thronehunters had reasons for wanting her dead.

They were predators, and she was nothing more than prey to them.

The four watched from the trees for a few moments longer before hiking deeper into the forest. They had trekked for two hours yesterday before night fell and they set up camp. Alexandria had taken the first watch. Carter insisted on staying up with her, but she forced him to rest. She did not get much sleep anyways, even after Leianna took over.

It would be four more days of traveling until they reached Regia's borders. From there, they would have to figure out how to cross the capital to get to the palace. Alexandria had never been required to travel through Regia on foot, so she did not have the first idea where to begin. She had simply been escorted to the palace with her parents during their past visits. It would not be so easy this time.

Alexandria quickened her pace to catch up to Leianna. "Did you hear anything about more blockades?"

Leianna shook her head. "As far as I heard, that was the only one. Then again, they think you're still hiding out in Hult somewhere. I'll set up the portable radio when we stop next."

As the sun lowered behind the trees, they came across a less-dense patch of forest. Fire raced through Alexandria's sore muscles, and she breathed a sigh of relief at the sight of a resting place. She winced remembering that they had four more days of this. Constant maneuvering around fallen logs caused her back to tense, her legs to cramp. When she looked back to Carter, she could not ignore his grimace as the steps jostled his ribs. He tried to hide it whenever he noticed her looking, plastering on the smirk she knew too well.

At least it was getting warmer as they journeyed toward the coast. Not warm enough to melt the snow entirely, but the layer coating the ground was only a few centimeters thick. Another week into winter and this area would be blanketed as the forest was in Hult, a half-meter deep. Alexandria was grateful for the minor reprieve from the harsh winds as they traveled through the woods, though traversing the rough terrain likely also played a role in keeping her warm. She was sweating underneath her coat.

"Here," Alexandria said, handing James the tent she carried. He began to set it up, Leianna taking the other side, as Alexandria followed Carter to one of the logs in the middle of the clearing.

He dropped onto it slowly, holding a hand to his side. "I'm fine," he said. Snow crunched as his backpack hit the ground.

"Let me see."

Carter unzipped his coat and pulled up his shirt, exposing the bandages beneath. "Don't stare too long or I'll freeze."

She ignored his comment as best she could. Heat rose to her cheeks all the same. Only a thin line of red stained the bandage right where his stitches were. If they weren't so exposed, she would take the time to rewrap it. She made a mental note to do so once the tent was set up.

Though she had done the exact same thing when she wrapped his wound before, this felt different. Her hands did not shake from the adrenaline of him bleeding out on her floor, but from something else entirely.

Her gloved fingers brushed against his skin as she set the hem of his shirt back in place. She reached for her canteen and handed it to him.

He held his hand up. "Save it for later."

"Just drink it, Carter." She pushed it toward him again. He sighed, unscrewing the cap before taking a few sips. When he finished, she put it back into her bag.

The cramps in her legs melted when she sat down beside him. She rubbed them up and down, releasing the last few knots. "If I ever have to walk again, it'll be too soon," she breathed.

"We could use some help over here," Leianna called to her. She and James were struggling to set up the tent. One of the metal poles stuck straight in the air. Alexandria groaned as she stood from the log.

"Too soon?" Carter smirked.

"You're lucky you're injured," Alexandria muttered. She walked over to the two, who were bickering about which side to put together first. They slid the poles into the plastic sleeves of the tent. It came together eventually, and Alexandria jumped on the stakes to wedge them into the frozen ground. After they finished with the tent, she and Leianna went on a search for logs and branches to start a fire.

Alexandria was fortunate that her parents had taught her about these things, especially when it came to the fire. They had camped a few times in colder autumns, but never in winter. It took her twice as long now to find logs that were not too frozen or wet from snow. Her joints were stiff as she climbed a tree to saw off higher branches with her knife.

She leaned back against the trunk, her legs straddling a branch, eyes closed. Whenever they settled around a fire, her parents somehow always ended up sharing the story of how they met. They would interrupt each other, finish the other's sentences.

"She snuck out to be at the party–" her father had started one time.

Her mother had immediately cut him off. "I did not sneak out. Alexandria, don't even think of doing that."

"You were the mayor's daughter. How else would you be at a party?"

"I wasn't locked up."

Her father raised his eyebrows and threw up his hands. "Anyways, we were at a party. It was after exams, and some students from the university were celebrating. I had just finished my second year and was going to start teaching in a week. This woman walks in, and she has the most beautiful eyes I've ever seen. I instantly fell in love."

"You did not," her mother laughed.

"If not then, it was soon enough. She started singing my favorite song. Knew every word…"

At that part of the story, Alexandria would think of Phillip, every single time. He knew her better than anyone else. Her favorite song, her favorite book. The time of night she preferred to be outside, and where she wanted to be. He appeared in all her best memories, the dreams she replayed in her mind countless times.

Her heart panged as she realized that was no longer true. Her favorite song had changed in the past two years. She had read new books and could not talk to him about them. The night was now a threat, the beach a lonely place. All her dreams had turned into nightmares. Phillip would not know what she had done in the Campaign. What had been done to her.

He would not recognize her. Would she want him to?

She shivered. Deep purple tinged the sky, bird calls dying out as the animals returned to their nests. Her descent was slow, her fingers frozen from sitting so long. She clutched the sawed-off branches to her side as she returned to their makeshift camp.

"We were starting to get worried," James said, "Carter was about to run after you." A mischievous glint shone in his eyes.

Carter shifted on the log. "Because it's my job, and Leianna didn't seem to care."

Leianna scowled and turned to him with concerning speed. "I'm here now," Alexandria interrupted whatever was about to occur. She held the branches out in front of her. "Let's make a fire."

James and Leianna dragged some logs into a circle around where Alexandria and Carter set the fire. The gloves made it impossible for Alexandria to grip the flint. She took them off to strike the starter, sparks falling onto the kindling as cold bit her fingers. As soon as the flame caught, she pulled her gloves back on, holding her hands over the heat.

The four dropped onto the logs, finally resting after hours and hours on their feet. Alexandria unzipped her backpack and handed each of her companions a package of dried fish. Leianna nodded her thanks, taking a bite of the fish before laying the portable radio on the log next to her.

She cranked the knob on the front of the small gray box until the static cleared. They ate in silence, listening to a woman narrate the events of the day in a soft tone. Alexandria tensed when she mentioned a fight at the blockade they had passed earlier in the day. A man did not take kindly to being stopped and figured he would take out one of his competitors for her throne.

"The man has since died from his injuries," the reporter said without emotion. Alexandria inhaled sharply, dropping her package of fish.

Carter rested his hand on her knee. "It's not your fault," he said in a low voice.

"Isn't it?" she replied. He was right. She did not shoot the man herself. Yet they were all looking for her. The tension was rising on her behalf. They were only fighting each other because they could not fight her.

"It'll end soon enough," Leianna said. "Once you're seen in Regia, they'll turn their attention to you."

Alexandria picked up her fish, though she was no longer hungry. "That's not even remotely comforting," she muttered.

The reporter transitioned to other updates, but Alexandria's mind lingered on the man who was killed. Did his family know he was hunting her? What happened to the woman he was with? She exhaled slowly, her breath turning to fog in the air.

A loud beeping sound echoed through the clearing. Another emergency alert.

"Breaking news," a different reporter interrupted, "The Dais has officially convicted the suspect charged in connection to

Queen Evangeline's death. William Olivier will be executed for her assassination tonight at midnight in front of the palace. There will be a celebration of Her Majesty's life directly following the execution."

A strangled noise tore from Leianna's mouth. Carter's hand stiffened where it laid on Alexandria's knee. His face had gone pale in the light of the fire. "Lei–" he started, cut off by Leianna's hand at his throat.

"This was you, wasn't it? You did something and it got him killed. You killed him." Her voice was unnaturally calm.

Alexandria tugged at Leianna's arm. "Carter had nothing to do with this. Let him go," she commanded. Leianna's arm went slack. "Who is William Olivier?"

The woman's eyes were blades, piercing her own as their gazes met. "My husband."

Carter rubbed his neck where her fingers had dug in. "I'm sorry, Lei," he said, "but I would never do anything to hurt either one of you. We're friends. We were, anyways."

Their history went deeper than Alexandria thought. She touched Leianna's shoulder, but the woman shrugged it off and marched to the trees. "I'll take watch tonight," she called as she vanished into the forest. She did not specify which of their four watches she would cover, but Alexandria knew the woman would stay awake until sunrise.

Her heart broke for Leianna. She would not be able to be there for her husband's last breath, his last words. It did not matter if he assassinated the queen or not, though Alexandria doubted that William was the true assassin. His conviction *had* to be another play in Mendoza's game.

Carter unzipped the tent and disappeared inside. She looked at James, who seemed just as shocked as her. His eyes widened as he looked back and forth between the forest and the tent.

Alexandria motioned toward the tent. "Could you give us a second?" she whispered.

James nodded as if telling her to go ahead. She inhaled and exhaled until her breath steadied and then followed Carter inside.

The tent that was usually sufficient for three people could not have felt any smaller as she zipped it closed behind her. Carter sat on a sleeping bag, his face buried in his hands. She kneeled beside him. He shifted, staring up at a space beyond her head.

She touched his chin with her finger, turning his face to hers. "What just happened?"

"Will was my first friend in the Argentum. As close to a friend as I could make. It was hard, when we were all fighting against each other for our superiors' favor," he said.

"Why would Leianna possibly think you were involved in him being executed?"

His eyes locked onto hers. "I didn't know any of this would happen."

Alexandria's heartbeat picked up speed. "What does that mean?" she asked in a hoarse whisper.

"I killed Queen Evangeline."

TWENTY-TWO

Alexandria's hand fell. She tried to jump to her feet but stumbled as the world spun around her.

"Carter..." she started, not knowing what to say next.

"She ordered me to do it. I had no choice. It was what she wanted." His voice pleaded for her to listen, to understand.

She was beyond comprehension.

For two weeks, she had been afraid of the queen's assassin finding her, killing her. She had told Carter those fears. He could have alleviated them and given her the answers that she longed for. But he hadn't.

"You lied to me." Her voice staggered. "Again."

"I never lied to you."

"You hid the truth," she whisper-shouted. James and Leianna could not know about this conversation. Still, it was difficult to keep her voice low in response to his confession.

"If I had told you the truth from the very beginning, would you have trusted me?"

"No, I wouldn't have."

"Exactly." Carter leaned forward, his hand extended toward her face, before he grimaced and leaned back.

Alexandria remembered her earlier vow to change his bandages. Though her head told her to leave him, she shoved past her anger for a moment. She knew deep down that he was right. If he had told her at the fuel station that he was ordered to kill Queen Evangeline *by* the queen herself, she never would have believed him. She would have run in the opposite direction and likely gotten herself killed in the process.

She wordlessly pulled the kit out of her backpack, the roll of bandages dwindling as the days passed. "Lift up your shirt," she said. It took effort for her to keep her voice calm. To trust him. She would have to, if she wanted to survive. She would remind herself, over and over, that she would be in Regia soon. That he was not a threat. It did not take as much convincing as she would have liked for her shoulders to relax.

He complied. Alexandria pulled off her gloves, tossing them to the side. She unwound the bandages from his ribs carefully, wrapping her arms around his back to pull the loose end through. Pure instinct made her hold her breath. She kept her skin from making contact with his, as if touching him would change everything. Her heart skipped a beat. And another.

Alexandria cleared her throat. "Why did the queen ask you to kill her?" It was too casual, obvious that her calm tone was a facade.

Carter shook his head. "I don't know for sure. I didn't ask." His lower lip trembled as he spoke. Such a tiny movement, but she was transfixed by it. "When Queen Evangeline gave you an order, you listened. Even if you didn't want to do it. Especially then. There were many people she did not trust in that palace, for good reason. Any flicker of doubt put you on that list."

"Why? How did she have so much control over you? I know she was the queen, but this is different. She had to have been controlling you, somehow. I just can't understand why you would carry out that order."

"We loved her." His brown eyes grew deeper in the darkness. "For those of us without a family, she was everything. Her people might have disagreed with her, hated her even, but she was like a mother to the agents who enlisted young. We grew up under her care."

Alexandria held her breath as the bandage came free, listening for his next words. His stitches were jagged, but they held. Stark black lines against the tan skin of his rib cage.

"I knew she must have had a reason. She always had a plan. The poison I was to put in her food, the time she would consume it, how long until she would be declared dead, she had it all laid out. I didn't even have a chance to think about it. Not until I was already in Kureya, watching you. Protecting you." He held her hand against his chest. It was shockingly warm, even through his shirt. Alexandria sucked in a breath.

Carter ran his thumb across her knuckles. A shiver crept up her spine. "I didn't want any of this to happen, Alexandria. Not her death, not the Campaign, not..." He exhaled shakily. "Any of it. I would take it back if I could."

"I wouldn't." Her voice would've been lost if the wind was any louder. "Don't blame yourself for the Campaign. It would have happened eventually, and I might not have had you by my side."

He squeezed her hand. "You finally figured out I'm not that insufferable. I knew you'd come around."

"No. I just realized I can't survive without you." *Can't survive the trip to Regia*, she corrected internally, though she could not make herself repeat the words out loud.

Her eyes caught his. They drew her in like the waves on Kureya's beach. A storm built between them, and that pull, that gravitational force, grew stronger by the second.

His other hand brushed a curl behind her ear. He twisted his finger in it, twirling it as if it was the most fascinating thing he had ever seen. She circled his wrist, guiding his hand to hold the nape of her neck, fingers entwined in her hair. His eyes flashed. The corner of his mouth raised a fraction. A dimple slowly appeared there.

The tent unzipped, and they both threw themselves backwards. Carter let out an audible gasp as he strained his stitches. "Let me bandage that again," Alexandria hurried to say.

James was barely inside the tent before he apologized for interrupting. Alexandria was not entirely sure what he had walked into, either. All she knew was that he had saved her from making a terrible decision.

Carter was an Argentum agent. She would, if all went to plan, become the queen. Very bad conflict of interest, even if they just kissed and moved on.

Alexandria shook the thought out of her head with such force that James asked, "Is there a fly in here?"

She hoped that the darkness hid her blush. "No–I–I'm just going to finish this." Adrenaline shocked her system, making her hands quiver as she wrapped new bandages around Carter's ribs once more. Whatever had passed between them was now long gone with James's entrance.

"How's Leianna?" Carter asked, his voice low.

"She's back. Not good company right now, but I understand why," James replied. He checked the watch on his wrist. "Her husband's execution is in an hour."

When Alexandria had finished with Carter's bandages, they all huddled into their separate sleeping bags. She imagined that it would be warmer if she was sharing with someone. With where that train of thought ended up, she wrapped her arms around herself tighter, resolving to freeze rather than explore that alternative.

That will never happen again. She promised herself that, even though nothing had really happened. Carter was her one source of true safety. Of course, she would get those feelings mixed up with something else. A knife twisted in her gut as she pondered what Phillip might think. But Phillip was dead, she reminded herself. Yet that was exactly why she could not be distracted, now that she was so close to Regia. She had to remember Queen Evangeline so that she did not become her. To do that, she must remember what exactly Evangeline did to her and countless other families across Kevelda.

She could not forget Phillip. Nor could she forget that the queen's assassin, Evangeline's most trusted agent, was sleeping right next to her.

Alexandria laid with her eyes closed, sleepless, but trying not to think. Thinking never brought her anything good, not after dark.

Soft cries sounded through the fabric of the tent. *Leianna.* Alexandria turned to look at James's watch, his arm sprawled across the tent floor.

It was a minute after midnight.

TWENTY-THREE

The bridge stretched so far that Alexandria could not see the end. It had to be at least two kilometers long. They would be completely exposed as they crossed it.

A chill ran up Alexandria's spine that had nothing to do with the weather. As they neared the coast, it was warm enough that the river remained unfrozen, though Alexandria doubted it would ever freeze with how fast it flowed.

If they had a boat to cross the river, perhaps they would be safer. But that was not an option. They would have to take the risk and run the bridge.

Leianna took the sleeping bag from Alexandria's shoulder. "If you need to run, it's better to not have the extra weight."

"What about you?" Alexandria asked as the woman shouldered the bag herself.

"They won't be looking at me," Leianna replied. Defeat laced her tone, her voice completely flat. Alexandria searched her face for any emotion, but Leianna hid her feelings well. That is, if she allowed herself to feel anything at all in that moment.

Alexandria nodded, unable to respond. Her mind raced, the image of Will being hanged joined rapidly by the thought of her dying on this bridge.

Leianna pointed at James. "I go first, then you." She turned to Alexandria. "Wait five minutes before you follow. If we don't shout, then it's all clear. Carter will take up the rear."

Leianna and James began to run before she could protest. Alexandria counted in her head, mouthing the numbers as they passed. After a few minutes, the two disappeared over the arch of the bridge.

She bounced from side to side, her legs shaking with anxious energy. Carter rested his hand on her back. "We'll make it," he whispered into the breeze. Alexandria stood still, her nerves on fire where he touched her. Her senses tuned into his every movement. She was acutely aware of where he stood, the shifting of his body in her periphery.

The countdown could not end soon enough. She braced herself, bending her knees slightly. "Are you ready?" she asked.

"As I'll ever be," Carter responded.

Alexandria took off running. Her lungs burned as cold air swept down her throat. She had to pace herself. They had crossed less than half of the bridge, and she already struggled to breathe.

She looked back, nearly stumbling in the process. Carter kept pace with her. He could have passed her, she was sure, but he clutched his injured side. The pained twist of his mouth intensified with every step.

"Keep going," he breathed, his voice ragged with the effort. "I'm fine."

She faced the bridge in front of her. He would not let her slow down, even if the run was torture for him. They cleared the top of the bridge in a few minutes. Leianna and James disappeared into the trees ahead.

"Almost there," she staggered out. It was more a reminder for herself than for him.

Humming rose from behind them. It started as a low rumble, growing louder with each step.

Someone was driving on the bridge.

They were too far away from the tree line to make it in time. There was still a quarter of the bridge left to cross. Alexandria slowed, her heart thumping so hard it felt as though it would shatter her sternum. Her thumb rested on the hilt of her dagger. Carter threw the hood of her coat over her head. She prayed it would be enough to disguise her.

He wrapped his arm around her shoulders, a shield between her and the road. A once-white truck, more covered by rust than its original paint, drove past them. Alexandria blew out a breath as they continued down the road.

The truck stopped at the end of the bridge and turned around to face them. Alexandria's heart skipped a beat. It stopped completely when the driver flashed the barrel of a shotgun through the window.

"We won't make it," she said, her voice taught. Every muscle in her body tensed. Her thoughts circled like buzzards, and she couldn't pick a single one of them out.

Carter latched his hand to hers. "Trust me," he said, as he climbed onto the ledge of the bridge.

"What are you doing?" she shouted.

"It's our only choice." He pointed to the water below. It was only about five meters from the ledge to the river, but with the speed it flowed...

Alexandria did not want to think about what would happen when they hit the surface. She gripped his hand like a lifeline. The truck came closer. Metal glinted as the gun pointed at them.

"Okay," she said, "okay, okay, okay." She jumped onto the ledge. Her eyes caught Carter's one more time.

He smiled tightly. "See you on the other side."

For a second, her feet touched only air.

Her skin stung as she hit the surface, like pure concrete on contact. All she knew was darkness. The current pulled her under, twisted her around.

A vise gripped her lungs as the pressure of the water forced the air from her chest. Her head spun as her body did, mind unraveling and spiraling. Popping filled her ears. She could not find the surface. All the while, the river kept running, and there was no light, no up or down, only the depths to which she was rapidly sinking.

An arm wrapped around her, dragging her back to the world above.

Air rushed back into her lungs, cold and clear and sharp. She kept herself just above the surface, gasping every time the water crashed against her mouth.

Once she had her bearings, she swam as hard as she could. Her arms burned. She clambered through the waves. The water chilled her to the bone. A few minutes in, her joints became solid.

So close. Gravel from the shore bit at her hands. Scraping her fingers against the ground, she grappled for purchase as the river threatened to carry her away.

Carter had already made it to the bank. His entire body shook. He reached for her hand, water dripping down his face. She threw herself at him, gripping his arm. Icy air stabbed her skin as she climbed from the water.

They ran for the trees. Her soaking wet clothes dragged her down, backpack slamming into her back. From the protection of the woods, Alexandria saw that they had been carried far downstream from the bridge. It was hardly a speck in the distance. She hoped that Leianna and James would not come to look for them.

Alexandria and Carter needed to find somewhere to stay, and fast. If they stayed in those wet clothes, they would freeze. Changing in the forest was not an option either, not with the temperature barely above freezing and the truck driver knowing where they were. They couldn't stop, couldn't rest.

Carter slumped against a tree, gripping his side. Alexandria realized that the drops on his face were tears, not river water. He unzipped his coat and pulled away the shirt that clung to his skin.

Alexandria gasped when she saw his side. The swim had torn his stitches. Blood gushed down the side of his ribs. It soaked through the wet bandages.

She dropped to the ground, rifling through the drenched backpack. To her surprise, the interior was only damp. The bandages in the plastic kit were completely dry. Wadding them into a ball, she held the bundle firmly against his open wound. He tossed the old cloth to the ground.

"I'm okay," he said through gritted teeth. His closed eyes and furrowed brows indicated otherwise.

"No, you're not. We have to find somewhere to go." Tugging his shirt down over the cloth, she wrapped her arm around him, putting pressure on the wound as they walked. They shivered in sync.

"Just keep walking." It sounded like he was reminding himself. She burrowed into his side, not daring to move the cloth keeping the blood inside his body.

They picked their way through the forest, muscles slowing with each root and stump they maneuvered around. Alexandria's grip on the bandage slipped further with time. Her limbs begged her to sit, to rest.

It couldn't hurt, she thought, *I just want to sleep.*

She stumbled, knees giving out. Her ankle twisted. A lightning bolt of pain shot up her leg, bringing her back to her senses. "This–this is going to be what kills me," she chattered. Her tongue was thick in her mouth. "The cold. Not a thronehunter. After all this time."

Give up, the voice in her head demanded. *You deserve to rest.*

"No, I won't let that happen." Carter's words slurred. His leg dragged slightly behind him.

"You can't st–stop it."

Alexandria could not discern how long they had been walking. Two minutes? Twenty? An hour? Time was irrelevant. They would die in these woods. She fell again, but this time, she did not rise.

Carter shook her shoulder. Her palms dug into her eyes, the darkness inviting. "Come on. Get up."

"Five minutes." She did not recognize her own voice. It was light, like a breeze on a summer day. Summer days on the beach with her friends. Kissing Phillip. His hands in her hair.

The memory roped her in, begged her to stay. She would relive it over and over and over. *Five minutes. Let me be there again for five minutes.* But when she pictured that day again, only Carter was there.

"Please get up," he pleaded, his voice jarring against the smile on his face as he stared at her on that beach like she was the only person in the world.

She tangled her hand in the short curls of hair behind his ear. His eyes matched the golden sunset. The dimple appeared next to his mouth. She traced it with the tips of her fingers. He pulled her toward him, his arm around her waist. When he held her face with his other hand, she did not hesitate to press her lips against his.

The kiss was a promise, a future. It tore her heart in two and pieced it back together again. He tightened his grip on the back of her neck, and she melted into him. His mouth was hot against her frozen skin. Skin too cold for summer.

Reality punched through the mirage.

"Alexandria Redmond, you are not going to die here. You are going to get to Regia, sit on the throne, and live a long life. You are going to become the queen and grow old and *live*." His voice broke, mouth pressed against her ear. "Don't you dare give up on me now."

It shocked her system enough for her to plant the palm of her hand against the ground. She shoved herself up, limbs shaking uncontrollably. *I will fight.*

Carter wrapped his arm around her waist and tugged her to her feet. "That's it," he whispered, breath hot against her skin. "Stay with me."

"I'm here," she replied weakly. Her blinks grew longer.

She stepped forward, her legs struggling to remember how to walk as he guided her. His breaths grew ragged. Carter was fading, too.

"Tell me a story," he said.

She could barely string together a sentence in her head. The first memory she could think of was the one where she told Phillip she loved him on the beach. And so she told Carter, recounting her and Phillip's friendship, the feelings that grew up alongside them. Whether she could distinguish between fact and fiction, between the memory of Phillip and the dream of Carter, she did not know, or frankly, have the energy to care. She simply spoke and spoke, carrying them through the forest as their legs failed.

Darkness rimmed her vision, growing steadily. Alexandria's focus faded. Her sight narrowed to a pinhole in front of her.

It was through that pinhole that she recognized the shape of a structure in the distance. Some kind of shack.

Stiffly, she craned her neck to catch a glimpse of Carter's face. His lips were blue. "Ahead of us," she croaked.

He nodded blankly. They stumbled toward the shack, half dead, half alive. Fatigue pressed in.

So close. You can sleep soon. The thought kept her moving. She and Carter dragged each other to the door, a dirt-covered wooden slab. A sign hung on the wall next to it, but Alexandria could not read the words. Her hand twisted the rusted knob. It opened easily.

Once inside, they both dropped to the floor. The interior was a few degrees warmer, but it would not bring their body temperatures back up. "Fire," she said. Carter's eyes did not flash with any recognition. By some miracle, he moved, crawling over to a fireplace on the other side of the room. A stack of logs laid next to it. He tossed a few into the pit.

Alexandria peeled off her gloves. She knelt in front of the fireplace and struck her blade against the flint. Her fingers struggled to grip the metal. Carter held his hands over hers, holding them in place. A spark flashed against the wood. The fire caught, slowly sending heat back into her skin.

She forced herself to stay awake as she reached into her bag, pulling out the slightly damp clothes. Carter followed her movements. He must have come to the realization that he needed to change out of his wet clothes, too, because he pulled an extra set out of his backpack. The Argentum must have supplied him with a bag even more waterproof than hers, because his clothes were completely dry.

Alexandria limped to a corner and stripped off her wet clothes. The chill threatened to set in again, but she moved quickly to throw her relatively dry shirt over her head. She turned to see Carter's side stained red with blood.

She scoured the room, her vision still fuzzy, for any kind of first aid supplies. A bright red box stuck to the wall by the door. *Stay awake,* she bargained with herself, *just one more minute.* Inside the box was a package of adhesive sutures. Her body screamed at her to stop as she shuffled back over to Carter.

Neither one of them spoke as she wiped away the blood around the wound with her sleeve. She pinched the two ends of the gash together. Carter did not wince. She prayed that his numbness was reversible. After she applied the sutures, she helped him pull his new shirt on.

They collapsed in front of the fireplace. Alexandria huddled against him and finally succumbed to the darkness.

TWENTY-FOUR

Alexandria awoke to the distinct feeling that someone had shoved a shard of glass through her skull.

As they slept, the fire had burned down to embers. Her joints were stiff as she crept over to the stack of logs and set another gently on the dwindling flame. It caught after a few moments. She held her hands out over the delicious warmth, weakness still permeating her sore limbs.

Carter stirred as she searched her backpack for the water canteen. It was nowhere to be found. The current must have ripped it from the side of the backpack. Her head throbbed as she stood.

They would not survive the day without water. Alexandria began to search the shack, praying that she would find something to help them. The room only had two doors, with four windows lining the walls, one on each side. One of the doors led to a small bathroom, but Alexandria quickly found that the running water had been cut off.

In the main room, pins stuck a map of Kevelda to the wall, with another map of the area hanging beside it. Upon closer inspection, she discovered that they were on the outskirts of Regia. Another day and they would make it to the suburban area.

A wooden desk jutted out from the wall below the maps. Piles of books rested beside it, ranging from wilderness survival information to a well-read romance novel. Alexandria skimmed it, stowing it under her arm. Light reading never hurt anyone.

On a shelf by the entrance laid a solitary can of preserved fruit, tilted on its side, condensation lining the inside of the jar. An expiration date written in marker noted that the fruit had gone bad three years prior. Whatever this place was, it had been abandoned long ago.

The tension gripping her chest eased. No one would find them here. They were safe, for the time being. They could finally rest. Get their strength back before running into the fray once again.

She nearly jumped for joy when she spotted a barrel in the corner. A faded label told her that it was, in fact, water. Ramming an old screwdriver under the lid, she opened the barrel with a *pop*. She took the can of expired fruit, dumped it down the sink, rinsed the container with some water from the barrel, and filled the glass.

Her head instantly cleared as she drank it, though it filled her mouth with a stale, metallic aftertaste. They had been preserving their water over the past few days, and Alexandria did not realize how dehydrated she was until she took her first sip. She downed the entire glass, then another, before filling it again and bringing it over to Carter.

He groaned when she shook his shoulder. "Rise and shine," she said, "I have a gift for you."

Redness rimmed his eyes. He stared at her bleary-eyed before registering her words. Shifting onto his elbows, he reached for the glass in her outstretched hand. "Thank you," he said, drinking it in a few seconds. He winced at the taste, but still handed it back to her for a refill.

"How are you feeling?" she asked.

"Never been better."

Carter did not say anything as she kneeled and lifted his shirt to look at the adhesive sutures she had haphazardly placed last night. Proof that he was still a little bit out of it. No joking comments.

The white strips held the wound together tightly. Only a slight trickle of blood leaked from it, now dried flat against his skin.

"I'll be good to go in a few minutes," he said.

She shook her head. "We'll stay here through the night." It appeared to be some time in the afternoon, if she could judge by the fading light through the windows. They could have been out for only a few hours or a whole day. The latter option set her heart racing. If Leianna and James had moved, there would be no way to find them. Still, another night would not change that. Traveling through the woods in the dark would be dangerous enough in itself, further compounded by their need to recover.

"I won't argue with that." He took another sip of water. Alexandria tracked the movement, her throat still raw with thirst. Even though it would make meeting back up more difficult, she hoped that their other companions had found water somewhere. James stocked up on some food from the pantry, so they would not starve. Beyond Leianna's own canteen, however, they would dehydrate quickly.

Alexandria rested her forehead against Carter's shoulder. The glass clicked against the wood floor. His arms wrapped around her, a hand holding the back of her neck. He trailed his other hand up and down her spine, almost absentmindedly. Her senses sharpened, attuned to every movement.

In that moment, she let go of every lingering question she had about him. The queen had taken advantage of him, using his loyalty to command him to do something he would regret for the rest of his life. Alexandria knew that the guilt he carried drove him to protect *her*. She had never felt safer than she did there, on the floor of the shack in the forest, in his arms. Not in the past two years. Maybe even before that.

Her skin tingled where he touched her, a hundred zaps of electricity waking up her nerves. She was not tired anymore. Even as her eyelids struggled to open, her mind lit up. His breath warmed her scalp as he pressed his face against her hair.

One more person she could let down. One more person her choices could harm.

Yet as long as he stood by her side, and even if he didn't, she would risk everything to protect him. That was their mutual promise, if unspoken. She would crawl to the ends of the earth, scrape her hands and knees, fight, beg, and die, if it meant the people she loved were safe. Against all odds, he was one of them.

With that thought, she drifted off to sleep, clinging to him like a tree in a storm.

~

Brightness seared through her eyelids. Alexandria lifted an arm over her face, but the light seeped through. She blinked her eyes open, her pupils painfully adjusting to the light.

Carter held a book up over her. He read it intently, not noticing that she had woken. She raised her head from where it rested on his chest. "I didn't expect you to be a fan of romance novels," she said, her voice still raspy from sleep.

"What can I say, I'm invested."

"Don't tell me what happens."

He closed the book and set it beside him. His hand rose to her hair, brushing curls off her face. "I think they're going to kiss soon. Though, if you ask me, I prefer the long game."

Alexandria was not entirely sure if he was talking about the book. A shiver trailed down her spine. She was reading too far into his words. "I just told you not to tell me what happens."

If they were just two normal people who met by chance in Kureya, Alexandria doubted the game would be very long at all.

But they were not normal people. He was an Argentum agent. She would be the queen. The thought made her move her head away from his chest and stand up.

"Have you eaten?" she asked. Her stomach grumbled in response.

Carter followed her to his feet. "I was waiting for you."

"How chivalrous." She tossed him one of the last packages of preserved fish. They would have to find more food in Regia before they traveled to the palace.

They ate slowly, enjoying the last moments of peace before they reentered the world. Alexandria wondered if she would ever feel safe again, even on the throne. Especially then, with the war in Thaertos raging. Perhaps Evangeline had wanted a way out of it all, and that was why she ordered Carter to kill her. The thought did not sit well in Alexandria's mind. Not when she would take the woman's place soon enough.

Their coats were dry in front of the fire. Carter must have moved them at some point while she was sleeping. "Did you get any rest?" she asked.

"Enough."

"That doesn't sound very promising."

Carter smirked, pointing the packet of fish at her. "You're a restless sleeper. You also talk in your sleep. Quite a bit, actually."

Heat rose to her cheeks. She did not recall what she had dreamed about, but it likely consisted of her parents, Phillip, or him. It was better if she did not know. "I'll keep that in mind."

"Good. For the sake of your future guards."

The Queen's Guard. She forgot that she would have to choose her own. Carter would be one of them, of course. She needed to keep an eye on him. "You had to watch the queen sleep?"

He shrugged. "How else would we protect against attackers?"

"Standing *outside* the door, for one."

"We never thought of that." His eyes widened sarcastically. "A story spread around the Argentum that an assailant had scaled the walls and climbed in through the window. Her Majesty had a knife hidden under her pillow and took care of him herself, but after that, the queen always had two guards stationed inside her bedroom."

"It looks like you'll have to deal with my sleep-talking for a long time, then." She realized the implication much too late. To cover her blush, she pulled on her coat and gloves, threw her steadily lightening backpack over her shoulder, and walked to the door. "Let's go," she said.

Carter followed shortly behind. She took her last breath in the safety of their shelter before opening the door and stepping into the real world. The one where everyone she came across would try to kill her.

On the way into the forest, she looked back to read the sign on the shack. It was a ranger station, from the days when people would explore these woods, not confined to their cities and struggling to provide. The Draft had likely taken the person who tended to it.

It was a miracle that they had come across it, hypothermic and half-dead. She silently hoped for another miracle, one that would help her survive the fight to come.

TWENTY-FIVE

Alexandria had grown accustomed to the feeling of someone following her: the sounds they made, the hairs raising on the back of her neck, the rapid heartbeat.

When a twig snapped behind them, she looped her arm through Carter's, tapping twice on his bicep with her pointer finger. "Someone's here," she whispered.

Carter nodded almost imperceptibly in response. The river had stolen his gun. He dragged his finger across the hilt of his dagger, ready to use it at a moment's notice. Whoever was trailing them did not come closer. The two picked up speed, the slight noise of leaves rustling growing quicker as they did. Still, the sounds stayed at a distance.

They reached a small clearing, pausing in the center. Carter whipped around and threw the blade. It lodged in the middle of a tree.

A girl cowered centimeters away from where the blade struck. Her pale skin made her look ghostly with the near-dead trees surrounding her. She went even paler when Alexandria locked eyes with her.

She's just a child, she thought. Mid-adolescence, at most. The girl gripped no weapons, just the back of her head as she shielded herself from the blows she expected them to deal.

Alexandria held the palms of her hands in the air. "We won't hurt you," she said. "Tell us why you're here."

Carter tensed behind her, his hand on her back as she stepped forward. Though her senses screamed at her to run, she could not ignore the child in front of them, scared and starved half to death. The girl's cheeks had deep hollows underneath them. Alexandria's heart panged at the sight.

She crouched in front of the girl. "Please," she said. Alexandria met Carter's gaze. He backed away slowly, careful not to startle the girl further. The girl had no blades on her, but even if she did, Alexandria would have no difficulty fighting her.

"I need the money," the girl whispered. "He hasn't eaten in three days. I don't think he'll make it much longer."

"Who?"

The girl blinked up through long eyelashes. A tear dropped from her left eye. "My brother."

"Where are your parents?"

"Dead."

Alexandria inhaled sharply. "How would you get money from this?" she asked.

"I–I heard it on the radio. They're rewarding anyone with information about where you are."

"The Dais?" She held her breath as she waited for the girl's response.

The girl nodded. "I'm sorry," she said, almost pleading, "I promise I won't tell if you let me go."

Alexandria touched the girl's shoulder, and she shrunk away. "What's your name?"

"Reagan."

They only had one package of dried fish left. Alexandria dug into her backpack anyways. She handed it to the girl, who grabbed it tentatively. "Reagan, how did you find us?"

"I'm a good tracker." A hint of pride glowed in her eyes.

The corner of Alexandria's mouth tilted upwards. "Yes, you are." She rose to her feet, her knees protesting with the movement.

As she turned away, the girl spoke again. "Remember us when you're queen." Alexandria saw only hope in the girl's eyes. Not ambition or greed. *Hope* that she and her brother would survive with Alexandria on the throne.

"I will," Alexandria promised.

Carter squeezed her hand as they walked into the forest, leaving the girl behind. "You'll make a great queen," he said.

The second time someone had told her that, and she still did not know if she believed it. She hoped he did not notice the tear that she wiped away.

~

They followed the river through the forest until they spotted a blue tent peeking through the trees. Alexandria would have run if her legs allowed. Though they had rested for a day at least, her body ached.

Alexandria could not stop thinking about their interaction with the girl. The Dais was rewarding people for information about her whereabouts. Even if someone did not want to kill her, they had the incentive to tell the thronehunters where she was. Everyone was a potential threat before, but now, they all could get her killed, if not by their own hands.

She sighed, breath clouding around her. How she wished she was in the shack again. It was impossible to ignore the cold now that she had known warmth.

James threw another log onto the fire as they walked up. His eyes brightened when he saw them. "We thought you were dead," he said, embracing Alexandria.

"Almost," she replied. "How long were we gone?"

"You don't know?"

"We had a minor hypothermia-related incident."

James shook his head. "Two days. We were about to pack up and head into the city."

So they had slept for a whole day after finding the ranger station. Alexandria certainly did not feel like she had.

"No one noticed the fire?" She was sure that the driver with the gun had reported them. They might as well get a reward if not the crown.

Leianna stepped out of the tent. "A couple came by. They thought we were thronehunters, too. We told them that you'd been spotted on the other side of Regia, that we were heading that way."

Alexandria sighed in relief. "That's good. They'll likely tell the reporters that."

"We should still be careful with the fire though," Carter said, "in case more people come to the area."

"I agree," Leianna replied. "We can last a night without it. Once we're in Regia, we won't need a fire."

They would be in Regia tomorrow. The final push to the throne. Alexandria braced herself against a tree to keep from heaving.

This is it, she thought. She could be dead within the next few days. With her friends protecting her, they could be, too. Claws of fear constricted her lungs.

"What's the plan?" she asked. She cleared her throat to cover for the shakiness in her voice. "What will we do when we get to Regia?"

"I know someone who will let us stay for the night before we go to the palace," Leianna said.

"I don't trust anyone in the Argentum. Not after Jason."

"He's not Argentum."

Alexandria raised her eyebrow. "Who is it, then?"

"Will's father. Bailey."

A knife could cut the silence.

"Won't he be under surveillance?" James said warily. Alexandria had the same suspicion. Will was just executed for assassinating the queen. No doubt his father would be investigated as well.

"Argentum agents won't kill Alexandria in a church. That's an unspoken rule even *they* won't break. Especially when it comes to Bailey."

"Why?" Alexandria asked.

"Because," Leianna said, "he performed Queen Evangeline's last rites, and King Tomas's before her." She smothered the fire with a clump of snow. "He is the only way you'll make it to the palace alive."

"There are tunnels," Carter said, eyes wide. "That's how Queen Evangeline said the priest would make it to her without alerting anyone to her death."

Leianna nodded. She locked eyes with Alexandria. "And that's how you'll get in."

Another miracle. Alexandria would be praying a lot in this church.

~

Alexandria, James, and Carter crowded into the tent, huddling inside their sleeping bags to fight the nightly chill. Alexandria was tempted to ask Leianna if she wanted to join them, but the woman had been particularly silent that evening. It would be difficult for her to see her deceased husband's father. Alexandria could not even begin to imagine what Leianna was feeling.

Alexandria loved Phillip, and when he was Drafted, it broke her so thoroughly that she doubted she would ever piece herself back together. Nights that she hardly remembered were the way she kept herself alive, her body at least. Her heart had stopped beating when Phillip left. Only when her friends intervened was she able to start picking up the shards, though she was still fragile.

But Phillip had never been *hers*. She longed for him to be, but to the world around them, they were just friends. They could have been more, if they had the time. If they had been married, Alexandria wondered if she would still be stuck in the daze that had trapped her in the months after.

Leianna might hide her feelings, but Alexandria did not doubt that they drowned her nonetheless.

Nerves about what the next day would bring shook Alexandria awake every time she tried to close her eyes. She sat up in her sleeping bag, clutching it to her shoulders. At her movement, James did the same. Carter remained still, his chest rising and falling steadily. At least he could get some rest, now that she was not tossing and turning.

She absentmindedly shifted closer to him, brushing his hair with her fingers.

"Are you going to keep doing that? If so, I'll close my eyes again," James whispered.

Her hand stilled as she realized what she had been doing. "Sorry."

"Don't apologize. It's good to see you like this."

"Like what?"

He cocked his head to the side and rolled his eyes. "You know what."

"I really don't."

"Even in the face of death, you're smiling. Because of *him*."

"You underestimate the wonderful impact of having a conversation with you."

"I haven't seen you like this since Phillip..." He didn't finish the sentence.

Alexandria pulled her hand back into the sleeping bag. A chill went up her spine. "This is nothing like that. It could never happen."

James stilled. "You loved him, didn't you?"

Alexandria nodded, tears welling up in her eyes.

"Did Amira know?"

"Yes. She was the only one who did."

"I've been a terrible friend to you. And now Amira's gone, too."

Her throat tightened. "You were never a terrible friend. You lost him, same as me, same as all of us. But you were the one to remind me of that. To pull me out of my misery long enough to realize that I still had you two." She brushed her coat sleeve across her cheek. "We'll find her."

"I don't know what I'll do if we don't."

James and Amira had always been close. Amira had an innocent crush on him when they first met, but as they grew older, she wasn't really interested in anyone in that way. She had Sam to take care of, and even if she didn't, Alexandria doubted Amira would pursue a romantic relationship. Still, she and James had a close bond, different than what Alexandria and James shared, perhaps stronger. While Alexandria and James bickered, he and Amira stood side-by-side. They were the closest of allies. Their hearts beat as one, even if his went on to beat for another.

"We will." Alexandria feared she had made too many promises that she could not keep already.

"What if it wasn't Mendoza?"

Another nagging thought she long tried to bury. "There's no one else." She did not know that, not for certain. Many other people could want to target the future queen's friends and family. The last queen had sent thousands of people to die. Alexandria would inherit numerous enemies. The problem laid in the fact that she had not yet uncovered their names. If Mendoza was not the one to take Amira, then she would have to face rivals she could not even begin to imagine.

"I hope you're right."

She laid on her back, settling down next to Carter. "I do, too."

With that thought in her mind, she did not feel like talking anymore. It prevented her from getting any real sleep, even as Leianna and Carter switched out for his watch shift. She stared at the top of the tent until he returned and James took his place.

Carter's eyes met hers before he laid down next to her. He slid a hand out of his sleeping bag, palm facing the ceiling. Alexandria took it with her own.

Everything would change when they got to Regia.

She tossed and turned, holding onto his hand as long as she could.

TWENTY-SIX

No trees covered them as they traveled through the manicured lawns of suburban Regia.

Multiple-story houses lined the streets in rows, roofs painted in primary colors. Red, blue, yellow. Red, blue, yellow. Alexandria became dizzy when she tried to take in the size of the homes. She resolved to keep her head down and stare at the road as they went.

It was too early for anyone to venture outside. The four had woken up long before the sun, none of them getting much sleep anyways. Their surroundings made even less noise than they did. All Alexandria could hear was the hushed breathing of her companions. She battled to keep her own breaths steady. It grew increasingly difficult the closer they came to the palace and the brighter the sky glowed.

An alarm blared, jolting them from their concentrated steps. Alexandria loathed the sound of the emergency alert. It would be the first thing she would rid the kingdom of when she sat on the throne.

Static crackled from the triangular speakers embedded into light poles every few streets. Leianna stiffened, scanning their surroundings.

Mendoza's voice carried across the silent neighborhood. "Good morning, Kevelda. We have an exciting update on the Campaign. Alexandria Redmond has been spotted in Regia."

Alexandria immediately dropped to the ground, as if the words alone would set hordes of people on her. She would find no cover here. They needed to move quickly.

"The Dais has decided to celebrate this development by inviting all the mayors and their families to the Ascension. Every citizen of Kevelda is welcome to gather in their town squares to view the televised event. We hope you will join us in welcoming the heir, whether it be Alexandria or another heir ascendant."

Tense silence flooded the air once more. Bile rose in Alexandria's throat. She was going to be sick. She kneeled in front of a perfectly square bush just in time. Carter rushed to her side, pulling her hair back.

"We have to go," Leianna said.

Alexandria vomited once more, her stomach on fire as she rose unsteadily to her feet. Her lungs stopped working. She heaved in and out, desperate to drive oxygen into her body.

James spoke next. "You can do this."

"Okay," Alexandria choked out. She swallowed hard.

And then she ran.

Leianna pulled in front, leading them through the streets of Regia. The houses became denser, sitting almost on top of each other, as they journeyed deeper into the heart of the capital. Regia's citizens were waking up. Cars populated the road. Drivers turned to stare. Pedestrians pointed. Alexandria did not look at them beyond a passing glance.

The four wove through the maze of alleys and passageways. With their speed, the city transformed into a sea of white plaster and glass. Above all the buildings stood the palace, a grey stone building that rose to a point, a clock set straight in the middle. It cascaded out in pillars, expanding into wings on each side of the main tower. Alexandria knew the building well. She had stared in awe of it before she had come to understand the court politics that corrupted within.

Beyond pointing and staring, no one attacked them. It made Alexandria uneasy. She had prepared for a fight at every corner all the way until they reached the palace. Why did they not try now, when she was so visible?

Perhaps the proposed spectacle of the Ascension satisfied their need for her blood enough to keep them at bay. It would be much more entertaining to see her fight dozens of mayors and their children than to take her out themselves. Alexandria might have been sick again if she had not been running so fast.

There had to be some in the capital who wanted the throne. Like Jason. He was from Regia, part of the Argentum even, but could not keep his daughter fed. Were there more in

Regia who faced the same challenges? If so, she was hopeful not to meet them at the end of a blade.

She had promised the girl in the forest that she would remember her. She would remember all of them. Reagan and her brother. Petra. James. Elsie. Mrs. Collins. Sam. Phillip. The people she watched get drafted as she sat on stage, the faces she had not studied, the names she did not memorize. They would all watch her from her mind, scrutinizing every decision that she made.

If she survived the Ascension, they would follow her for the rest of her life.

Leianna ducked into an alley. Alexandria nearly crashed into her as she slowed to a stop in front of a dark wooden door. It was attached to a building that looked much like the others: white, only two or three stories tall, with a multitude of small windows. Leianna knocked three times.

The door cracked open an inch. A pair of steel grey eyes stared back at them. Then, it opened wide. The four shuffled into the safety of the church. An elderly man locked the door behind them.

"Bailey, we need your help," Leianna said.

The man surveyed Alexandria. His lined face was friendly, though his mouth was flat as he evaluated the situation. "I see," he said, voice softer than Alexandria imagined it would be, "You're always welcome here, Lei."

Leianna turned her face to the altar at the end of the sanctuary as if scrutinizing it. She looked back a few moments later, eyes glassy. "I'm sorry," she said. "I wish I had been there."

The man's mouth quivered. "It is a lonely thing, outliving one's child."

Leianna nodded. Her expression neutralized again. She shifted, motioning toward Alexandria. "I assume you know who this is."

Alexandria held out a hand. Bailey shook it, clasping his other hand over hers. "I do."

"Nice to meet you, Father Bailey."

"Just 'Bailey' is fine, unless you need confession."

She chewed her lower lip, all too aware of the shame that settled at her core. It had become familiar to her, an old friend she fell back on whenever she reached her lowest points. "I might."

He examined her face for a long moment. After she broke their eye contact, he shook Carter and James's hands.

"Would you all like something to eat?" Bailey asked.

Alexandria had never followed someone faster.

~

Bailey watched Carter as they ate. He gave them each soup and a slice of bread. With their diet over the past few days having consisted of preserved fish and minimal water, Alexandria nearly drowned herself in the bowl. It burnt the roof of her mouth as she sipped the broth. The hunger was like nothing she had ever known.

When she emerged from the bowl, Bailey's eyes were still focused on Carter. Surveying. Scrutinizing. Alexandria wondered what it could possibly be about. He wouldn't know Carter, would he? Carter was one of the queen's personal guards, but Alexandria doubted the queen called on the priest very often. Maybe she did, and Alexandria misjudged her. The queen would have had a lot on her conscience.

"Carter," the man finally spoke. "Did you know Queen Evangeline?"

A spoon clattered against a bowl. Carter looked up warily at Bailey. "I did," he said.

"I believe I have a message for you."

Alexandria rested her hand on Carter's knee, hoping to give him some semblance of comfort. He gripped her fingers in response. His entire body tensed beside her.

"From the queen?" he asked.

"Yes," Bailey said. "When she died, I was the only person there. The Prime Minister had left moments prior." His soft voice shook. "It is a tragedy to watch a woman you blessed at birth meet such a terrible end. Mendoza thought her last words were naming Alexandria as the heir, but they were not. They were an apology. To you, Carter."

Carter stayed silent. He kept his face unnaturally neutral. Where there always shined a hint of humor in his eyes, only a blank stare remained.

Bailey continued, "She told me to tell the boy named Carter she was sorry, though she supposed you were not much of a boy anymore."

James caught Alexandria's eye. He did not know about the role the queen played in Carter's life, nor about her order that he poison her. She nodded slightly, a sign that she would talk to him later. Leianna's brows furrowed as if she was trying to put a puzzle together. Alexandria did not doubt that she still sought a connection between Carter and Will's execution.

The silence grew tense. They all waited for Carter to speak, to move, but he did not. He returned to his bowl of soup, stirring the spoon around and around.

Bailey was the first to speak again. He turned to Alexandria. "Queen Evangeline did not stand by her father's side as he took his last breaths. She waited outside of the throne room, preparing to fight. I witnessed how that broke her. No matter how much she hid her pain, I could not forget the look in her eyes as she left his deathbed. Regret and determination, all at once."

"Why are you telling us this?" she asked. Her intention was not to be rude, but she did not want to think about Evangeline any longer. Not when she would face the throne soon.

"I tell you this so that you know what kind of woman she truly was, behind the crown," he said. "Forgiveness cannot be earned, but it can be asked for. And she did just that, right before she passed."

"She sent thousands of people to die. Those who remained either starved or labored themselves to death. Kevelda cannot forgive her. I cannot."

"'I let them down. I will not do it again.' Those were some of her last words."

"Far, far too late," Alexandria said, rising from the table. She breathed, settling her racing pulse. "Can I help you clean up?"

The priest rose and picked up his bowl. After gathering everyone else's, he motioned for her to follow him. They washed and dried the dishes in silence. Alexandria knew he was evaluating her the whole time.

~

The four settled into the back room of the church. They began to plan for the Ascension. A fight Alexandria knew she could not win.

"We should stay here for a few days," Leianna said. "Get your strength back."

Alexandria bit down on her tongue to avoid a snappy comment. As the hours passed, the fire in her nerves grew and grew until it threatened to consume her. She balanced on the edge of a blade; one wrong step and she would be skewered.

The one person who could calm her down had not spoken more than three words since their meal. She wanted to argue with Carter, just to feel something other than suffocation as she fought to pull air into her tight lungs.

Mendoza had signed Carter's contract. The thought made it even harder for her to breathe. "You knew about the Ascension, didn't you, Carter?" she asked, an edge to her voice. She shouldn't blame him. On another day, she wouldn't have. But she needed a target, and Mendoza was safe in the palace. For now.

Carter stared at her for a moment. The seconds lengthened into hours as their eyes locked. A storm flickered in his face. His jaw clenched and relaxed, his voice raw. "I tried to convince you to stay at the cabin."

He knew. From the very beginning, he had been aware of Mendoza's plan to set the mayor's children against her. To make her death a spectacle. Carter had been so determined to take her to

Regia, and suddenly, he changed his mind. Alexandria did not focus on the latter fact. Her anger boiled over, hands clenching into fists. "You *knew*," she spit, "and you didn't tell me."

She expected him to be just as angry as her–*wanted* him to be–but instead he slumped against the wall. "I trained you. I made sure you were prepared."

"It doesn't matter. I'll be dead before I'm halfway across the throne room." Venom dripped from her words. Her heart and mind waged war against each other as he strode out of the room. He did not slam the door. Alexandria would have.

"I don't trust him," Leianna said, "but even I know that he would not put you in danger of his own accord. Agents in the Argentum cannot argue with orders."

Alexandria braced herself against the wall. Hot tears stung her eyes.

James stepped toward her. "Think about it, Alexandria. The Campaign was never real. Sure, people could find and kill you on their own, but why send a Protector if Mendoza wanted that to happen? And not one Protector, but two."

"I don't know." She pressed her hand against her forehead. "I've stopped trying to figure it out."

"The Ascension is what Mendoza wanted. A battle between the mayors' children so that the people could be invested, feel like their cities would be represented. A war the people would wish they could fight."

PART III

THE HEIR ASCENDANT

248

TWENTY-SEVEN

Alexandria knelt before the altar of carved wood. She prayed that she would survive, but even if she didn't, that her friends and family would be okay. That her parents would live, far out of Mendoza's reach. That if she did make it on the throne, she would not destroy Kevelda, even as it already laid dying.

Footsteps sounded next to her. She whipped her dagger from its sheath.

Bailey stood beside her unfazed. Alexandria had forgotten Leianna's promise that no one would attack her here. Adrenaline coursed through her veins regardless.

"I do not wish to be the king," Bailey said.

Alexandria remembered her weapon and put it away. Heat rushed to her face. "I'm sorry," she said, "the Campaign has taken a toll on me."

"You are forgiven." His statement weighed heavy with meaning. "I apologize for interrupting."

She rose to her feet. "No, it's okay. I should go prepare some more."

If she was being honest, there was nothing else she could do to prepare besides eat regular meals and rest. Mostly the former, since every time she closed her eyes, her potential fate played behind her eyelids.

"What worries you?" he asked.

Alexandria blew out a breath. "Everything." There was no sarcasm in her tone.

"Dying?"

"No. The pain, maybe, but beyond that, not really."

Bailey dropped onto a pew with a sigh. He patted the seat next to him. Alexandria hesitated. She eventually joined him, not having anything else to do.

"The crown does not change people. Not entirely. It simply amplifies a person's core, what drives them. What drives you, Alexandria?"

"My family." Adopted and bonded. All those she cared about. "I want to protect them. If I hurt them in any way, like Queen Evangeline did, it would kill me."

Bailey nodded as if coming to an understanding. "Your people will become your family. Every choice you make will be for them."

"That's what I'm afraid of," she whispered.

"This world will never be perfect, regardless of the choices you make. The one thing you can do is point your people toward a better one."

"What if I can't?"

"You may have to make decisions they cannot comprehend, but you will right wrongs. You will save us all, I have no doubt."

Alexandria hoped that he was right. Saving her people did not seem possible, not with the overwhelming number the war with Genea had already killed. If Kevelda stood any chance, they would have won already. The conflict had begun a half-century ago, and in the aftermath of the attacks on Regia seven years prior, Thaertos would not be the only thing she risked to lose. If Alexandria withdrew their forces, Queen Natania might very well flood Kevelda with her army.

Send her people to die or let them be killed by the enemy.

A hopeless choice. Futile.

Loss had ruled her life for the past two years. Waves bringing people into her life, letting her care about them and dragging them back out to sea, never to be seen again. Ever since Phillip had been stolen from her, she held onto those she loved with all her might, her fingernails clawing into the sand as if the tide would pull her away with them.

Who would tether her to the shore as the current towed thousands of her people away?

~

A bullet tore through Alexandria's thigh.

She jolted from her sleep, leg still burning from the imagined pain. It took a moment for her to remember where she was. The room was dark, the two small windows letting in a sliver of moonlight. Stacks of boxes created shadows in the corners.

Her heart raced as she crawled out of the sleeping bag. Darkness suffocated her. She had to get out, had to get out, had to get out—

She crept down the hallway, out onto the balcony that overlooked the city. If anyone was awake, they would see her. That thought did not stick. She couldn't breathe until she stepped outside.

Alexandria pulled the cold air into her lungs, gasping in the night. Eyes squeezed shut, she slid down the wall. Familiar arms wrapped around her and pulled her close.

Without opening her eyes, she knew it was Carter. Guilt tugged at her instantly. She should apologize for accusing him of something he had no control over. He was her safe space. This whole time, he had been. Her anger should have been pointed elsewhere. The thought of losing him because of her words tore a hole in her chest.

But he was here. No matter what she said, he still held her.

Her lifeline. Her anchor.

She did not want to let go, but she pulled back to look at his face. "I'm sorry," she said. "I say a lot of things I don't mean when I'm scared. And I'm terrified right now."

"It's okay." He pressed his forehead against hers. "I meant what *I* said. Everything I've done since the cabin has been to protect you. I don't care about orders, about Mendoza. Not anymore."

I care about you. The words remained unspoken. Yet that truth had been displayed in the way he fought for her, how he watched her back. How he tried to convince her to stay at the cabin. If not for Mendoza threatening to execute her parents, she would have. It wouldn't have been so bad, spending the rest of her life with him.

She *would* do that, technically, on the slim chance that she survived the Ascension. He would be on her guard. Perhaps it would be easier if she assigned him somewhere else, but she could not bring herself to do it. She needed him. She could not have him, not in the way she wanted to.

Her people would be her priority. When every decision could hurt them, could hurt him, she could not be distracted. It was easy to understand, now, why Evangeline never married.

Alexandria leaned back against the wall, putting a space between them. One she could not cross again. Carter settled next to her. His shoulder brushed against hers.

"Tell me about her," she said. "The queen."

"I had known her from a distance, but when I joined the Argentum, she was different. She took notice of every recruit, especially the young ones. If we were doing well, she would bring us gifts. Things that reminded us of home. Of family." He paused, staring out at the skyline. "Sometimes I wondered if she was just trying to get us under her control. I still wonder that. But I couldn't shake the feeling that she wanted to make up for the people we all had lost because of the war. Mothers. Sisters."

Alexandria's chest tightened. "Did you have a sister?"

He nodded. "Three years old when the bomb hit. It haunts me, thinking about who she could have been today. I couldn't protect her."

Alexandria did not know what to say. She broke her promise to keep her distance from him. Her hand found his in the darkness. He had not told her about his sister when they were in the cabin, but then again, she had not asked for specifics. Still so much she did not know about her Protector.

"I don't know what Evangeline was apologizing for. Maybe the war, maybe because of what she ordered me to do. I'll never know. I'll just spend the rest of my life regretting that I obeyed." He rested his forehead on his arms, crossed over his knees.

When his body shook, she held him without hesitation.

~

The next morning, the five sat around the table, eating a breakfast of eggs and toast. Bailey raised chickens on the roof of the church. Just a bed of hay in a wood and wire coop. Alexandria had wondered where the priest lived, and she discovered that one of the rooms on the second floor was his. The building used to be a set of apartments before the first floor was converted into a sanctuary.

"The tunnels are not here," Bailey said. That answered another one of Alexandria's questions. She had not seen any hidden doors that would indicate secret passageways on the first floor. "The church's original building was turned into Rosalia

Station nearly twenty-five years ago. You'll find the entrance to the tunnels through a maintenance door across from the second line."

Alexandria tensed. They would have to travel through a train station. She pictured it now, a bustling, cramped area where she was the only target. It would be impossible for her to go unnoticed there.

"How busy is it at night?" Leianna asked.

"It was not very busy when the Prime Minister called me to come for Queen Evangeline. You will not be alone, however. People do not tend to question a priest, but they will certainly notice you."

"What do we do, then?" Alexandria asked.

"You'll need some kind of disguise," James said. He looked to Bailey. "Do you have any bleach?"

Alexandria shifted uncomfortably. "Planning on killing me yourself?"

"When Elsie was fifteen or sixteen, she hated having red hair. She used bleach to turn it blonde. Or, at least, yellow."

"I think I'll stand out more with yellow hair."

Carter chimed in. "He's right. It could work. You wouldn't match the description. On the slim chance someone recognized you from a television, we would be long gone by the time they realized it was you."

"You are welcome to use anything you find around here," Bailey offered.

"Fine," Alexandria huffed. "Make me over."

"Make it quick," Leianna ordered. "We'll leave tonight."

Alexandria waited patiently in the bathroom while Carter and James searched the church. Leianna did not seem at all interested in *how* Alexandria would be disguised, just that she *was* in time for them to leave. Alexandria's reflection in the mirror stared back at her, gaunt and exhausted. Dark circles wrapped around her eyes, her freckled brown skin tinted grey. She did not recognize herself. Soon, it would be even worse.

The springy curls that reminded her of Evangeline would be gone by sundown. Perhaps that was a good thing. The less Alexandria looked like the dead queen, the better.

Alexandria opened the bathroom cabinets and stumbled across a pair of scissors. *Less damage for them to do*, she thought. The scissors snipped cleanly through the first curl right under her jawline. She continued working, avoiding the mirror as much as possible. It did not matter if it looked good. Better if it looked bad—it would keep eyes away from her face.

There were so many things about Alexandria that she was no longer familiar with, far deeper than her appearance. But when she saw the pile of hair on the floor, tears rolled down her cheeks. She rested her elbows on the bathroom counter. The edge dug into her skin. Her fingers tangled in her hair before falling into free air at her chin. A completely foreign sensation.

Someone cleared their throat behind her. Alexandria blinked back the tears and straightened. In the mirror, Carter leaned a shoulder against the doorway, the corner of his mouth tugged upward in a playful smirk. "You got started without us," he said.

"I'm not a patient person," she replied. The lump in her throat made her words sound thick. She tugged at her curls, some pieces sticking out longer than the others.

"Do you want me to fix it?"

"Do you have a second career I don't know about?"

"No, but I do have eyes."

Alexandria smiled tightly and handed him the scissors. He tapped an empty space on the counter. She pushed up on her palms and slid onto it, legs swinging against the side of the cabinet. Carter set his hands on either side of her knees.

Distance, she had promised herself.

That vow never stood a chance.

He surveyed her for a second before cutting the first strand. His fingers brushed her skin as he worked. By the time he set the scissors down, she needed air. *Always making things difficult,* she chastised him in her mind.

Tucking one side behind her ear, he leveled her face to his, finger under her chin. "It suits you," he said, completely oblivious to the heat that rose to her cheeks. She twisted away, gazing into the mirror behind her. Her hair sat evenly a few centimeters past her jaw.

"Maybe you should take up that second career," she muttered.

"I'll be a little busy saving your life."

"I can protect myself."

"I'm aware. Doesn't mean you have to, though." His hands were on the counter again.

"You could retire. I'll make sure you get paid well. You've done more than enough for me."

"I'm not done with you yet," he said. "Besides, what would be the fun in that?"

Alexandria laughed, tears drying against her skin. "I would retire with you, if I could."

"Is that a promise?"

"It's a dream. That's all it can ever be." The space between them grew taut. Alexandria froze in place. A heaviness shrouded the air, the weight of her words settling in. "Queens never rest."

"Eventually, you will. Your heirs can take over, and you'll be free."

Heirs. Her children would be forced to reign. To run the Campaign.

No, she promised herself, *that won't happen.* She would not have any children. Let the Dais figure out who would take her place. It was a price she was willing to pay to not rest this weight on another generation. If they grew up in the palace, they would be more prepared, but she could not in good conscience set them up to fight and possibly die. Would the Dais allow her to dismantle the Campaign if she tried? Was that power even in their hands?

The Campaign was ingrained so thoroughly into the history of Kevelda that she could not remember learning about a time before it, not since the Fall set the rest of the earth ablaze. For the past century, the kingdom's leaders have had to pay for their throne in blood. To prove they were strong enough to deserve it, protect it. Who would they be without it?

"I will never be free," she said.

"Then let us pay that price with you. Let me."

James walked in with a jug of bleach. They both snapped their heads toward him. "I have no idea how to do this," he said, lifting the bottle.

Alexandria could not help but laugh as her heart broke inside her chest.

TWENTY-EIGHT

Her hair was more yellow than blonde and almost completely fried. James at least had the sense to dilute the bleach, so as to avoid burning off the top layer of Alexandria's scalp.

Definitely succeeded in making me look different, Alexandria thought. The color was startling against her skin. After she survived the Ascension, she would have to dye it another color. Someone in Regia must sell coloring solutions. Half of the Dais ministers did not show a speck of grey, despite their ages warranting it.

Another task on her to-do list once she became queen. Her mind already buckled under the weight of all the responsibilities she would have. Keeping up with the court, withstanding hours-long meetings with the Dais, making allies, ending the war. It would be impossible for her to do it all alone.

She could appoint her mother as an official in the palace. The mayor had the experience that Alexandria so desperately needed, yet she felt as though the Dais would not look very favorably upon her giving a relative a position in her inner circle. She also feared the risk that her parents might face in Regia. It was safer to keep them right where they were in Kureya.

The sight of Leianna striking Carter tore Alexandria out of her thoughts.

They were attempting to teach her some last pieces of fighting strategy before she entered the throne room. Leianna's expression, a tight-lipped smile and narrowed eyes, told Alexandria that she was far more invested in this fight than was probably safe. A hint of enjoyment flashed in her eyes as she struck Carter in the side with the hilt of her dagger.

He kept his left arm down, which gave Leianna an advantage. Alexandria begged him not to tear open his wound *again*. Carter refused to back down to Leianna's challenge, however. Thus, Alexandria was forced to watched as the woman nearly knocked him to the ground.

His right arm flicked to block her as she aimed the hilt at his chest. He twisted away and drove his own at her back. She ducked and rolled with incredible form. Though Alexandria worried Carter would get himself hurt while his injury was still fresh, seeing the woman match him hit-for-hit filled her with mild satisfaction. At least someone could knock him on his back.

Leianna did exactly that. Crouching down, she swept her leg out at his feet. A split second later, he was on the floor, clutching his side.

"Good one," he said breathlessly, reaching out to shake her hand.

She hesitated. Then, she gripped his hand. He immediately pulled her down, kicked out at her stomach, and flipped her over. She fell onto her back behind him.

"Okay, you both won," Alexandria said, "Stop before I have no one breathing left to protect me."

They both laid still on their backs, chests heaving. Carter gave her a thumbs-up from his spot on the ground. Leianna rose first, jumping gracefully onto her feet. She made fighting, and recovering, look easy. Alexandria wished she had that strength and skill. If she had trained for the Campaign her whole life, perhaps she would. She hoped that no one else in the throne room was as disciplined as an Argentum agent.

Alexandria walked over to Carter and helped him up. "So, what'd you learn?" he asked.

"That Leianna's a better fighter than you."

"I'm injured," he said, before shrugging his shoulders, "but she's been around longer, so I supposed you're right."

Leianna's eyebrows raised. "I'm two years older than you."

"One year more Argentum experience," Carter replied.

"You enlisted at sixteen?" Alexandria asked.

Leianna nodded. Her eyes went distant. She sheathed her dagger and left the back room, shutting the door behind her.

Alexandria turned to Carter. "Can I trust her?"

"Yes." Carter dropped down against the wall, sipping water from a glass.

"She doesn't trust you."

"I don't trust her. That's just how being in the Argentum is."

"You just said I should trust her."

He set down the glass. "She's dedicated to the throne, no matter who sits on it. If that ends up being you, then yes, you can trust her with your life."

Alexandria weighed that for a moment. "I'm assigning her to my guard."

"I'll try my best to keep her from killing me, then."

"Something tells me that won't be easy."

"How so?"

"For starters, you stole her promotion."

"I did not steal anything. Queen Evangeline gave me my position."

"And there's no reason why she would do that?" It came out as an accusation, though Alexandria intended it as a joke. "I'm sure you don't know," she quickly added.

Carter straightened his shoulders. "I don't," he said, a mischievous glint in his eyes, "but I do know that even if Leianna can beat me at sparring, I'm still a better fighter than you."

Alexandria crossed her arms. "Is that a challenge?"

"Do you want it to be?"

The corners of her mouth lifted. "As much as I would love to fight you, *you're injured*. And you have almost a decade more experience than I do."

"Excuses."

"*Not* excuses. Valid reasons."

"Sure about that?"

Truthfully, if Alexandria crossed the distance that she had vowed not to cross–but had already crossed multiple times, much to her dismay–she feared she would do something that she would regret, something that would complicate her decisions much further, when there would already be hundreds of demands on her attention as queen.

Being close enough to Carter to spar with him? A terrible decision.

"Call it what you want, but I'm not fighting you."

"You're just afraid you'll lose."

"I beat you that one time."

Carter put his palms up in the air. "Okay, whatever you say."

Alexandria turned away before she reconsidered her decision. "I'm going to see what James is up to. We leave at dark," she called back.

If he gave a response to her statement, she did not hear it. She only heard him whisper as she rounded the door frame. "She's going to be the death of me."

Maybe Alexandria was not the only one thinking about the distance.

Before she reached the kitchen, she noticed whispering coming from the room. James and Bailey huddled around the stove. Her friend turned around, holding a pot of boiling water by the handle. He almost dropped it when he saw her.

"How was training?" he asked, hand on his chest.

"Leianna nearly broke Carter," she said. "Can I help?"

"Figures. And you can drain this for me."

She held the pot over the sink, water dripping over the side. There were dumplings in the bottom, a savory smell arising from them. "This looks amazing." She set the pot back on the stove. "Thank you, Bailey. I know it was a risk to have us here."

"Anything for my daughter," he replied, "and for the future queen, of course."

The way he said *daughter* melted part of Alexandria's heart. They were not related by blood, but Leianna and the priest had formed a bond out of their shared love for Will. A man they would never see again. Leianna had not spoken a word of him since they had been in the church.

"I will do my best to honor the sacrifices you have made on my behalf."

Bailey held up a finger. "You do not have to prove yourself worthy of a sacrifice, nor do you have to repay it."

Alexandria simply nodded, though she vowed that she would find some way to give back to the priest once she was on the throne. Her list grew more extensive by the second.

"Where is Leianna?" Bailey asked.

"I don't know. I assumed she was with you," Alexandria said. The man's brows furrowed. "I'll go find her."

She wandered through the sanctuary before moving onto the second floor. Three doors that Alexandria had not yet opened lined the walls, joined by the door to the room they slept and trained in. One led to a storage closet, even more full of boxes than the back room. Another looked to be Bailey's office. It held a desk and shelves upon shelves of books. A circle of chairs crowded in the third room, a thick layer of dust on each of them. No Leianna.

As Alexandria cleared the third floor, she wondered if Leianna did not want to be found. If not for the worried expression on Bailey's face, she would have given up long ago. Let the woman come down when she was ready. Yet the sun was starting to set, the sky changing from blue to orange. They would have to head to Rosalia Station soon.

Alexandria was met with sobs when she opened the door to the balcony. Leianna immediately jumped onto her feet. "I'm sorry," Alexandria said, backing away. "I'll go."

Leianna ran her sleeve across her eyes. "It's fine. We should start getting ready."

"Leianna, if you need time–"

"I said it's fine." Her eyes had already hardened, her mouth set in a flat line.

Alexandria did not back down. "I don't just mean now. If you need time away from the Argentum, I will make sure you always have a place."

"I appreciate that." She locked eyes with Alexandria. "But I do not know if I can return while the man who executed my husband walks those halls."

"Mendoza will never be welcome in the palace again," Alexandria promised. It was more complicated than that, however. He had done nothing he could be charged with. There were rules, an order she had to follow. She could not simply oust him, not without proof of any crime. The Dais would only see a stranger, an amateur, coming in and overthrowing them, one by one. They would mutiny.

The thought stuck in her mind as they both set out to join the others.

Silence sat like a storm cloud over their last meal. Alexandria wondered if she would see the morning. Would she have any regrets as she lay dying? It was an impossible question to answer. There was still a chance she could live–slim, but there. She worried more about surviving as the queen than being killed in the throne room. Arguably, falling in the Ascension would be the easier option.

Yet there were promises she had to keep, and surviving would be the only way to do so. Her challengers would not know Reagan's story, nor Phillip's. She could not guarantee that they would care. They were all grappling for power, even her. What they would use it for, Alexandria did not know.

It was her duty to protect her people, even if the crown never rested on her head. She would have to fight, if not for her, for them. Their names would race in her mind as she faced her challengers. If by sunrise Alexandria spoke her last words, they would be of those names, begging her killer to fulfill the promises they stole her ability to keep.

The four said solemn goodbyes to Bailey and to each other. Alexandria did not know if she would be able to give a proper one to any of them before she was killed.

She embraced James, the friend who had always been by her side and across the hall, even though they did not always see eye to eye. "When you see Amira, tell her I love her," she said.

James shook his head. "You'll tell her yourself." Alexandria argued in her mind.

Leianna and Alexandria looked at each other awkwardly for a moment before she wrapped her arms around the woman.

"Keep them safe," she whispered. "If I don't make it on the throne, take my family somewhere safe. Carter, too. Whatever Mendoza's plans are, I don't think he'll stop once I'm dead." When she pulled away, Leianna nodded, perceptible only to Alexandria.

Her heart lurched when she locked eyes with Carter. He pulled her against his chest. She squeezed her eyes shut, savoring her last moment of peace, of safety. His heart raced, the sole indication of his fear. Neither of them said anything. No words would ever suffice. Nothing could capture what they had gone through, what they now felt about each other. Alexandria regretted letting him go.

Before they left, Leianna hugged her father-in-law. "You always have a place here, Lei," he said. "You are my child, too."

Alexandria turned away, not wanting to intrude on their moment. She gripped the door handle. It kept her upright as the world spun around her.

They ran into the cold night, through the streets of Regia, all the way to Rosalia Station.

Though more than three weeks had passed since Mendoza named her the heir, Alexandria could not help feeling as though the Campaign had just begun.

TWENTY-NINE

Two Argentum agents guarded every entrance to the station.

The exterior of Rosalia Station remained unchanged from its origins. White corrugated siding with a green sloped roof, a steeple rising tall on one side, though the cross had likely fallen off or been taken off when it was transformed into the train station. Windows with pointed arches lined the sides in two rows. It towered over the four as they scouted a way inside.

"There's no way I'll be able to make it inside with them standing there," Alexandria whispered, huddled behind a bush. She would have found the situation laughable had her senses not been primed for threats.

"James, distract them," Leianna ordered. "We'll run in while they follow you."

"Why me?" James asked.

"Because Carter and I know the palace the best. If you're detained, we'll still be able to help her."

James resigned to the order, and after taking a moment to think of a plan, he started running toward the agents. They both reached for their guns, though only one pulled hers. James threw his hands up in the air.

"The heir attacked my partner," he said breathlessly. "Please, help me get her to the hospital."

The female guard holstered her government-issue gun. Annoyance flashed across her face. "That's the risk of thinking you can win the Campaign," she said to the other agent.

He, at least, had more sympathy for James's imaginary partner and immediately started following James. The woman seemed to hesitate before trailing behind them. Her eyes flickered back to her post once before they rounded the corner in the opposite direction.

Alexandria did not want to consider what would happen when the guards realized he had tricked them. How long would they follow him before they realized there was no injured partner? Would they arrest him? The female agent seemed particularly trigger-happy. Alexandria shook the image of James being shot out of her mind.

With no one else in sight, Alexandria stood. She pulled her hood over her head, a few stray yellow-blond curls peeking out from underneath. It would have to do.

Her sight pinholed on the doors. She took steadying breaths as she walked across the pavement to the station. Carter and Leianna both followed, each keeping their distance, pretending that they did not know her or each other. The reporters would likely know by now that she was traveling with companions.

Act normal. The thought repeated in her head, over and over and over again. Almost like thinking the words would keep eyes off her.

The inside of the station still had pews lined in rows on either side of the aisle. At the other end, a ticket station replaced the altar. She paced herself, relaxing her shoulders as if she simply wanted to catch a train. A few other passengers sat in the pews. One turned to look at her, surveying her longer than made her comfortable. Her skin tingled. There were eyes everywhere.

Alexandria read the timeboard as she waited to speak to the attendant. The next train would run to Kureya, but that was on the first line. They would have to wait for a train to board from the second line before the door leading to it would open.

She shifted from one foot to the other to avoid shaking. A man came out from behind the ticket counter and rearranged the letters on the timeboard. Another person finished with the attendant, leaving only one more before Alexandria.

When the man walked away, the sign displayed that the next train on the second line would be departing in an hour. She cursed under her breath. Anyone could recognize her and kill her by then. The agents would come back, and if she was unlucky, would put together that James had been distracting them from something. They would search the pews. They would find her.

Alexandria wondered if they were under special orders to bring her to the palace, now that the Ascension had been announced. Mendoza wanted her there alive, that much was certain. But the longstanding rules of the Campaign could not be broken. There would be no repercussions if those agents decided to kill her and risk the Ascension themselves.

After all, she did not need to be the one to face her challengers. It only mattered that someone did. There was no reason why Mendoza would need her over anyone else. She had not even been aware that she was the heir prior to Evangeline's death, boasted no special training, and kept no allies. Her one advantage was that she was the daughter of the Mayor of Kureya, but even then, he had taken that away from her.

Right now, she was no one. Her death would not be special to the people watching the Ascension. If one of the agents killed her, the people of Kevelda would still tune into the fight. She was nothing but a pawn for Mendoza to use to spur citizens to fight once more. That is, if James was correct in his assumption about what the Ascension was truly for.

None of it made sense. A thousand little puzzle pieces that Alexandria had yet to put together. Two Protectors. Mendoza's threats against her parents. The queen asking Carter to kill her. They had to fit together, somehow. Alexandria feared that she would not live to uncover the answer.

Her fingers tapped nervously against her leg. "Next," the attendant called, and Alexandria walked up to the glass.

She ordered her ticket, hoping that the last of the money in her pocket was enough to cover it. The bills slipped through her fingers as she counted. Not enough. Counted again. Still not enough.

Sweat slicked her palms as she looked up at the attendant. "I'm sorry," she said, "I don't have enough."

A hand pressed against her shoulder. "Let me get that for you," Carter said, still pretending that he did not know her. She prayed that the woman behind the glass would not give it a second thought. He passed the money under the window.

The woman nodded, giving Alexandria a pitying glance before she slid her the ticket. "It'll be through the door to your right. We'll call out once the train is ready," she said.

Alexandria said a quick "thank you" before nodding in appreciation at Carter. She sat down in one of the empty middle rows. Too close to the back and the agents could spot her. Too close to the front and the attendant might give her a second glance. Her life was a balancing act, and it would take everything to remain upright.

Carter took a seat a few rows in front of her. Leianna positioned herself right across the aisle. The two had very different strategies for looking inconspicuous. While Leianna crossed her legs and rested her chin on a hand, Carter yawned loudly and pretended to go to sleep. Alexandria noticed Leianna's eyes moving on a swivel around the room, though her head remained perfectly still. Carter slumped down against the pew, his head leaning back against the top of it.

Alexandria would have pretended to read the romance novel she swiped from the ranger station, but she had left her backpack at Bailey's church. The extra weight might have slowed her down. When it was a matter of seconds between life or death, she did not want to take the risk. Besides, they would not need food or water or extra clothes to sustain them.

As the seconds passed, stretching out into their own eternities, she really wished she had brought the book. It was bad enough to sit in the same spot for an hour after she had been running from would-be assailants for the past three weeks. Let alone having to feel eyes flicker to her, then politely look away, without any distraction.

James crossed her mind again. She pretended to stretch, twisting to look at the doors behind her. The Argentum agents had not yet returned to their posts. He was either leading them far, far away, or they were busy dealing with him. Ideally, he would have found a random injured person on the street and pretended to know them. The chances of that were slim.

Focus. That was what she needed to do. Her senses sharpened to the tiniest of movements. The woman diagonal from her shifted slightly. A young girl wiggled next to her. Her rust-orange hair was plaited tightly in two braids. She fussed, picking at the woman's sleeve. Alexandria assumed the woman was her mother, or older sister, perhaps.

A man slept on the pew a few rows behind her, but aside from what she saw when she searched for the guards, she could not keep an eye on him. *Stay asleep.* He was not a threat, not yet.

A few more people bustled in and out, catching the train on the first line. Everyone in the pews must have been waiting for the second line. Surprise hit Alexandria as she realized how empty this train out of Regia would be. No one would leave the city, not when she was here, about to make her final appearance.

She wondered if her parents had come to Regia. While her mother was not the Mayor of Kureya anymore, would she have come anyways? Alexandria hoped that they had stayed far away. Dying brutally would be bad enough in itself, let alone with her parents watching from a few feet away. With Mendoza so easily threatening their execution to spur Alexandria toward Regia, she hoped they would never come to the capital again. Especially if she did not survive the Ascension.

The little girl stepped into the aisle. She jumped up and down, shaking out all her energy. Her mother watched as the girl spun around and around. When she stopped, she made eye contact with Alexandria. Alexandria quickly looked down. Her hood would not cover her face entirely. If the girl had seen Alexandria on a television or in a newspaper, she might recognize her. *Children always verbalize any thought that comes into their minds.* Would she tell her mother about the woman whose face she saw on the screen?

Alexandria counted to sixty and lifted her eyes up. The girl sat back in her seat. Every few seconds, however, she glanced back at Alexandria. Her mother tapped her arm and whispered something in her ear. Before the little girl could look at her again, Alexandria gathered her last semblance of steadiness and strode casually down the hallway that led to the restrooms.

Once out of sight, she let out the breath she was holding. She entered the restroom, glad to find that it was a private room with no one else in it. She locked the door behind her.

At least forty-five minutes had passed since Alexandria bought her ticket. She doubted that she could lock herself in the bathroom for the rest of the time. For the moment, she allowed herself a chance to breathe. No one could hurt her in there. She shook out her arms and legs. Her nerves were a jumbled mess, electricity zipping through her fingers.

She jolted at the sight of her reflection before remembering her bleached hair. A completely different person stared back at her, far beneath her skin. Never again would she be the Alexandria she was before the Campaign. The one who would become the Mayor of Kureya, following in her mother's footsteps. The one that Phillip loved.

A knock reverberated across the room. Alexandria tensed. "One second," she called, turning on the faucet. The water froze her skin as she splashed it onto her face. She reached for the dagger at her belt, hand hovering over it.

Head down, she opened the door, ready to slide past the person on the other side. Carter pushed her back inside. He pressed the door shut. "The agents are back. They're searching everyone."

Alexandria braced herself against the wall. They were *so close* to the tunnels. "What do we do?"

"Leianna was going to distract them, but we figured they wouldn't fall for that again. I just had to warn you," Carter said.

Her thoughts raced as she attempted to arrange some kind of plan. There were two agents. It would not be that difficult to take them down, three against two. But they could not do it in front of everyone in the train station. If any other agents were called, they would not make it out alive.

His eyes brightened. "I'll get them to come in here. Once they do, we'll knock them out, lock them inside."

"What if they wake up before the doors open?"

"They won't."

Her heart pounded furiously in her chest. "That's not a very good answer."

"It's the only one I've got." He squeezed her hand. "Trust me."

"You know I do."

She held her breath as he ventured out into the waiting room. The seconds ticked by in her mind. Five minutes passed before the handle twisted. Alexandria crouched down, squeezing into the space behind the door.

"I swear I saw her come in here, Jackson," Carter said as he and the two guards walked into the now-cramped space. She jumped up, pushed the door shut behind them, and locked it.

They turned to face her, guns drawn. "I wouldn't do that," she said, putting her hands up in front of her.

"Why not?" the female agent asked. By the time the words came out, Carter jammed two of Leianna's tranquilizer darts in their necks. The two slumped to the floor, their guns clattering against the tile.

"Quick question," Alexandria said. "Everyone in the waiting room saw those two come back here with you. Won't they be concerned when they see us come out without them?"

"We'll stay back here until Leianna comes and tells us the train is boarding." He examined one of the guns before putting it into his holster. "Don't worry. We planned everything out."

Alexandria rolled her eyes, though grateful. "Imagine how quickly I could have made it to the palace if you two worked together to begin with."

"As far as I'm concerned, you didn't want to go to Regia when we first met."

"My point still stands."

"Well, I'm glad it was just me and you," he said, "even if you're not."

"Who said I'm not?"

"You implied it."

"My life certainly would have been easier if we hadn't been running from Leianna."

"You're right, but it wouldn't have been as fun."

Carter smiled when Alexandria hit his shoulder. A dimple appeared on his left cheek. Though thinking about their relationship left a complicated, knotted mess in her mind, she would give anything to see that dimple again.

She looked down at her hands, fidgeting with the edge of her sleeves. With her sudden silence, Carter leaned against the wall. Alexandria could feel him watching her, see him staring out of the corner of her eye.

They did not say another word until Leianna knocked on the door.

THIRTY

Slamming the door shut behind them, Alexandria stumbled as the maintenance tunnel landing was instantly bathed in darkness.

A dim light shone from below. It vaguely outlined a series of steps going down, down, down.

The three staggered forward, near-blindly following the stairs until the light faded. And then there was nothing. Each step they took based on faith alone.

A hand brushed against Alexandria's. Familiar callouses lined his skin. She fumbled for Carter's hand and caught it, interlocking their fingers.

The darkness stretched longer and farther as they descended, until suddenly, the light began to grow, giving them a vision of the stairs' outline until the bottom step became completely visible.

Dimly lit by a flickering fluorescent light, the tunnel stretched so far that Alexandria could not see the end. Her throat tightened at the sudden thought of them running out of air. The passageway thinned, only room for them to walk single file. Concrete walls that could cave in and crush her to death.

Alexandria had never really been claustrophobic. Yet the thought of someone following them into the tunnel, with nowhere to run or hide, constricted her lungs. She drew in a steadying breath, forcing herself to calm. The wall froze her fingers as she ran her hand against it. Carter still had a hold on her, his hand stretched out behind him as he and Leianna took the lead.

Walking at the back of the group would not be her first choice, but there was no room to change their positions. Even if they could, she would not want anyone else to be at more risk than she was. Her ears homed in on the ambient noise. Complete silence, other than the fabric of their coats rustling, their muffled footsteps.

A staircase appeared at the end of the tunnel. It rose beyond the ceiling, the upper landing hidden. The walls widened slightly as they moved forward. Alexandria's breaths evened out, the crushing weight on her chest now just a nuisance.

Carter looked back at her, flashing a reassuring smile as he squeezed her hand. She would have given anything to hold onto him for a second longer. Yet as they inched closer to the stairs, she knew her fight was coming at last. She had to face it alone.

Her heart lurched at the thought that this might be the last time they touched. If she survived, she and Carter could not continue down the path they were following.

He might not feel the same butterflies in his stomach that exploded in hers when their eyes locked. It could all be in Alexandria's head, a result of him saving her life repeatedly. Bonded by trauma, rather than true feelings.

None of that rang true. She could not deny the electricity that ran along her skin when he brushed against her, or the tightness in her diaphragm when he smiled. Like holding a breath while it was being taken away.

He would be both her greatest weakness and her most important ally. She trusted him over anyone else. She had to keep him close, but that also meant she could not complicate things between them further. She would break her own heart repeatedly if it meant that he would be the one to watch her back in that court.

Alexandria dropped his hand, gripping onto the hilt of the blade at her waist to keep from reaching back out to him. His eyes flicked to hers. She stared straight ahead at the stairs that would lead to life or death.

Distance, she promised. The word had become more a plea than an oath.

Footsteps whispered behind her, and she could barely turn before a sharp pain tore into her shoulder blade. Fire lanced through her bones. She screamed, a guttural gasp tearing from her throat.

Carter shoved her forward and stood between her and her assailant. Her knees buckled. Warmth trickled down her back. A line of crimson blood trailed to her right fingertips, but she could not feel it. She pushed off the ground with her other arm.

Her eyes followed the line of Leianna's arms as she pointed her gun at Jason. The man's eyes burned with a ferocity that made Alexandria's stomach tighten.

"How does it feel?" Jason spit at her. Leianna's finger tightened on the trigger. "Go on, shoot me. Make him happy. Take her to the throne room, see if she survives there."

"Make who happy?" Alexandria hissed through clenched teeth.

"You know who." He locked eyes with Leianna. Alexandria swore his face softened as he looked at her. His friend. Someone he trained and served alongside. Pity flickered in her mind before the throbbing pain in her back boiled over, threatening to buckle her knees again.

A gunshot blared through the tunnel as Jason lunged at her. The sound punched into Alexandria's ears. Ringing echoed in her head while she watched Jason slump to the ground, his knife clattering beside him. If she could hear anything, she knew the thud would haunt her for the rest of her life. Leianna flinched and holstered her weapon.

Alexandria gritted her teeth as she used her left hand to press her other arm up to her chest, holding it in place. Her wrist went slack as she cradled it toward her. Nausea bubbled up in her throat at her arm's limpness, darkness creeping along the edge of her vision. The ringing subsided, replaced by the sound of her blood rushing in her veins.

A whimper escaped her lips when Carter caught her. She had not realized she was falling until she felt the cold press of concrete against her knees. Warm water crept through the fabric there.

Not water. Blood.

Carter's arm tensed around her midsection. "She's bleeding too much," he said. The words came through an ocean of water. Waves crashed against her skull. If only she could lean back and float on them.

Her head rolled to the side. She tried to pick it back up, but fatigue washed over her. Leianna cursed quietly, or perhaps at a normal volume that Alexandria could not hear right.

Someone mentioned something about an artery. She was being carried now, floating through the tunnel. Pain seared in her shoulder again. Through slitted eyes, she caught a glimpse of Carter nestling her lifeless arm against her chest. He held her with an arm cradling her back, the other underneath her knees.

Her nerves dulled. The room grew dark, footsteps silent. She was being rocked like a boat at sea. Like the fishing boats on the beach in Kureya, anchoring for the night. They swayed side-to-side, antsy to be free once more. She did not want to be free, not from the anchor of his arms, the one line connecting her to reality.

"Stay awake." Carter's voice came from somewhere above. His arms pressed against her tighter. She opened her eyes, having closed them unknowingly. Ice ran along her veins.

Her head bounced against his arm as he ascended the stairs. She pressed into his chest, until all she could hear was his heart racing. His breaths turned shallow. Pain washed over his face as she slammed against his ribs.

"They'll kill her as soon as you walk through those doors," Leianna called. "She's in no position to fight."

Carter stopped–or, judging by the jolt, Leianna stopped *him*. "Mendoza will make sure no one hurts her, not before the fight. He has to look strong, prove that the Dais should listen to him after he takes the throne."

"And what if you're wrong? What if he doesn't care about the Dais or need their approval? He's already served as the Prime Minister under two monarchs. Carter, think about this."

"Then he'll have to care about his son!" Carter shouted. "And his son needs her alive."

THIRTY-ONE

Cold water dragged along her arm.

Alexandria squinted against the bright light. Once she could finally get her eyes open, she took in her surroundings. Confusion washed over her as she stared at the blank white walls around her. She realized soon enough that the icy sensation came from the IV line in the pit of her elbow.

An ache deep in her shoulder sent her memories spiraling back to her. The tunnels. Jason. Fire burning through her bones. She tried to move her right arm, but nothing happened. A void spread below her arm socket. Complete emptiness.

Her heartbeat quickened. There were no threats to be found, but there could be. And there she laid, unable to move her arm. She wrote and fought with her left, but now her body felt unbalanced. She pushed up onto her elbow. Instantly, her head felt light.

Whatever pain medications they had her on were strong, though the longer she was conscious, the sharper her senses became. She contemplated squeezing the IV drip, making the medicine flow faster, but she decided against it. She needed to be alert.

There was one person with the power to keep the hospital staff from killing her, and she did not trust Mendoza's reasons for doing so. Seconds ticked on the clock.

I need a plan, she thought, despite her body's pleas for her to lie back down. It was impossible to know how long she had been in that room. There must have been some kind of surgery to stop the bleeding. She brought her hand up to her shoulder, noticing a bandage at the front of her chest. The knife had gone clean through.

The thought sent her vomiting over the side of the bed. Embarrassment flooded her before quickly resolving. She would have to apologize to whichever nurse was assigned to clean that up, if they did not try to kill her first. Supposedly, that would be against their oath to do no harm. Alexandria wondered if that vow still applied in the Campaign. Everyone else seemed to think it was okay to kill her for the throne. Maybe she didn't count as a person in this situation, just as the heir.

Alexandria chewed on her lip to keep from throwing up again. The liquid in the IV dripped. More coldness washed over her arm where the needle dug into her skin. The medicine likely nauseated her too, though the thought of her injury would have done it all alone.

And where was Carter? She wanted him by her side. Desperately. Her stomach tensed, chest unable to pull in enough air. The first time she had been without him in three weeks, and it was when she was at her most vulnerable. Even when they were on the run, she felt safer with him than she did in this room on her own. If both Carter and Leianna were nowhere to be found, that was very, very bad.

I need to get out of here. She could not disconnect her IV, not with her other arm paralyzed by her side. Blowing out a breath, she braced herself for the only thing she could do. Her teeth clamped down on the IV line. A pinprick of pain dragged slowly under her skin as she tugged on the line. She squeezed her eyes shut to avoid watching the sharp plastic withdraw from her arm. The adhesive holding it in place tore at her skin as she pulled her head back.

The IV tore free in a final lance of pain. Blood bubbled up on the inside of her elbow. She forced herself to look away, nausea again threatening to spill the meager food in her stomach. Her last meal had been at Bailey's church, but who knew how much time had passed since.

She swung her legs over the side of the bed, wincing at the dull pain that throbbed down her spine as she twisted. Her feet planted firmly on the ground. When she rose, her legs nearly gave out. Gripping the arm of the bed kept her upright until her muscles were strong enough to hold her steady.

A set of cabinets ran along one wall. She staggered over, catching herself on the counter. Cold air blew against her bare legs. All she wore was a flimsy paper gown. Despite her instinct to cover herself, she had no means to do so. She gritted her teeth and began searching the cabinets.

She reached for the handle with her right hand only to remember that it could not move. Worry trickled in the back of her mind. *What if I can never move my arm again?* As long as she survived, she supposed it would not matter. Her real fear was making it across the throne room with only one arm. The challengers would already be more skilled than she was, but without full use of her body, her odds of survival were slim to none.

It would be faster if she ended it herself. Less painful. Mendoza would not get his spectacle. If she found a way to do it, the throne would be his, no doubt. Let the Dais question his motives. She wondered how he would spin the situation if they suspected him of killing her in secret. That idea wouldn't be too outlandish.

I will fight.

A lump formed in her throat. The room closed in, her vision focusing to a pinhole. Nothing in the cabinets could help her either way. In fact, the cabinets held nothing at all. Her bare knees froze as she sank against the tile floor. The bottom cabinets, too, held nothing of use.

She pressed her palm against her forehead, her head hitting the cabinet as she rocked back and forth against it. The pain in her shoulder shifted from dull to searing.

The door slammed open. She shuffled backwards toward the wall. Her heart pounded. Sweat slicked her hand. It slipped against the floor, sending her sprawling onto her back. Fire scorched her shoulder blade.

"I'm not here to hurt you," Mendoza said, his mouth twisted in a smile.

Alexandria shifted onto her elbow and locked eyes with him. She spit onto the floor.

"Come on now." He shook his head. The light reflected blindingly off the grey streaks in his hair. "You used to be such a nice girl."

Blood rushed to her face. Her nails dug against the floor as she clenched her hand into a fist. "That was before you threatened to execute my parents." Even before that, she disliked him, ever since she watched him hit his son.

His son. The words gave her pause. Her brain told her that they were important. Whatever it was, she had forgotten. His son was dead.

"Did you really think Kevelda could last without a ruler? How selfish of you to hide when your people needed you most."

Though she did not want to give him any credit, guilt turned her stomach. "Considering you set up an arena for me to die in, I would say it was a smart thing to do."

"The Ascension has always been tradition, just without a name. I invited the mayors simply so that they could watch as I take the throne, regretfully killing the heir so that someone with Kevelda's best interest in mind could reign. At least this time, the Dais had the sense to keep other citizens out of the throne room. Poor Evangeline had to fight a rebel."

A rebel. Alexandria stored that piece of information in the back of her mind. "Kevelda's best interest," she laughed scornfully, "I doubt it."

Mendoza crossed the room and crouched down in front of her. He was impeccably dressed in a grey suit jacket with a matching waistcoat and trousers. From far away, she could understand how he would charm people. Up close, it was impossible to ignore the cruelty in his smile or the sickly pale tint to his skin. "*They* won't. And after today, your opinion won't matter at all."

She spit again, hitting his cheek this time. He wiped it off with his hand. His golden-brown eyes bored into hers, narrowing as if he was examining her soul. It felt familiar, but her body recognized his threat.

He rose again and turned toward the door. "I'll have the nurses bring you new clothes," he said.

Alexandria spoke before she could stop herself. "Why me?" she asked. "Why not order someone to kill me and then take the proof of my death from them?"

He stopped in the doorway. "You are far more important than you will ever realize."

His words played on repeat in her head as she slumped against the wall. So many questions that she might never get the answer to. In that moment, she did not feel *important* at all. She was as insignificant as a bug, and she would be crushed the second she walked–stumbled, rather–into the throne room. Tears stung at her eyes. She blinked them back. There was no time to cry, to despair about her fate.

With the determined strength of a woman pushed too far, she rose. Alexandria had already lost far too much. The weight of Phillip's death pulled her forward instead of dragging her down. She made promises to his memory, to the children who went hungry, to the families who lost homes. This was the cross she had to bear, and if it meant clawing her way to the throne, body broken and bleeding, she would tear herself apart to do it. Only divine will would send her to her grave today. If that was her fate, she would not let her loved ones see her falter as she met it with open arms.

Bracing herself against the counter, she watched as a nurse set a bundle of clothes on the bed. The young woman flashed her a meek smile before walking out of the room. "Be careful when you unfold them," she said as she went.

Alexandria's brows furrowed as she examined the stack. When she lifted the first item, a knife tumbled out. It nearly sliced her hand open. "Thanks for the warning," she whispered into the air. She unfurled a small piece of paper that fell beside it.

"Good luck," it read.

Perhaps she had allies in the palace, after all. Just not in the way she expected.

Several minutes passed before Alexandria figured out how to put on the black shirt and trousers with one working hand. The jacket was another challenge entirely. She stared at the zipper for a few moments, wondering how she would hold the bottom down while she zipped it up, before realizing that it was an Argentum uniform. If it was Mendoza's idea, she had no clue what he meant to do with it.

She pressed her paralyzed arm against the fabric and pinned it in place with the bed's railing before tugging the zipper up. Though a small win, it made her feel slightly more capable than before. Fighting her challengers would be much more difficult.

Her leather boots rested on the other side of the bed. She had never been more grateful for the zippers on the side. Shoelaces might have killed her before she ever had the chance to face the Ascension.

The thought sent adrenaline through her limbs. She could never be ready for what was to come. Yet she had to move. She had to face the fight ahead of her. There was no use waiting for her nerve to fail. Her fate would be determined by nightfall.

Alexandria cracked open the door, scanning the area before exiting the room. It was eerily empty. No movement or noise trailed through the fluorescent-lit hallway that stretched in either direction.

She passed through a set of metal doors at the end. They opened into a larger hallway, this one lit by sconces and stained-glass windows set into the greyish-white stone walls. The floor changed from tile to a black-stained wood.

The medical wing in the palace, she thought. Though she had never been there herself, she had passed by it on her late-night explorations. She knew exactly where to go from here. It would not be a long journey to the throne room. Not long enough to prepare herself for what she was about to face.

Carter had trained her. She forced herself to remember every trick and step he had taught her. To look past the memories of his comfort, the comfort she desperately needed as she strode through the hall, and memorize the patterns that would save her. He protected her from the very start, yet he was not by her side now.

The thought tied her stomach in knots. Her breath caught as her wound stung from the force of running. She did not have time to stop. If she did, she might never start again.

A set of wooden doors appeared as she turned the corner. Her fate laid beyond them.

She pondered how many prayed for her death just through those doors.

THIRTY-TWO

Her heart hammering in her ears was the only sound as she opened the wooden doors. The entrance was not at all spectacular as she struggled to pull the heavy door open with one hand, but Alexandria had no interest in theatrics.

Her fight was finally beginning.

Spectators filled the pews lining the walls. Alexandria recognized most of them from her time in the palace. Marlowe stared daggers at her, her mouth twisted in a smirk. Alexandria's stomach lurched. If Marlowe tried to fight her again, she feared she would not make it out alive.

That fear continued as she surveyed the rest of the attendees. Some watched her with pity, others with determination. A few were the children she had grown up alongside, now adults preparing to take over their parents' duties. Quinn. Taylor. Erwin. She would never have called them friends, but they were not enemies, not before today. Soon enough, her challengers would reveal themselves. Any moment now.

"Let go of me," a woman said sharply. Alexandria found Leianna to her left, her arms held behind her back by two Argentum agents. Warning flashed in Leianna's eyes. "Alexandria, run."

Shock hindered Alexandria from responding. She had nowhere to run but the throne.

A hush settled over the spectators. They sat still like the statues in the palace's courtyard. Had these faces watched Will's execution as motionless as those stone carvings?

She strode down the middle of the hall, wondering why no one rose. Finally, she spotted Carter. He stood at the base of the steps leading up to the throne.

A lump formed in her throat as she ran toward him. If anyone were to come at her, she would not have noticed. The room blurred around her, a mass of gray walls and jewel tones from the stained glass. He moved toward her, a half-smile forming on his face.

They collided in the center of the room. He wrapped his arms around her, burrowing his face in her neck. She held her good hand against the back of his head. They stood frozen for a moment, basking in each other's warmth.

He pressed his lips against her ear. "He knows about Queen Evangeline," he whispered. "He knows I killed her, and he's going to tell the Dais."

Alexandria fought hard to keep her expression neutral. "But you were under orders. He must know that."

"The Dais suspects him. If he kills you now, it'll just add more fuel to their investigation. He'll make sure I take the fall if I don't..." His voice trailed off.

"If you don't what?" As soon as Alexandria asked, she realized the answer.

Mendoza spoke, his voice echoing across the throne room. "Fight well, Alexandria."

Another memory came back to her, crashing into her thoughts. The golden-brown eyes. The same sharp jawline. The boy in the palace hallway who looked eerily similar to the man with his arms around her.

His son. Carter was Mendoza's son. The man who had protected her all this time, wanted to bring her here to die and then changed his mind.

Mendoza would not be her challenger, after all.

For the first time, Alexandria did not know whether Carter would go through with it.

She pulled away, drawing her dagger. His eyes softened. "You have to kill me, Alexandria. If you don't, he'll find a way to blame you, too. He's already put the thought in their heads that Leianna and I were working with Will. The only way out is to show them that I'm not your ally."

The Argentum uniform weighed against her skin. Mendoza wanted to make it seem like they had conspired together, far before she was ever named the heir. She cursed under her breath. "I won't," she said through gritted teeth. "He has taken far too much from me. I won't let him take you."

"You can do this. Don't let him take the throne. I can't watch him turn into even more of a monster."

Tears blurred her eyes. "No."

He covered the hand on the hilt of her blade with his. "Please." His voice broke.

She could not do it. Every time she had dared to imagine a future in which she survived and became the queen, he was always by her side. No matter in what way, whether guard, friend, or something more, he was there. They would both make it out of this, or neither of them would.

"If he wants a fight, we'll give him a fight," she said, "but we are both leaving here alive. I'll knock you down, but make it look real. You can help me convince the Dais that he killed Evangeline, not you."

Carter locked eyes with her. His eyebrows furrowed as if he was thinking over her proposal. Then, he let go of her knife. "Remember what I taught you?"

Alexandria nodded, her mouth turning up into a smile. "You'll wish I hadn't."

They stared at each other for a long moment before Alexandria lunged at Carter with her blade. She narrowly missed his shoulder, glad for the control over her muscles.

He unsheathed a dagger from his belt. His left arm hugged closely to his side, likely because of the healing wound along his rib.

They were evenly matched. Both unable to defend one side.

Metal grazed her ear as she spun away from his attack. He sucked in a sharp breath as she winced. Worry flashed in his eyes.

She slid across the floor, twisting to face his back. Her arm curved around his neck. He threw his head back into her nose, softer than necessary to inflict any real pain, but she squeezed her eyes shut and jumped back, pretending injury.

Carter spun and slashed at her jacket. The dagger sliced only through the fabric. No pain. She shielded her side anyways.

When he lunged at her, she dropped to the ground and kicked out at his ankles. He slammed onto his back.

She held her arm against his throat. "Sorry," she whispered close to his face.

"I'm more proud than hurt," he said. The grimace on his face indicated otherwise.

One final touch. She stabbed her dagger into the fabric of his jacket, pinning it to the floor.

Alexandria pushed off the ground and ran toward the throne. If she sat on the throne before the challengers came after her, she would not have to fight them. She did not care if she looked weak. Even that short fight with Carter had drained her. The stab wound in her shoulder seared like a brand.

Steps away from the throne, something slammed into her side. She collided against the floor. Pain tore through her shoulder, through her head, through her whole body. Her assailant grabbed her hair and tugged her head upwards.

She twisted to face her attacker. Quinn, who had become the Mayor of Kefla a year ago, after her father's passing. Alexandria gritted her teeth. Her scalp burned as she tore her head away from the woman's grip.

"I hate to do this," Quinn said, "but you know how few choices we have."

"We could be allies," Alexandria spit out.

Quinn shook her head. "The only person I trust to take care of my people is me."

"We have more in common than you realize." Strategies rolled through her head. None of them were viable. She no longer had a dagger. Quinn wouldn't be moved with words.

The throne sat only meters away. She had come *so close.*

"Not enough." Quinn whipped a gun from her side and pressed it against Alexandria's forehead.

Alexandria wondered how the woman acquired a gun. They were rare for anyone besides Argentum agents, so it must have been passed down in her family.

Is this the last thing you're going to think about before you die? she scolded herself.

Shouts rang out from the pews. Quinn glanced toward the noise for a split second. Just long enough for Alexandria to swipe the gun away from her face.

Leianna stabbed a knife into the crook between Quinn's neck and shoulder. Alexandria's stomach turned at the gurgling noise that erupted from the woman's throat. Her body slumped onto the bottom step.

Alexandria pushed herself onto her knees. No matter how hard she tried, her fingers would not reach for the blade protruding from Quinn's neck. Leianna faced the other direction. Her eyes narrowed.

As Alexandria got to her feet, she followed Leianna's gaze.

Five more people stood in front of them, weapons out. One had a sword gripped in his hands. *How dramatic.* She choked on a nervous laugh as Carter limped over to her side.

A hand brushed against her arm. She jumped away, holding her fists in front of her. Marlowe stood next to her. The girl handed her a silver dagger before saying, "I like to be on the winning side. Keep that in mind."

Alexandria did not have the chance to thank her before metal flashed in her periphery. The blade sang through the air. She dodged. Her blade caught a man's wrist. His sword clattered against the ground as he pulled his arm to his chest. A deep gash in his skin sent blood dripping to the floor. He withdrew to the pews.

She sheathed her dagger and snatched the sword up. It weighed heavily in her hand. Though she was not used to that big a weapon, it gave her an advantage against the other four assailants. They all gripped short blades, but a glint of black metal on Erwin's hip suggested a gun.

The mayor's son wanted to appear strong by fighting hand-to-hand, but if she or Carter took his blade, he would not hesitate to shoot them.

Carter fought next to her, lunging toward the two challengers who stood side-by-side. He slashed his dagger through the air. The young woman across from him blocked his blow. Alexandria could not remember her name, though she recalled the girl's sheet-white skin.

The woman next to her was obviously her mother. Alexandria recognized her as one of the mayors. They had formed a team. Two chances to get the throne.

Alexandria tried to slash the sword at Erwin, but without her second hand to support it, she could not get a strong enough swing. She threw it onto the steps and drew her dagger again. If she survived, she would learn how to swordfight one-handed.

Erwin threw his dagger at her. It must have missed as she dove toward him. Just as he gripped another dagger from his belt, arrogantly ignoring his gun, her blade found his chest. She stifled the gasp that rose in her throat. His fingers closed around the hilt. Pain clouded his wide eyes.

Erwin collapsed to the ground, his young daughter's screams piercing the tense silence. Alexandria clutched her stomach. When she looked down at his body, her eyes caught onto something sticking out of her arm. The dagger he had thrown stuck into her skin.

She did not even have time to get nauseous before the mayor turned her attention away from Carter and onto Alexandria. Her daughter's blade staggered centimeters from his neck. His arm wavered as he blocked it from driving farther.

Alexandria scrambled to grab Erwin's gun from his holster. She thought back to how Jason handled it, cocking it and squeezing her pointer finger against the trigger. The bullet lodged into the mayor's thigh. A mix between a scream and a growl came out of the woman's mouth. She pressed her pale hand against the blood bubbling out of her knee and limped away.

Her daughter was the last challenger standing. Leianna had easily taken down the other two. A woman with short auburn hair paled further as blood leeched out of her neck. The other man's body laid halfway across the throne room with a dagger in his back. He had tried to run.

No one else dared to move from the pews. A few whispered underneath the sound of the young girl screaming for her father. Alexandria's gaze drifted to his lifeless body. Another pair of open eyes to haunt her nightmares.

Carter groaned as he was forced to flex his injured side to block the mayor's daughter's blow. Alexandria snuck up behind her and held her dagger against her throat. A small bead of blood formed underneath it. The girl released her blade.

"Smart," Alexandria said in a low voice. A voice that did not sound like her own. "Now go."

Alexandria withdrew her dagger and shoved the girl toward the pews. She and Carter looked at each other, both breathing heavily. He held out his arm to her. She braced herself against his side as they both stumbled toward the throne.

So much for convincing the Dais they weren't conspiring with each other. She would deal with that later. All she needed to do was sit on that cursed throne.

A gun cocked at her left. She cursed loudly. Gasps sounded from the pews, though whether they were in response to the gun or her mouth, Alexandria was not sure.

Mendoza held a gun to Carter's head. Alexandria's dagger was out and raised in less than a second. "If you sit on that throne, I'll shoot him," Mendoza said. His face burned red.

"Don't you dare," Alexandria bit back.

"I am saving the people of Kevelda from a queen with no experience and no concern for this kingdom." He looked out at the crowd, trying to connect with his audience.

"You are only saving yourself from having to work under another queen after you killed the last." More gasps. Though it was partially a lie, the people bought it for the moment. She had to point everything back to him. She had to save Carter.

Her hand shook as she continued. "You would kill your *son* to take more power." The crowd stood speechless now. She locked eyes with Carter, begging silently for his forgiveness. "I am saving Kevelda from *you*."

The Dais ministers sat in the pew behind her. She turned toward them, praying that they listened closely, and that they believed her. "Mendoza killed Queen Evangeline and is now trying to cover his tracks. Will you let him get away with his crimes?" Her gaze found several of the mayors' as she scanned the room. "Will any of you hold him accountable?"

Though she meant the question about the queen's assassination, her heart longed for justice for the boy who had grown up under this man's cruelty. The boy who had become noble and compassionate, even with Mendoza as a father.

The Minister of Development, Priyanka Agate, called for the Argentum agents at the back of the room to detain Mendoza. Alexandria had not named any real evidence, but the revelation that Carter was his living son must have shocked the ministers into action. It did not matter that Mendoza was convicted now. She only needed the distraction to keep Carter alive.

Mendoza lowered his gun.

Leianna got to him before the agents could. She stabbed her last knife through his shoulder, forcing him backwards. His scream joined hers, a ballad of rage and grief that she had avoided singing for far too long.

"You killed my husband." Alexandria had never been more terrified by four words in her life. She would have felt bad for anyone else at the receiving end of Leianna's fury.

"William was collateral damage," Mendoza replied through gritted teeth.

He bellowed again as Leianna twisted the knife. "Don't say his name! You don't deserve to stand here while he's lying in a grave!" Sobs drowned out her last few words, tears streaming down her cheeks. It did not stop her from yanking the blade out and stabbing the Prime Minister. Again. And again. And again.

Agents swarmed her, pulling her away from Mendoza. To Alexandria's surprise, the man still stood. The agents forced his hands behind his back, crimson stains spreading across his white shirt, and carried him out of the throne room.

Carter drew a sharp breath. She did not realize how still he had gone, how truly afraid he had been with his father's gun to his head. He must have been in shock. Her hand found his, and together, they climbed the steps to the throne.

She slumped down onto it. The cold metal failed to soothe the aches wracking her body, both dull and sharp. To the audience, she must have looked like some kind of undead creature. Bloody, bruised, with a knife sticking out of her arm.

It did not matter. She was their queen at last.

The audience watched her as she sat there, their eyes wide. They wanted her to speak. She was faintly aware of the little girl screaming somewhere in the pews. Nothing she could say would comfort her, would give back the life that Alexandria had taken.

Only five words passed her lips before she succumbed to the darkness.

"I did this for you."

THIRTY-THREE

Alexandria awoke to the smell of cinnamon rolls. Her eyes flicked open, taking in the white spackled ceiling.

She pushed up onto her elbows. Light lined the room through the slit in the curtains, highlighting the pattern on her quilt. *The cabin.*

Sniffing once again, she knew she was not mistaken. Someone was making cinnamon rolls. Her favorite. A delicacy to only be expended upon for the most special of occasions.

Voices drifted through the walls, growing louder as she opened the bedroom door. When she entered the living room, Amira's eyes met hers. Alexandria ran to her best friend.

"You're here," she breathed, embracing Amira tightly.

"I am," Amira replied, "and you're crushing my ribs."

Alexandria squeezed her one more time before pulling away. "Sorry."

A smile spread across Amira's face. "I knew you'd make it."

"Really? I didn't." They both laughed as Alexandria caught James's eye. "Nice distraction."

James brushed his shoulder. "Only spent a few days in the palace cells." He rose from the couch and gave Alexandria a hug.

"Thank you," she whispered. Once he let go, Alexandria took in the sight of her two closest friends. Her eyes grew hot with tears. Amira noticed and pulled her in again. James wrapped his arms around them both. She closed her eyes, settling into the moment of peace.

"Cinnamon rolls are ready," a familiar voice called from the kitchen. Alexandria broke away from her friends. Carter carried a plate full of the pastries toward them, the warm, spiced scent filling her nose.

For a moment, Alexandria could not tell whether she was more excited to see Carter or the cinnamon rolls. She decided the answer was *both* and nearly knocked the plate out of his hands as she hugged him.

The plate clicked against the counter. Then, he held her, as if there was nothing more important in the world. She buried her face into his shoulder. Briefly, she felt as though there was something she was supposed to be angry at him for. The thought left as soon as it came. He smelled like cinnamon.

Her stomach grumbled, breaking the silence. Carter laughed and handed her a roll off the plate. "Come on," he said, "you can be excited to see me after you eat something."

Alexandria rolled her eyes, failing to hide the smile on her face. She took a bite of the roll, savoring the taste. It had been years since she last had one, back before the bakery next to the city square closed because of the Draft.

The Draft. Reality shoved its way to the forefront of her mind. She was the queen now. Why was she in the cabin?

"Alexandria?" Carter waved his hand in front of her face.

She shook the thought out of her head, resolving to enjoy the last few moments of peace. She raised the pastry. "Very good," she said.

They sat down on one of the couches, and soon, Amira and James joined them on the other. Before thinking about it, Alexandria rested the back of her head against Carter's shoulder. He nestled her into his arms. She tucked her legs up underneath her, enjoying the last of her cinnamon roll as he trailed the tips of his fingers up and down her arm.

If she had the choice, she would live in this moment forever.

A knock sounded at the door. She groaned, moving to her feet. "I'll get it," she said, when Carter began to rise from the couch.

When she opened the door, cool metal pressed against her forehead. The gun cocked. Mendoza stood on the other side of it, fury in his eyes.

"Good luck, Alexandria," he said as a gunshot shattered her eardrums.

The nightmare repeated.

Over.

And over.

And over.

Until finally, the cabin's spackled walls turned into plain white ones.

Fluorescent light burned into her eyes. Pain erupted from every part of her body.

Besides her right arm. Alexandria's gaze shifted to her shoulder, her neck sore as it twisted. New bandages lined her upper arm. She recalled the sight of the knife embedded in it. Yet, she did not feel anything at all.

Her brain screamed at her fingers to move, to no avail. Alexandria drew in a sharp breath, her heart racing too fast for her chest to handle. It would cave in unless her pulse stopped first.

"Even sedated, you still talk in your sleep," Carter said.

She turned her head, another sharp pain slicing through her neck. He sat in a chair next to her, facing the hospital bed. His skin had darkened around his eyes. Alexandria tried to come up with a response, but her heart continued to drum viciously. When their eyes locked, his teasing smile fell.

He swiftly moved to the edge of the bed and took her hand. Alexandria shifted over to make room for him to sit. Her legs were stiff as boards. It took a few tries for her muscles to regain consciousness. Carter gently moved the IV line out of the way and sat down beside her. As he stroked her hair, her body finally began to relax.

"You're his son," she said. The hoarse words scratched against her dry throat. Alexandria felt Carter nod next to her. "Why didn't you tell me?"

"You hated him from the beginning. I couldn't bear it if you hated me, too."

The crack in his voice dampened her resolve. "I could never hate you," she whispered, "but I can't trust you."

"I understand." Neither of them moved.

He had hidden his part in Evangeline's death and kept his assignment to bring her to his father a secret. The entire time they had been together, he had concealed who he truly was. What hurt the most was the thought that he had not let Alexandria in, even though she had revealed almost all her pain and fears to him.

He had told her about his mother and sister. He had comforted her after her first kill. He had protected her in the throne room.

There was no one she trusted more to keep her alive, yet the thought of the secrets he kept gnawed at the back of her mind. Now that she did not need him to keep her alive in the Campaign, she could not as easily gloss over his lies. An entire side of him she did not know. That could be dangerous. *He* could be dangerous.

Mendoza had made his son pretend to have died in the Genean attacks. He forced Carter into the Argentum for his own gain. Alexandria did not know what the man's strategy was, only that it put her and her people in danger. How far had Carter gone to serve his father?

"Tell me the truth. For the final time, Carter. I need to know everything."

His hand stilled. "When the bombs hit, I was buried in rubble. My mother was gone. My sister's body had been so badly damaged that Mendoza could barely identify her. It wasn't unbelievable, then, that they could not find my remains. He told me the only way to avenge their deaths was to join the Argentum and work my way into the palace until he had a plan.

"Everyone thought I was dead. I cut my hair, changed the way I walked and talked. No one suspected I was Mendoza's son. They had never interacted with me beyond watching me stand by his side. I shouldn't have trusted him, but he's all I have left. Or he was, until I met you."

Silence stretched tight between them. Alexandria's mouth opened to speak, but her mind would not give it the words. Carter's voice quieted as he continued.

"He avoided me so that the rest of the Argentum would not question our relationship, but I knew most of my assignments were from him. My first kill, the man who told the Genean soldiers how to sneak past our defenses, was at his order. Every day since Evangeline died, I have asked myself whether he told me the truth then, or if I have an innocent man's blood on my hands.

"When she laid out the plan for how I would kill her, I told my father. I begged him to find me a way out of it, to talk *her* out of it. If I disobeyed, I feared she would cast me out, and I couldn't bear that. While my father ignored me for seven years, she watched over me. I would have lost her either way. She was so sure that everything would work out, that her death was the only way to save Kevelda.

"Mendoza signed the contract before she succumbed to the poison to make you believe I was really your Protector. He wanted to keep my movements a secret, so that it was just him and I once more. We were a team again. After all these years, he had come up with a plan to take down Genea, but he needed to be the one on the throne. And so, my mission was to bring you to Regia and watch him kill you."

"What changed?" she asked. "Why turn your back on him, after everything you had done?"

"I could not let you die. It didn't matter that you hated me. You kept fighting to survive, against all odds. Not just survive. Live. And you reminded me there is a difference between the two. Ever since my family died, I have been surviving, lying in wait day-by-day, waiting for the man who was supposed to protect me to find another way to exploit me. Mendoza never cared about me. You made me realize that, and that my life could be so much more than he wanted it to be."

"I just wanted you to stay with me in the cabin. That hardly seems like living."

"Life with you would have been so much better than anything he had planned for me. Doesn't matter where. In a cabin in the middle of the woods. Even in a prison cell. I'd choose you anywhere."

Alexandria's heart lurched at the words. If they were still back in the cabin, everything would be different. In another life, she would choose him, too.

But she was Queen Alexandria of Kevelda, and Mendoza's son could not have a place in her court. Not when he could betray her, though she longed to believe that he wouldn't. And especially not now that everyone knew who he was. With Mendoza under suspicion by the Dais, his son would be, too.

Alexandria knew all of this to be true. Her mind could not be changed. She was aware that she would have to send him away, that she could never see him again, and if she did, she could not open up to him anymore.

But she could not bring herself to pull away.

For the past month, his arms had meant safety. They had been her home.

She would never go home again.

~

Alexandria could not let go of the feeling that the interim Prime Minister strongly disliked having a twenty-year-old woman as her superior. Vada Scottsdöttir led her and Carter down to the cell where Mendoza was being held. Her sharply cut white hair glowed in the dim below-ground light.

While it might have been easier for Alexandria to make a clean cut and send Carter away before she left the hospital room, she would not deny him the opportunity to speak his final words to his father, whatever they were.

Whereas the halls of the castle had been lined with stained glass and sculpted stone, the palace cells were straight concrete. The windows were level with the ground outside. If anyone passed, all the prisoners would see were shoes.

Alexandria's stomach twisted at the thought of being imprisoned down here. She wondered who the former queen had taken prisoner and what had been their punishment. Her thoughts turned to Will, to the gallows that still stood in front of the palace. Leianna was nowhere to be found. Alexandria supposed that was a good thing.

A woman with shoulder-length blonde hair stood in front of Mendoza's cell.

"Agent Watson," Vada said, "Her Majesty is here to speak with the prisoner." The word *prisoner* was filled with such venom that Alexandria was surprised Mendoza did not flinch.

He watched them through the bars, brown eyes piercing against his ever-paling skin. Alexandria thought he grew sicklier every time she saw him. He was deteriorating, but from what, Alexandria did not know. Unless it was the wasting sickness.

She shook the thought out of her head. That did not happen in Kevelda. Only in the eastern or western regions of the mainland could the wasting sickness be found, a side effect of the Fall. Before the war with Genea, when Keveldan leaders visited allies in the southern countries, they did not catch the disease. One would have to be exposed to it for a very long time before the illness manifested, according to her late grandmother.

No, the wasting sickness did not cause his pallor, but the multiple stab wounds scattered across his shoulder. Courtesy of Leianna. The outlines of his bandages were visible through his shirt.

Watson nodded, unlocking and opening the cell door. Alexandria straightened her shoulders as she walked into the cell.

Mendoza stared past her, his eyes settling on Carter. "Are you here to apologize?"

Alexandria clenched her fist to avoid screaming at him. She exhaled steadily, waiting for Carter to speak first.

"I regret nothing I have done. I only did my duty to protect the heir." Carter's mouth drew into a tight line when he finished speaking. A tense moment passed. "Would you have liked me to do anything else?" he added sarcastically.

Vada and Watson stood outside of the cell. While their backs were turned, Alexandria knew they could hear every word. Any answer that Mendoza gave could add fuel to the investigation.

The former Prime Minister, wisely, remained silent. Because Alexandria wanted real answers, she ordered the two to leave.

"Your Majesty–" Watson began, but Alexandria held up a hand.

"We'll be okay. I need to speak with him alone."

The agent nodded and walked up the stairs to the main hall, Vada following behind. She glanced back at Alexandria briefly before disappearing from sight.

Alexandria ground her teeth to level her head. "Why did you really want the throne?"

"Why wouldn't I want the throne?" His gaunt eyes flashed with arrogance. "Between myself and a girl with no idea what she is doing, I would be foolish to allow the latter to rule Kevelda."

Carter crossed his arms over his chest. Alexandria looked at him, but his eyes were on the wall. "I didn't believe that the first time you said it, and I definitely don't now," she said. "I order you to tell me the truth, or I guarantee this will be much more painful."

Alexandria did not have the stomach to torture anyone, but she figured the threat would be enough for the man to cave. After all, he only ever had his best interest in mind.

"Everything I did was for my son," he said. "Believe that."

She stepped toward the man, and to her surprise, he shifted away. "You don't get to call him that. Not after you threatened to pin Evangeline's assassination on him, and especially not after you held a gun to his head." Her tone rang as sharp as a blade as she spit the words at him.

"I did not kill Evangeline. Whoever did tried to frame me for her murder. It was done in a way that could only have been possible if I committed the crime. The poison was bought in my name."

Evangeline had given Carter the poison, which could only mean one thing: the queen had wanted Mendoza out of the picture.

Why die for that? Alexandria asked herself. *Unless she knew she was going to die and wanted to take him down with her.*

Wheels spun in Alexandria's head, until finally, something clicked. "You were going to kill her anyways," she said. "That's why you hid the fact that Carter was alive all these years. You wanted an inside agent when the time finally came. But she beat you to it. She was in control."

Making Carter kill her was Evangeline's test to see what side he was on. She had to have known he was Mendoza's son when she promoted him to her personal guard. Doubt flickered in her mind. Something still did not add up about Evangeline's motives.

Mendoza smirked. "You think you're so smart, don't you?"

She continued, ignoring his comment. "Why would you want Evangeline out of power, when you saw firsthand the war

Kevelda was in? Why risk so much to be in charge of a fight you could not win?"

"Think, Alexandria. Those soldiers Evangeline sent became nothing more than slaves for Natania's activities on Thaertos. What would you do, if you were in my position?"

Alexandria's stomach fell. *Slaves?* A thousand questions ran through her mind all at once. The only one she ended up asking was, "What is Natania planning?"

Mendoza opened his mouth to say something before his body convulsed violently. He slumped to the ground. His arms and legs thrashed until he went limp as quickly as the attack had begun.

Carter kneeled at the man's side, a passing moment of him being his father's son. Alexandria yelled for the guard. She felt Mendoza's wrist for a pulse, but none could be found.

She pulled Carter away from the body as a group of guards rushed in. "Go upstairs," she ordered. He took one final look at his father, face devoid of emotion, before walking out of the cell.

One of the guards shouted. Alexandria rushed to see what he was looking at. Burn marks crawled along Mendoza's wrist where his shackle had been. Inside of the metal was something that looked like an electrical circuit.

"He was electrocuted," Watson murmured.

Alexandria's heart pounded as she inspected the device. "How could that happen?"

She already knew the answer. Someone had been listening to them, and they did not want Mendoza to reveal anything else.

He had been murdered.

THIRTY-FOUR

Alexandria paced back and forth, her boots clicking on the tile of her new bedroom. The queen's suite had not been remodeled after Evangeline's death, a thought that turned Alexandria's stomach. Vada assured her that the space had been completely cleaned and that her ladies-in-waiting had bought a new quilt in the week that she had been in the hospital after ascending.

At least they had tried to quell her unease at living in the room the former queen died in.

The room was located on the third floor of the palace, which had been added onto the building some time after the Fall to keep the reigning monarch secure. She had the entire wing to herself, and it was only accessible by a highly guarded staircase that rose from the throne room. And of course, a secret tunnel that opened into the hospital wing, and another that let out in the forest outside of the capital.

Alexandria wished she had known about that during the Campaign. It would have made her life much easier. She would likely still have use of her arm, which now pressed against her chest, held in place by a black molded sling that secured with snaps over her left shoulder. The palace tailor, who made the queen's clothing as well as designed Argentum uniforms, had pieced it together out of a bulletproof fabric. Flexible, yet protective. It would not keep a bullet from tearing through her stomach, but at least she wouldn't take any more damage to her shoulder and arm.

Finally, the guard at her door announced that her parents were entering.

Alexandria ran to her mother, her shoulder stinging as they embraced tightly. She hugged her father next. Tears streamed down her face as the emotions overwhelmed her. "I thought he was going to kill you," she cried. With only her parents and the guards in the room, she did not hold back the sobs that had built inside her chest for the past month.

"I would like to see him try," her mother said, wiping the tears from her cheeks.

"He won't be able to anymore." Alexandria paused, glancing at the guards. They already knew that Mendoza was dead, but no one outside of the palace did. With the Dais investigation ongoing, there was no news to share to the citizens that would not incite panic. All Kevelda would know was that two high-ranking people had been killed in a month, with no explanation for the second death.

It would raise even more concern that Will had not been Evangeline's assassin, a revelation that the Dais was still mitigating after Alexandria had announced to everyone in the throne room that Mendoza was the queen's killer. The cameras and microphones broadcasting the Ascension were on a delay and had been shut off as soon as Mendoza pulled his gun on Carter. No one besides the mayors and their families were aware that Will's conviction had been called into question. To renounce it after having already executed the man would send the cities into chaos.

Alexandria could tell everyone. She could turn her people against the Dais, shut down the Draft, and rule on her own. But she had hardly been the queen for a week, and she did not know how to run a country. Soon, she would reorganize her cabinet and regain allies, both within Kevelda and outside of it. Until she had her feet underneath her, she could not do anything drastic.

"Mendoza's dead," she whispered.

Her father's eyes widened in shock. Her parents had been traveling to Regia when she entered the throne room, so they did not know anything that happened after the broadcast cut off. "Did he challenge you?"

"Technically, yes, but it wasn't then." She led her parents toward the windows, out of earshot from the guards. "He was murdered. We don't really know how, only that the attack was remote. Some kind of electronic device tucked into his shackles that electrocuted him."

Her parents shared a concerned look, the former mayor's eyebrows furrowing. "Someone inside the palace must have put it there."

"Exactly, but we don't know who." Alexandria sighed. This job was already exhausting her. She thought all her questions would be answered when she became the queen, but now, only more surfaced. "Something is happening. Something dangerous. We still have not found Amira or her kidnappers, and now Mendoza is dead. You need to get far away from this palace. Go back to Kureya, get Elsie and Mrs. Collins and Sam and go somewhere safe."

"We can't just leave you here to deal with this on your own," her mother said.

"This is my responsibility to handle, and you are part of my people now, which makes your safety my responsibility, too. If not as your daughter, then as your queen, I order you to get out of the capital before you get wrapped up in this."

Her father set his hand on her mother's shoulder. "She's right. If there's a conspiracy in the palace, then we'll only be fuel for the person behind it to use against Alexandria."

Alexandria chewed on her bottom lip, waiting for her mother to respond. "Okay," she said, her eyes glassy. "We'll go."

She squeezed Alexandria's hand before Alexandria wrapped her arms around her again. "I fought." Her voice cracked in the whisper. "I'll keep fighting."

"That's my girl," her mother responded.

They all embraced one last time before her parents were escorted out by the guards. "We'll see you soon, Alexandria," her father called back. Alexandria returned his sad smile before the door shut behind them.

She vowed to hold back her tears for a few more minutes. There were two final people she needed to say goodbye to.

Carter and James entered shortly after she sent the guards to find them. Carter had gotten James released from the palace cells during her hospital stay. She felt guilty for forgetting that her friend had been captured for her, but considering she had been unconscious from her injuries, she knew her friend would forgive her, even if he gave her grief for it.

Both of their expressions were heavy as they walked in. The dark circles around Carter's eyes had gotten worse in the day since his father's death.

James did not hesitate to ask about Amira. All Alexandria could do was shake her head. He hugged her for a moment before asking, "What now?"

"I don't know," she said. She locked eyes with Carter. "But I'm hoping you can help. You're Argentum. You know how to find people. I hate to ask you this with everything that has happened, but–"

"I'll do it," he interrupted. His mouth moved into a smile, but his eyes remained emotionless. "I'll find her."

"I'm going with you," James said.

Carter did not bother to argue. "We'll stock up tonight and head out in the morning."

"When you find her, James, bring her here first," Alexandria said. "If you run into *any* trouble, I want you to go home."

James set his jaw. "I'm not coming back until I find her."

Alexandria knew that he wouldn't. As long as his mother and sister were okay, he would look for Amira forever. "Then be safe."

James nodded and backed toward the door. "You be safe, too," he said, before leaving her and Carter alone with the guards.

She was tempted to tell the agents to leave, but it was for the best that they were not completely on their own. Her head reminded her that she could not trust him, even though her heart pointed to all the evidence otherwise. Though he had protected her, he had lied to her. Repeatedly. She replayed that thought over and over in her head as she examined him.

"I won't be coming back," he said, though it sounded more like a question.

"I know."

"Tell me to stay." He cupped her cheek with his palm.

She tried to step back, but her legs betrayed her. "I can't."

Even if he was not Mendoza's son, he needed to go far from here. People close to her would die. There was a storm brewing just under the surface of the war they were already fighting. She could not bear watching another person she cared about get killed. If she told him that, he would stay, regardless of what she said.

Let him think she hated him. It would keep him alive, even if it killed her inside.

"You can."

"I won't." Her legs moved now. "I can't say that I trust you. I can only say that I forgive you. You get to decide what you do with that."

Something shattered behind his eyes. Alexandria fought the urge to turn her face away. She had to look strong, even if she was anything but that. To her surprise, he got down onto one knee. "I will serve you as my queen, even if I no longer deserve to be called a friend."

Alexandria blinked quickly and took a steadying breath. "Oh, get up."

"That was a little dramatic, wasn't it?" A smile spread across his face. Alexandria wondered how much of it was forced.

"You always are."

"One more thing," he said. "If you're going to keep saying my name in your sleep, I'd prefer if you called me by the right one. Isaac."

Alexandria straightened her shoulders. "Isaac." Her voice came out like a whisper.

"The name my mother gave me, not the one my father made me use."

In an alternate universe, she stopped him as he turned away. She begged him to stay. She slammed the door shut before he could leave. She ran away with him, left the palace in shambles.

But this was reality.

In the real world, she kept her feet planted to their spot. She watched his smile fade. She memorized his last glance as he peered back from the doorframe. She remembered the sound of his footsteps, his voice, his laugh.

And she let him go.

"Goodbye, Isaac," she whispered at the doors.

The next morning, her guards informed her that Carter–Isaac–and James had set out from the palace. They took two guns, a few daggers, and a weeks' supply of preserved food. In a week, a month, a year, James would return. She would have her friends back and gain answers about one of her adversaries.

Isaac would be nothing more than a memory to keep her up at night.

EPILOGUE

The growing winter chill bit at Alexandria's skin as she waited outside of Bailey's church. Her two guards, Prior and Lawton, surveyed the streets around her. Since she had awoken in the hospital bed over two weeks ago, her heart had not stopped racing. Anxiety laid below every emotion she felt, simmering underneath the surface, waiting to strike.

Fortunately, most of the attacks came at night. She woke up screaming some nights, others in a cold sweat. Her guards had rushed to her side at first, but after three or four nights, they just watched her with concern.

The nightmares mostly revolved around real events, like the man in the ravine, Mendoza, and the little girl's screams as Alexandria stabbed her father. Alexandria preferred these. They had already happened, and Alexandria could tell herself that they were over, that she had survived. But sometimes the image of her parents and friends being killed startled her awake. In those moments, she could do nothing but remember that they were still alive and avoid counting down the seconds until they were not.

Alexandria snapped out of her thoughts when the door creaked open. Bailey stood on the other side. When he saw her, he bowed.

"You don't need to do that," she said, motioning for the priest the stand.

"To what do I owe the honor?" he asked.

"Is Leianna here?"

The priest glanced at the guards warily before he responded. "Yes."

"Can I see her? They'll wait out here."

One of the two started to protest, but Alexandria held up her hand.

Bailey nodded and Alexandria followed him inside. She found Leianna sitting at the table, reading a book. Her heart panged when she realized it was the one she and Isaac had found at the ranger station.

"I hope you don't mind that I took this out of your bag," Leianna said. She closed the book and stood to her feet. "Your Majesty." Alexandria rolled her eyes as Leianna bowed.

"You *especially* don't need to do that. You saved my life."

"It was my assignment."

"I'll ignore that you just said that." Alexandria cleared her throat. "I came here to tell you that my offer still stands. You have a place as the head of my personal guard, when you're ready to take it."

"I can't go back if Mendoza's there."

The corner of Alexandria's mouth raised. "Mendoza is dead."

Leianna's eyes widened, and she stood straighter. "I'll come back today, then."

"No, not yet."

"I'm ready."

"Your queen says that you're not. Besides, your first assignment won't begin until winter is over." Alexandria tossed a letter onto the table.

Her guards had given her the letter that morning. It had been addressed to her and the Dais, delivered by a young boy who had no idea what it contained or who had paid him to do so.

The letter was from Queen Natania, inviting Alexandria to a meeting in Genea.

"From one new queen to another. Let's end this war. Come to Genea when the ice has thawed." The queen had written nothing else besides her signature.

Once Leianna had read the letter, she handed it back to Alexandria. The woman's eyes watered for a moment before she blinked rapidly. "I will be ready, then."

Initially, the Dais argued that it could be fake, or worse, a trap. Alexandria gathered that they knew nothing of Kevelda's position in the war. They did not know their queen had failed them, that their soldiers had been working for Genea for who knew how long. The ministers still argued for increasing the Draft numbers.

This would be no meeting for peace, Alexandria knew. Natania had a plan, but Alexandria refused to fall prey to it. She had too many questions and not enough answers. A flicker of hope sparked in her chest, despite the dangers that laid ahead.

If the soldiers were sent to work, not fight, then Phillip could still be alive.

That thought carried Alexandria all the way back to her room in the palace, where she ruminated over strategy for her meeting with Natania until a knock sounded at the door.

She had told her guards she wanted some time alone and that they could station themselves at the stairs, so she stretched out her legs and went to open the door herself.

There was no one in sight. Alexandria craned her neck and saw only a guard's boot past the last step. Her heartbeat thundered in her ears. She palmed the knife she kept on her belt and moved to investigate.

Before she could take a step, the sound of crinkling paper stopped her in her tracks. Alexandria picked up the crumpled note, the print of her boot stamped on the top. As she unfolded it, the initial on the bottom of the page made her heart stop.

Hello Alexandria,

It's good to finally speak to you. Say hello to Natania for me. I'll send another message when you return. Whatever she offers, keep this in mind:

We can finally win this war, but only if we work together.

Much love,

E

ACKNOWLEDGEMENTS

I started writing *Paper Castles* in 2019, but the inspiration came long before that. My adolescence was filled with dread at not being able to solve any of the world's problems—a heavy weight for anyone, but especially for a teenager.

The people in my life have shown me that, while I cannot fix the world, I can be a bright light in my own community.

There are a few certain bright lights I would like to thank, who supported me long before I ever decided to write a novel, and for whom I will continue to be grateful long after.

To my husband, who goes above and beyond to express how much he loves me, even when I make mistakes: Thank you for waiting for me. Maybe I'll write a book about us someday.

To my family, who probably didn't know I was writing a book when I shut myself into my room during the COVID-19 lockdown: Thanks for loving me even when I only responded with noncommittal nods every time you tried to speak to me.

To the "friends" who I might as well call "family": You probably didn't know I was writing a book either. Oops. Either way, thank you for being there for me, whether we've known each other for over a decade or met in the past few years. Thanks for coffee runs and brunch dates, for watching my thesis presentations and listening to my book ideas.

To my writing friends, beta readers, and ARC reviewers, I am so grateful for your encouragement and wisdom in everything from publishing to worldbuilding to writer's block. A special thank you goes out to Manda, Dela, Courtney, and Maliyah for all their wonderful beta feedback. Sera, I seriously wouldn't have published this if you didn't keep asking me for the printed copy of the first draft (which I apologize for never giving to you—it's staying locked away).

To my readers—wow, I didn't know if I'd ever have you! It's been a long journey to get these characters out into the world, but I hope you love them just as much as I do.

Most importantly, I give all credit and honor to God, who kept me here long enough to get this book on paper. From the highest of highs to the lowest of lows, I have peace knowing He is in control.

ABOUT THE AUTHOR

Ellie Ember is an author who will read just about anything. From young adult fantasy to classic mystery novels, Ellie is always looking for her next favorite book. This variety of interests doesn't end with genres; after changing her major between political science and psychology, journalism, communications, and anthropology, Ellie finally graduated with a Bachelor of Arts in English. She completed a thesis on the political implications of language in dystopian literature, writing double the required number of pages (*cue "Non-Stop" from *Hamilton**). In an alternate universe (from 9AM to 5PM), Ellie is a grad student pursuing a Master of Science in Library and Information Science. Yes, she writes a lot for that, too.

You can find her on Instagram @ellieemberwrites.